T0162511

THE MANY REVENGES OF KIP FLYNN

Sean Dixon

Coach House Books, Toronto

first edition

 Canada Council   Conseil des Arts    ONTARIO ARTS COUNCIL   Canadä
for the Arts   du Canada   CONSEIL DES ARTS DE L'ONTARIO

Published with the generous assistance of the Canada Council for the Arts
and the Ontario Arts Council. Coach House Books also acknowledges the
support of the Government of Canada through the Canada Book Fund and
the Government of Ontario through the Ontario Book Publishing Tax
Credit.

This book is a work of fiction. Names, characters, incidents, historical
accounts, newspaper reportage, burial grounds, construction sites, living
spaces and misadventures are either products of the author's imagination or
are used fictitiously. It would be inadvisable for the reader to allow any criminal and/or investment decisions to be inspired by this book. Any resem-
blance to actual land speculations, illegal activities, or persons, living or
dead, is purely and unequivocally coincidental.

LIBRARY AND ARCHIVES CANADA CATALOGUING IN PUBLICATION

Dixon, Sean
    The many revenges of Kip Flynn / Sean Dixon.

ISBN 978-1-55245-242-4

    I. Title.

PS8557.I97M35 2011   C813'.54   C2011-901014-3

For my father, Bob Dixon, who reads all the Toronto books.
And for Kat, always.

'In the Ford factory, everything is collaboration, unity of views, unity of purpose, a perfect convergence of the totality of gestures and ideas. With us, in building, there is nothing but contradictions, hostilities, dispersion, divergence of views, affirmation of opposed purposes, pawing the ground … Let the hitherto contradictory currents line up in a single procession … Let the ghosts stop blocking the road!'

— Le Corbusier

'The outcome is in the balance, although the fight takes place in the air.'

— Pliny the Elder

It has a subway, with two lines – one that runs like a U down through the centre, and another that bisects the first about a third of the way up, like this: U̶. There are also streetcars. The downtown area is not porous with catacombs or old mines – it's a relatively new city – so there can be tall buildings. It has a couple of rivers, one of which could be said to be as mighty as the Thames, but these are not culturally significant in the same way because they're at the sides instead of the centre and there is a huge lake that runs all the way across the bottom. A little way out, still part of the city, there's an island. Several islands, really. Alongside the islands, a spit, created by earth and stones displaced by the building of the subway.

There are rich and poor people here, who, as in other places, generally stay out of one another's way.

If you've got a bit of money, you can occupy spaces that float above the city, where you might stand at your high window and say, 'What a view! Get rid of that blight right there and it would be perfect!' and point your finger way down to a small red brick garage with a rusty roof, still standing among all the titans, itself surrounded by demonstrators holding placards, trying to preserve it.

But if you're on the side of the small red brick garage, and if you're young and poor and don't mind a precarious existence, there's no better place to live than Kensington Market, where food is cheap and rent is low due to a certain relaxation of municipal regulations. That's where I live. Long live

9

One

NOT A CITY
BUT
A ROSE

1

Spring. A young couple, clad in black, crouched in front of the door of an old bay-and-gable house a mile or so northwest of the Market, as the crow flies. Pendrith Street. In the area of Shaw Street just south of Dupont, not far from Christie Pits. The houses in this particular area of the city follow an up-and-down wave pattern along some of the streets, like this

since they were built over a creek called the Garrison, buried not entirely successfully in the late nineteenth century. But the house that was the focus of current interest was in better shape, having been constructed on landfill of greater density and depth. It sat square on the top of a hill, with the subterranean creek running just behind, a sidewalk in front, and stairs climbing up to a front porch that offered a view of the whole neighbourhood – an overexposed destination for the two thieves who were breaking in.

The boyfriend was down on one knee, trying to pick the lock. The girlfriend, presumptive heroine of our tale, was more opaque and dreamy, easily distracted and, at the moment, a source of great annoyance to him. Still, she seemed to have hidden talents and abilities that could surprise even herself. Case in point: she tried the door. It was open. The boyfriend glared at her. His name was Mani. Hers was

KIP

and she existed mostly below the surface of herself.

Then they were inside a dark front room, Kip closing the door gently and watching Mani. They just stood there for a moment, overwhelmed by lack of experience, wondering whether they should turn around, grab their bikes locked together at the corner of the street and go home.

'Tell me what you told me before, Mani.' (Whispering.)

'What's that.'

'That this isn't wrong.'

'This isn't wrong, Kip. He had it coming.'

'He had it coming,' said Kip, trying to convince herself.

'You can't just do what he did and get away with it.'

'Right,' said Kip. And then she looked around. 'I don't see any-thing to steal, though.'

Just to their right, a load-bearing wall had been taken down, exposing some remnants of brick and newly supported up above by a brand-new eight-by-eight beam. Across the jagged divide, there were piles of dirt, as if someone didn't know it was the inside of a house. There was no furniture. Nobody seemed to live here, a fact that made Kip almost giddy with relief. The only valuable thing in sight was the front door, which was teak and featured a bas relief carving of the whole earth.

'Maybe we should just take the door,' whispered Kip. 'I could start a whole new enterprise with it.'

'What enterprise?' asked Mani, without enthusiasm.

Kip played the part in low tones: 'Heeha, ladies and gentlemen, our blind Market swami will feel out your future on this door of the world …'

'Where do we get the blind Market swami?'

Kip pointed at him and shrugged. He told her to shut up and let him do the deft work of a prowler.

Mani may not seem to be a particularly likeable character, but he is not going to be in this story for very long. Which is itself a tragedy because Kip loved him. And he generally deserved her love. It just so happens that at this particular moment, he was feeling foul. Case in point: the words *shut up*. Their careless employment pushed a button in Kip, who was in a bit of a bad mood herself, though she didn't like to admit things like bad moods. But she had cause today.

She was pregnant, you see.

And she wanted to tell Mani but couldn't quite come out with it.

Maybe the timing was bad. They were robbing a house after all. Then again, it was an empty house, undergoing renovation, with an unlocked door. Maybe even now she was being characteristically unassertive. She asked herself, *What is there to steal?* She asked herself, *Why are two inexperienced thieves robbing a house in which there's nothing to steal?* She told herself, *Look on the bright side: at least nobody's here.*

Except she was wrong about that.

The house is owned by a developer named J. Cyrus York, who is not particularly likeable either, but who is also not going to be in this story very long. Still, he has some interesting hobbies. He's been digging in the basement here. Though urban preservationists are a collective thorn in his side, he's paid attention to one of their more epic interests: the buried creek.

At the moment, he's down there toasting his successful (historic!) containment of the Garrison's seepage – the house having been picked and purchased for this very reason – in the company of a distracted and moody son. The father is so spirited you would never consider him to be a dangerous man. But he's also armed.

On the business side of things, Cyrus York has recently embarked on an ambitious project to redevelop the city's Kensington Market, a ramshackle collection of vegetable stands and drug dens sitting on top of the most eligible real estate in the city. His associates have been applying gentle pressure on the Market's landlords, compelling them to part with their properties. The threat, barely whispered, is that he is prepared to make formal complaints to the fire marshall about all the regulations currently being flaunted. Thus will come crippling renovation expenses to destroy them all.

Ninety percent of these landlords have been rolling over. But there's one – a small-time Vietnamese gangster type named Joseph Luong – who has informed Cyrus that he will not respond well to threats. Research has pointed to this man having fingers in a lot of Market pies – some are fruity, some are savoury, most are treacherous.

And so the old man has taken the precaution of arming himself with a small Glock which he likes very much and which he's going to register very soon. There was a time in his life when he would have employed bodyguards. But these days, he's feeling more than a bit set in his ways, not keen on the company of strangers.

For Kip, presumptive heroine of our tale, the Market is just a sweet place where she can live and shop her wares. She has no idea she occupies ground zero in a war of dark against dark, a war for the city's soul. She has a bit of a blind spot for the dark, in fact, having lived in so many ramshackle places that she has developed an instinct to look towards the light.

If you want to see Kip (or, rather, her type), travel down to the Market at seven o'clock on a warm summer evening. Get to what seems to be the bottom of Augusta Avenue, a short block above Dundas Street. There's a smallish park there called Bellevue. You'll see a statue of Al Waxman there, and Kip and Mani too, in the flesh, sitting on the grass with all their worldly possessions – stuffed army knap-sacks, beat-up guitars, short-haired dogs or just themselves. They won't be alone either. You might have heard some expert on urban demographics tell you they've all come from Peterborough or the suburbs and are merely in the throes of youthful rebellious ecstasy, but there are more than a few – like Kip, and even more like Mani – who just sprang up there like mushrooms after the first spring rain.

Kip wasn't born in Bellevue Park or even the Market, but she wasn't from Peterborough either. She was the daughter of one of the city's many living urban ghosts, the type that can drift over the streets of a city for almost a century without leaving a mark of any kind; the type who would not be able to bail you out of a spot of trouble, no matter how much he might want to; the type with a daughter left to her own devices.

Kip was a hard worker. She didn't look like your standard work-ethicist, not even in silhouette, but it's what she was, right down to the bone. Since her primary property and living space had always been her own body, she kept it adorned in the way you might decorate your home – with glittery baubles, pretty lampshades, old keepsakes, shrines, hidden closets, drawers, tool racks, nooks, windows, stashes of feathers and stones, pressed roses, pure colours, and private letters creased and recreased. If you can imagine transferring everything you treasure from within four private walls to the secure surface of your person, then you'll start to recognize Kip. You'll see her completely only when you understand these bits as architecture and not deficiency, mental illness, rebellion or lack of cohesion. To get to know her is to take the tour. Otherwise you'll confuse her with your own opinions about bits and baubles, torn cloth, piercings and dreads.

Kip lived hand to mouth, pretty much exclusively. And so, given this reality, every meaningful relationship she forged in her life had to be encountered and sealed somewhere between the hand and the mouth. Mani, for instance: she'd met him in the course of her working life and he stuck because he got involved in her schemes. Here's an example: for a while, she ran a guerrilla bar out of the back of a station wagon – totally illegal, you understand, but you might be surprised at how many respectable people will accept an outdoor drink in exchange for cash when it is presented with brio and a hint of class. No paper-bag business here. The idea had come in a flash when Kip had, by chance, come across six tumblers of Bohemian crystal (a $360 value) sitting in a box by a dumpster. This was a decidedly finite number for any conventional drinking establishment, but Mani proved such a wizard with the washcloth, despite the limitations of the station wagon, that you could swear there were up to ten people being served at a time. He also mixed the drinks and kept a keen eye out for prospective thieves. Bodyguard, bartender, dishwasher, pocket-warmer. What was not to love?

For the last several months, Kip and Mani had been engaged in the surprisingly lucrative business of producing BLACK ROSES FOR SALE – hanging fresh red ones up to dry and then dipping them in hot tar, allowing them to harden, painting the leaves green again and then selling them in the streets and goth bars of the city.

This one had been Mani's idea. He had recognized the beauty of tar-fixed plant life one night the previous spring while pissing in a laneway where someone had been repairing the leaky roof of a garage. The weeds poking up from beneath the foot of the wall had been thoroughly tarred, yet retained their shape and even the delicacy of their veins. Despite his drunkenness, Mani had declared it the most beautiful thing he'd ever seen, plucking several of the leaves and waltzing out onto Spadina Avenue to show them off to strangers.

Since Mani was a bit of a natural-born alchemist (having once turned a few bits of base metal into enough gold to fleck Kip's eyelashes), it was no time at all before he'd whipped up a burbling laboratory on the back roof of Kip's building, behind the gable that blocked it from a view of the street – beside the fifteen pretty potted marijuana plants he kept there.

'Genius,' as Kip was wont to say in those days.

The cauldron stank badly and sometimes Kip and Mani stank too. But at least, Kip thought, they stank together. Otherwise, Mani smelled like cinnamon and tea tree oil and sometimes sulphur, which was not a bad smell to her because it reminded her of her father and his perennial skin problems.

You might think there would not have been a market for black roses outside the goth community, but the two of them hit pay dirt when a popular musical, *Beauty and the Beast*, came to town. Black roses appealed, for some reason, to the audience of this show, a cuted-up version of an old legend about spousal abduction. Kip happened to be walking by at intermission one night with an armful of wares. Then, before they knew it, she and Mani had a kiosk in the outer lobby of the Princess of Wales Theatre, and were spending all their off-hours hovering like hecates over the bubbling cauldron. The demand had been so great, they'd been unable to prevent inferior mimics – two of them – sprouting rickety structures, on each side of theirs. Unscrupulous men who used fake roses and spray paint.

Still, our innocent heroine and her loyal sidekick stayed above the fray, even if it was clear that 90 percent of the patrons could not distinguish a difference in quality.

Then, just a couple of weeks before this night of prowling in an empty house on a hill with a creek in its basement, came the fateful moment when Kip handed a particularly fragile specimen to a small, silver-suited young gentleman whose only physical blight was a delicate silver scar running down the centre of his nose.

Perhaps this one flower had been too delicate to withstand its plunge into the boiling tar. And perhaps someone opened a door to the lobby just in that instant, it being intermission, at the same moment when an actor was stepping back into the wings from stealing a smoke on the fire escape. Perhaps this created a unique draft through the building, slipping under doors and around corners, lifting a strand or two of Kip's hair, and beginning a storm of escalating vengeance that would only come to an end eight months later in the much bigger firestorm of a burning, three-storey pit.

Whatever the cause, it was a very simple effect: the flower tumbled off the stem, snapping off a couple of petals as it bounced off the young gentleman's sleeve, rolled past his elbow and fell to the carpet.

That was all there was to it.

Kip snorted goofily and the man flashed her a look she could not interpret. Then his eyes rolled up into his head for a moment, like he was having a seizure. It was over in a moment but it clearly embarrassed him and then sharpened his anger. He snorted something about elite arty hucksters and would not accept a replacement. It soon became apparent that nothing would convince him that one rose's lack of integrity was a fluke. He was more than indignant, he was enraged, explaining that he was advocating on behalf of those whose roses would collapse closer to their cars. Which of course didn't make any sense since it was intermission and there was a whole other act to come. But this dude was on a rhetorical roll.

He made it his mission, accomplished within ten minutes, to get Kip and Mani escorted from the property forever – checking the other kiosks and pronouncing their synthetic knock-offs entirely more durable.

And so a grudge was born. In Mani, if not in Kip.

Not wishing to return to the indignity of trolling goth bars, no longer consumed by the gargantuan alchemy project and possessing two weeks' worth of savings before the wolf came to the door, Mani devoted all waking hours to ascertaining the identity of the man in the silver suit. He would not have gotten anywhere – detective work not being his calling – and his rancour might have faded away in a few days, had it not been for a brief encounter with Kip's flatmate,

NANCY,

who knew how to take advantage of a grudge.

Nancy was an urban explorer, builderer and anti-development activist who took pleasure in infiltrating new condo towers for the purpose of liberating collections of cockroaches and mice, also staining the whitewashed walls with tea to create the illusion of water damage from faulty pipes. She had a team of shadowy allies, many of whom worked in the city's downtown as innocuous tour guides, who gazed out every day upon a city razed and replaced, spinning bitter tales about its former beauty, like a tag-team Scheherazade.

You'll see Nancy in that park at the bottom of Augusta too, but she fits more with the demographic. She had not always been a Market-dwelling activist. It just so happens that Kip met her on the day – the very moment, in fact – of her metamorphosis.

Nancy grew up in Etobicoke with nice, responsible parents, went to a good school, said *please* and *thank you*, understood the importance of keeping proper accounts and going to church on Sundays, smiled sweetly, took a General Arts BA at a nearby university and then moved downtown to Cabbagetown and took a job as a tour guide in the tall concrete structure of City Hall. She excelled in the position, cycling to work along the bike lanes in the summer and switching to the streetcar in the fall, embracing the rhythm of city life with a studied contentment, observing the thousands of strangers who travelled with her every day as if they were all part of a single whirling ornament.

In her job too, she displayed a near empathic understanding of all the various interests of people who came through. One of her tricks for eliding the interests of conservatives, progressives, development buffs and conservationists was to praise the bold innovation of the City Hall design and then point out that concrete structures like it, far from being urban blights, should now be seen as historic monuments of their era that need to be protected against the latest architectural fashions. They were vulnerable, she said, an oversized endangered species like the blue whale or the African elephant. When asked how such sturdy concrete could possibly need protection, she would simply reply, mysteriously, 'I don't know. Ask the Romans.'

In lighter moments, she told the tourists that its pair of curved concrete towers were as fragile, in their way, as the petals of a flower.

But in the month before she first met Kip, Nancy had experienced a seismic shift. In her work, she was as dimply and patient as ever with her charges, but she seemed frayed around the edges, something was crumbling or leaking somewhere. If asked, she would have claimed not to know the source of her dilapidation, but if it had a homing signal, it would have led you, intrepid investigator, up the City Hall stairs and into the 4,000-tonne council chamber (whose weight is here noted because this same chamber has the interesting architectural feature of being supported by a single circular column in the floor below, a place, Nancy told her followers at the start of each tour, known as the Hall of Memory.)

In short, Nancy's problem was the new mayor.

She would never have confessed it at the time, since she'd actually voted for this longstanding councillor from her parents' ward. She thought she'd liked his common touch, had not liked the way some of her friends made jokes about his girth. She'd found him handsome and charismatic and was quietly impressed by his forthrightness. Admittedly (this being her pre-activist life), she hadn't paid much attention to his proposals. But there had been a moment in a public forum in Nathan Phillips Square where she had witnessed him be at a loss for words in front of a microphone while still clearly in the grip of feelings, convictions, the desire to express something he could not express. 'He's just like me,' she'd thought, in that moment, conjuring the whirling ornament. And so she cast her vote.

But the mayor turned out to be a different sort of beast than the one she'd conjured. When the time came for him to express himself more clearly, with policy, Nancy felt compelled to stop her ears for fear of getting upset and displaying some less than civil emotions. Specifically, he declared that her beautiful, gliding streetcars were impeding the progress of the city's movers and shakers: car commuters were tired – so tired – of spending forty-five minutes stuck behind such a vehicle after an hour or more racing through the arteries that brought them into the city. Nancy sympathized with the commuters, they made her think of her parents, haggard after a lifetime of driving. But ... but ... the mayor sought to replace her iconic trams with farting, greasy buses. He sought to supplant them by digging down and running subways through subterranean tunnels, the oiled darkness below the city. Such digging would require funding deals with building developers who would eradicate height restrictions throughout the city and see a new heyday in highrise development.

Still, she lived close by in Cabbagetown. She could shut her eyes to the new shadows rising, the pits being dug and the diesel uglies farting by. At least she still had her bicycle.

Then, one day, a few years before the events being here depicted, Nancy decided to break with protocol by giving her small City Hall tour group a gander inside the council chamber itself, even though it was in session. She tiptoed the four of them up the stairs of the central building and opened one of the doors just as the mayor, standing at his podium, was declaring to the assembled councillors that the city's roads were built for cars, trucks and buses. Nothing else. And she closed it again just as he said, 'My heart bleeds when a cyclist gets killed, but it's their own fault at the end of the day.'

Then she continued her tour out into Nathan Phillips Square, where it just so happened that her small group of four tourists was joined by a fifth, a certain pierced, tattooed and dreadlocked marginal type you happen to know by the name Kip Flynn.

Kip was working that day too, conducting research on the possibility of becoming a tour guide herself. She'd been reading up on the city's architecture – cultivating an interest that hearkened back to the fallout of a scheme from one snowy winter when she was nineteen: She and a beau had tried to set up small igloo-movie-viewing rooms for lovers with laptop computers in Trinity Bellwoods Park. But the igloos all collapsed so they were forced to give the admission money back and, in one case, run for their lives. The experience gave her a new appreciation for the rules and forms of architecture. Recently, her reading on the subject (in a particularly well-designed library on College Street just east of Spadina, fronted by a lion and a griffin) had led her to think it was possible she might be able to talk about it to people in a formal capacity. She'd come down to City Hall to seek out an example and joined a small cache of tourists standing with a cherubic guide, dressed in a particularly alienating colour of blue. She followed the pack into the building and was just arriving at the conclusion that the work would require an unfathomable transformation of personal style, when the guide, just coming abreast of the huge white column in the centre of the floor, suddenly rounded on the group with a sharp change of tone: 'You know, I used to love the Romans,' she said. 'I used to love concrete. I used to think the time of concrete and the Romans was in the past and should be preserved despite its brutality. But ... I mean, I'm not sure what's come over me, but I ... It's occurred to me lately that, right here, on this spot

where I've been preaching every day, there used to be a neighbourhood called St. John's Ward. It was a vibrant place, densely populated by people who didn't live like the big besuited dudes who ruled the city, the arrogant men who, claiming to speak for the weakest and poorest among us, took their diggers and their rollers and their Jurassic construction equipment and knocked down the ward, which they had declared smelly and dangerous, and whose blameless occupants – the city's weakest and poorest, if I may belabour the point – were thus driven out, making way, eventually, for this behemoth we're currently standing in the belly of, being slowly digested ourselves. Anyone who survived took up their bits of schmatte and their cans of herring and their pushcarts and lamps and they trudged over to the location of what is now known as Kensington Market, where they set up their livelihoods again. And these ... these ... fat cats, they're never going to stop, are they? They're never going to stop ...'

Then, in what Kip would later understand as an unprecedented moment that would never be repeated, Nancy burst into tears. 'I'm sorry,' she said, still speaking perfectly despite the emotional display. 'I don't know what's come over me. I'm just a little upset. I feel a little betrayed. I feel like I've been stick-handled through City Hall like a puck made of frozen gravy. I think this is my last day on the job.'

And that was all. She didn't say any more. Just continued to stand there, staring, wide-eyed, teary and open-mouthed at the collection of tourists, who eventually turned and fled just as Kip stepped forward to offer her a hankie.

'What's that for?' asked Nancy.

'You're crying,' said Kip.

'Am I?'

Nancy took it and wiped her eyes. 'Oh yeah,' she said. And then: 'Thank you. I really don't know what's come over me. I'm not even political, necessarily. I just –'

And then she noticed the monogrammed stitching on the hand-kerchief Kip had given her. 'Does that say *snot?*' she asked, appalled.

Kip nodded. 'I also have ones that say *sputum, phlegm, smegma, jism* and *tears.*'

'That's so gross!' Nancy shouted, and then started to laugh.

Kip told her she used to sell them for five dollars a pop but they took too long to make.

'Then you should totally charge more,' said Nancy, sniffling. And then: 'Wait a second. Don't you want to sell this one? You look like you could use the money.'

Kip said, 'This one is for my own personal use. But,' she added, 'it's clean.'

And then, after a bit more encouragement from Kip, Nancy finally blew her nose.

'That was an interesting speech,' said Kip.

'You call that a speech?' asked Nancy. 'I was thinking it was more like a meltdown. I feel weird,' she went on, looking around, Kip gazing at her with some fascination – she looked like a typical cus-tomer for one of her doodads, only different somehow. 'It's ugly in here,' Nancy went on. 'Wow. Look how ugly it is here. Where are all the windows? Can we get out of here?'

'Sure,' said Kip. 'But I wanted to tell you I had no idea about St. John's Ward even though I live in Kensington Market.'

'Really?' asked Nancy, embracing serendipity. 'Can I see your place?' She was still teary, wiping her nose, flushed, but sticking hard to the path that would lead to her new life.

'Sure,' said Kip, shrugging. 'I was sharing it with a guy, but I don't think that's going to work out.'

'I feel,' said Nancy, starting to move, 'like I've spent the last six months walking around inside a clock that just broke.'

So Nancy went home to the Market with Kip. And soon after that, she moved into her place.

And they became friends of course, that goes without saying. Close friends, like twins almost. Mirror images of one another. Kip wished she could be neat and organized like Nancy. Nancy wished she could be a goddess like Kip. That's how she saw her. Not that she'd ever come out and say something like that. But she felt – could not really help it – that Kip was – oh, what's the word? – *authentic*; that her movements hummed in the same key as the deep heart of the city.

Kip felt Nancy's admiration too, although it was never expressed, and although it mingled more and more with the spottier evaluation that began to emerge.

Nancy assumed, because Kip was poor and lived in the Market and looked the way she did, that she must be a rabble-rousing political activist. But Kip was no such thing. This was, at first, a cause of surprise for Nancy, and then – once she began to see her own value as a potential leader in her new community – disappointment. She was quiet about it at first, but, growing into her role, she became more teasy, goady, interventionist. Kip tolerated her friend's behaviour because she could always see, very clearly, the old Nancy embedded in the new. Her friend liked to keep clean, dress nicely, and became concerned when people didn't keep their finances in order or were not properly considerate of others face to face. Kip was charmed by the contradictions. She'd never known anyone like Nancy before and she loved her. So she didn't mind when her new friend tried, valiantly, to indoctrinate her to the cause.

The most memorable effort had taken place already during that first winter together, when Nancy dragged Kip out to a place called Guildwood Park, in far eastern Scarborough. Nancy called it 'the boneyard' because someone had partially reconstructed the buildings that had been torn down from the vicinity of King and Bay in the sixties, neoclassical structures of stone festooned with stern watchers, cross-armed and stripped to the waist, or lion heads flanking the cracked face of a child. A recent snowfall, melted, had left the stone steeped in hues of purple and green.

'You should know better than anyone how we're at war,' Nancy said, that day in the park, pointing to the archway behind her. 'And this is the cemetery for the honoured dead.'

'Not really a cemetery, though,' said Kip. 'It's a park!'

'Look at the address above the archway,' Nancy commanded.

Kip looked: 39 King Street West.

'Most of these structures,' said Nancy, 'were swept away by the erection of the Mies Tower and her sooty black sisters.'

Kip said, 'But I'm sure if someone threatened to pull down those towers, you'd be trying to stop that too.'

'No way,' said Nancy. 'I learned my lesson there. It houses one of the enemies in this war.'

'I don't believe in war,' Kip replied. 'I'm a merchant.'

'What does *that* have to do with anything?'

'Jane Jacobs says that merchants follow a different code than guardians like you.'

'Where does she say that?'

'*Systems of Survival*, it –'

'– was a completely unimportant book from an otherwise –'

'It was important to me!'

'If you're just about selling, then everything's for sale!'

After that, the two of them had made the long journey back downtown and Nancy didn't speak to Kip for a week. Kip only managed to break the ice, finally, by offering entertainment for some of Nancy's newly formed workshop rallies – a combination of stilt-walking, high-wire balancing and fire-breathing, all skills Kip had learned under the tutelage of a pre-Mani beau. Nancy called these entertainments 'bourgeois distractions,' but seemed pleased about them nonetheless.

And so everything settled down in their little Manichean universe for a while – Kip letting Nancy burst out with the occasional speech, Nancy allowing Kip to be her authentic self – until the day Kip was escorted (with Mani) off the grounds of the Princess of Wales Theatre before intermission was even over.

One morning, just a few days later, the vengeful Mani happened to be sitting in the Kip/Nancy kitchen, reading the newspaper that had been left there by a third flatmate, when he just happened to spot a photograph on page A7.

The shot was of a distinguished elderly man shaking hands with a prominent architect on the front steps of a Toronto house. The architect, Frank Gehry, was turning down a condo proposal just as the photo was being snapped and the old man was attempting not to betray his feelings on the matter. But Mani was more interested in a young face behind him, almost in the shadows at his shoulder.

'This is the guy. Hey Kip, is this the guy? This is the guy.'

 Kip didn't look at the top picture. Her eye had been drawn to the one beneath it, of one of the architect's famous projects: a building from a faraway city that looked like a man and woman dancing, though in an architectural kind of way. It reminded her of herself and Mani, in an idealized scenario, with Mani being manly and square and Kip leaning into him all curvy and spiky. Except she was more spiky than curvy and it was a building. Still she liked it. Its permanence attracted her. Especially since she was feeling vulnerable, mortal, fertile, pregnant. And Mani was clued out.

And she was disappointed that the female half of the building looked mostly like it was offering a tray of drinks.

She said, 'What do you think the baby building would look like?'

Mani said, 'Kip! Is this the guy?'

Kip said, 'I ... don't know.'

And then Nancy happened through. Happened to look over Mani's shoulder.

'What do you want to know about that guy?' she asked. 'I've got a whole dossier on him.'

'What's a dossier?' asked Mani.

'Newspaper articles, projects, medical histories – anything you can name.'

'Don't pay attention to her,' said Kip. 'She has an enemies list. She wants to change the world.'

'Not the world,' said Nancy. 'Just the city.'

'I have an enemies list too,' said Mani, pointing to the paper. 'This guy's the only one on it.'

'Great,' said Kip, rolling her eyes.

'He wants to tear down the Market,' said Nancy. 'He surely does.'

'Really?' said Mani, sitting up. He was really interested now.

'Really,' said Nancy. 'And he hatches his plots downtown at the top of the sooty black Mies Tower.'

Kip to Nancy: 'Just to be clear, you're talking about the old guy in the photo, he's talking about the young guy.'

'Like father like son,' said Nancy.

Kip gave her flatmate a dubious look and said, 'You're just trying to radicalize my boyfriend.'

Now that they had finally embarked on their revenge project and were inside the house, Kip suddenly found she wanted to ask Mani whether he might ever be willing to give up the self-destructive practice of seeking vengeance for what, in the grand scheme of things, was the merest of slights. Where daddy-material evaluation was concerned, it was just, she told herself, a theoretical question, since she was definitely not going through with the pregnancy. She would drop in at the Planned Parenthood (read, abortion) centre the next day.

Oh wait, no. She was waiting till the day after – right after the strangely early ultrasound appointment that had been scheduled for her by a cagey (presumably Catholic) doctor last week at the walk-in clinic, when Kip had gone in a teary panic and confessed her condition.

All this contemplation was keeping Kip quiet as Mani prowled around the gritty ground floor. She followed him around the front stairs where there was again nothing and she finally said, 'I really don't think there's anything here you can take.'

'Yeah, funny that,' he whispered. 'Considering you were so passionate about choosing this place.'

'I wasn't passionate about any of it. Nancy –'

'Nancy suggested the mansion on the Bridle Path –'

'Which features a snare and a net inside every window. Not to mention locks. You should thank me.'

'For talking me into robbing a house with nothing in it? I'm supposed to be wreaking havoc.'

'I'm not stopping you,' said Kip. 'Wreak away.'

'I'm wreaking,' said Mani.

'You stink too,' said Kip, 'speaking of reeking.'

'What do you mean?'

'Like, you haven't put on clean clothes in –'

'More important things to think about here,' protested Mani, his voice rising a bit.

'Why are you so bugged?'

'I'm not bugged.'

'Yes you are. You're bugged. I'm bugging you.'

'Just shut up. I'm trying to concentrate.'

'Your concentration has the look of a man who's bugged.'

Mani emitted a grumble that sounded suspiciously again like *shut up*. Believe it or not, it was only the third time he'd ever used such words with Kip, the first being just outside the door. Kip was beginning to wonder whether she wasn't telegraphing her indecision.

Or was he just being an asshole?

She opted to change the subject. Bring up the pregnancy.

'Mani –'

A bit of unearthly scuffling. There was a man there. Standing in front of them, in the middle of the far room. He hadn't been there before. Dust had been raised. Now a second man beside him, half his size in the half light. Had they come from the floor? Yes, from below. The second, older, pointing. There was something in his hand.

And then Kip saw that Mani had something in his hand too. Pointing it in the direction of the …

At the other end of the room, the dust came to a point. A flash of light.

Mani said something. And then, impossibly late, there was the sound of a shot and Mani was already falling. He had pointed his gun (*what was he doing with a gun?*) and then he had fallen. And then the sound. And then he had said what he had said. He'd said, 'He-ey.' Admonishing. As if some kid had just narrowly missed him on his bike.

Kip's eyes had gone blind with the shock of it. Her hands went to the floor. Filthy. Any second, that gun was going to go off again. She was choking from the dust. Coughing. There were voices. One low, staccato and soothing, controlling. The second choked and weeping. Two men. At least that much was clear.

The first thing she heard (or remembered hearing, since the shock placed her ahead of the action somehow, a few moments into the future, or maybe an hour, perhaps a century) was, 'What the fuck?' in the tones of an old man who sounded unaccustomed to cursing. Then there was a frantic exchange about 'How did they get in?' and 'I think I might have left the –' and 'Jesus!' and 'Just have a look see if anyone's put on a light somewhere.' And then, after a long pause, a pair of sentences, directed towards her:

'Who sent you? Why are you here?'

'Wh –' said Kip.

Followed by an argument, swift and hushed, between the older and younger man. She could not follow it. Then a pause. Looming faces. Soft, wrinkled wrist sliding from a sleeve. A firm grip on her forearm. The old man's tone was changing, though. It was taking on an august regret.

'It's all right, young lady. Nobody is going to hurt you.'

And then, the whole brief dust-raising cacophony having lasted no more than a few seconds, 'Let's move this conversation downstairs.'

Later, Kip was outside, standing in the darkness of an empty laneway. Feeling a bit like nobody. She looked down. There was a worm crawling over her shoe. She started to walk. Her lungs were pumping, her face flushed and hot, clothes wet. Now suddenly she felt woozy.

Still, she knew what they had done.

She knew what she had done too.

If you're all about selling, then everything's for sale.

Later still she was wandering through the city. Her feet didn't even get tired. Pendrith to Christie. Christie to Bloor. Sliding down Grace like a hillside, to College, where she should have turned left but didn't. Floated instead further down that street to Dundas and then over to Trinity Bellwoods Park. Felt the pull like her body was a divining rod carved from a tree that had sent roots down to the buried creek, and Mani was seeping away down it to lodge in landfill north of the lake. She ended up walking the minimalist grounds of Fort York, with its guns and grass and spartan stones. It was bothering her that Mani was wearing stinky clothes. And there was an old conversation running endlessly through her head. Mani once telling her she was an excellent salesman. Except in her memory now Mani was talking to her and holding the gun, casual-like, with Kip thinking, *I didn't sell him that.*

Eventually she came to her home, realizing, as she ascended the stairs, that she had forgotten her bike. Up there, near the death house, it was locked to a post, together with Mani's. They were locked together. This was going to bug her too, along with the fact that he was wearing dirty clothes. As if she didn't have enough to think about. All the little things that helped her keep her fingers in the dam.

The special illegal feature of Kip and Nancy's apartment in Kensington, one of the city's hundred thousand illegal flats, was the fact that the only access was up the back fire escape above a bar. The Last Temptation.

Kip had the whole third floor, underneath the roof, plus a hidden deck whose only access was through a window. Nancy had the front room on the second floor, below Kip's.

There was, incidentally, a third flatmate too, who was around some of the time and went about his business in the kitchen and the bathroom and the common room off the kitchen, but not in any way that was relevant to this story. He was some kind of grad student in the classics, ostensibly living there to save money to marry a girlfriend who never came by at all, and he seemed to be easily distracted by the drama of the apartment, often listening with a glass through the wall of his little hallway room. Kip and Nancy called him the Ghost, though he was corporeal enough to save the two of them $400 a month.

The two girls loved this regulation-breaking claptrap of a home above a bar. There was nothing classier than having a fire escape for a sole entrance. And it had a lot of floor space. Nancy especially liked the high volume of bodies that came in and out of this building (downstairs) and walked around inside it, drinking beer, playing pool, having animated conversations and listening to music that made the floor (and her futoned head) vibrate. She adored the company, so foreign to her former experience; it confirmed her metamorphosis and made her feel like she was part of the flower arrangements on the tables, not so much a whirling ornament as a stationary one. Sometimes their apartment would be full of people too, and then there'd be lit candles in paper bags and shadows on the wall, ukeleles, mandolins and pizza, or a big pot of chili that someone made, or beer puddles on the floor and food spatters on the wall, both pre- and post-consumption, sorry to say, that happened too, though not as often as you might think. Sometimes their apartment would be full of animals – mice (or rats), squirrels and once, memorably, a raccoon and a pit bull that someone had left overnight fighting at 4 a.m.

But if the tenants were feeling bereft (or overrun), there was, just next door, vintage clothing to try on. Just up the street, fruits and vegetables, cheeses, bread, fish, nuts, tofu, bongs and Akram's Falafel Shoppe.

This morning Nancy was in the kitchen, her soothing alto voice blending with the low stoner tones of Henry, who did not live there but liked to drop in from time to time. Nancy knew it had to do with his addled attraction for her, though he himself seemed unaware of it. She had the impression 12 Kensington was the only place where he got treated with a bit of affection. At the moment, though, he was standing just inside the door looking jittery. He was a big guy. When he was less than comfortable, it shook the kitchen.

Nancy was glad Henry was there. She found his presence comforting. She was feeling a little anxious because she had succeeded the day before in getting a handgun to Mani. It was just a pop gun, but it had looked real and so it made her nervous. She didn't think she was against violence in principle, in theory, but even this inert symbol made her uncomfortable. It represented a new step in her activist development that she wasn't sure she was ready for: experience told her the pace of change could be hard on a person; when the city changes too fast around you then you can start to lose sense of who you are. Could that also be true for individuals? Was Nancy breaking her own preservationist rules by making too many changes within herself? If so, she was a walking contradiction and a first-rate hypocrite. And it would mean the gun was really, truly a bad idea. Even though it was just a toy gun. It was just a toy gun. And a person has to be able to change, she thought, otherwise we'll all be stuck within our roles forever. Still, it gave her a bad feeling. She decided the best way to deal with the uncertainty was to put the thought out of her mind. That's what activism required: living in two realities at once.

'Why don't you sit down?' she said to Henry. 'Have some Turkish coffee. Have a glass of water. It's got fluoride in it.'

'That's because the government wants you dead,' said Henry.

'But at least they're killing you slowly,' said Nancy. 'There's time to sit down.'

'Got to keep an eye out the back,' said Henry.

About Henry: he was the type you might spot manning the front desk of a dingy boxing gym on old Yonge Street for eight dollars an hour, the sort of guy who could be shot eleven times and buried alive in the woods somewhere but still come back out of sheer dumb luck to haunt his tormenters. It was a mode of life that didn't do him a lot of good in the city. But he was doing his best to adapt.

Henry was trying to make it as a musician, an upright-bass player. Which is not to say he was himself always upright, though he tried to be, despite his habits. Some paranoia the girls knew nothing about had induced him to wheel his bass around in a hard-shell flight case that was bigger than he was and almost too wide to pull up the fire escape. When Henry came by on his way to a rehearsal or a gig, or for no reason at all, he'd lock his case to the iron bars at the bottom of the stairs. Up in the kitchen, he'd lean against the open doorway and poke his head out to yell at the punks who came out the side door of the Temp to recline against it and smoke. 'Hey man, do you mind?' With a pained, nice-guy expression that was well-honed, as if to say, 'I really hate the thought of kicking the shit out of you dudes,' a plausible notion to any stranger who clapped eyes on Henry. He was a beast. A lion practically, with his hunched, hulking size, wispy sideburns and intense glare. Nancy wished he'd get rid of the sideburns though, since he was constantly yanking at them with his fingers, as if checking to make sure they were really growing out of his face. She was mildly attracted to him despite his considerable flaws, imagined herself scaling him like a building. Viewing men as architecture was her precursor to flirting. If he got rid of the sideburns, and if didn't use the eye drops quite so much – i.e., if he didn't smoke so much dope – and if he maybe signed onto the cause a little bit, at least to show that he was present among the living, he might be a bit of a catch.

In other words, Nancy was simultaneously trying to radicalize Henry and also trying to turn him into more of a gentleman of the sort she could take home to her parents for dinner. This didn't quite work as a tactic, but Henry liked the attention and didn't notice the contradictions. He just loved the soothing sound of Nancy's voice, though he rarely had the first clue what she was on about.

Now, for instance.

'People are losing their edge,' she was saying, 'in this stupid building boom. Everyone's getting a fucking job.'

'Jobs are good,' said Henry. 'Wish I could keep one.'

Sudden concern: 'I thought you were concierge of your building.'

'Let's not talk about that,' he said.

Growing concern: 'What happened?'

'Nothing,' said Henry. 'I answered the door to my apartment in my underwear. Wasn't supposed to do that in my official capacity, so the official capacity is no more. I don't give a shit though. I just want to play.'

'Man,' said Nancy. 'You have to take care of yourself. You're too big to fail.'

A bag hit the bottom of the steep staircase to the third floor.

'Whoa,' said Henry. 'Epic laundry day.'

Kip followed it down a little more slowly, bent over the bag, picked it up like a hay bale and hoisted it over her shoulder. Her face was hollow, rings around puffy eyes. Nancy tried to direct her towards the coffee. She called it Turkish coffee. Kip kept going.

'Later,' she mumbled, moving the enormous Henry out of the way and heading down the fire escape. *Thunk thunk thunk.*

He followed her with his eyes. When she'd rounded the bottom step and headed off down the sunny alley he turned back to Nancy, satisfied that Kip had not tripped over his case.

35

'If you want,' said Nancy, 'I could find something for you to do.'

But before Henry even had a chance to respond – before, indeed, he could determine whether it was a flirt or a job offer – Kip was coming back up. *Thunk thunk thunk.* She appeared in the doorway looking shaken and pale, like her wings had been clipped. (Or did she look that way before?)

'Guys,' she said, in a small, high voice. 'I …'

She was still holding the sack over her shoulder.

'I just …'

She sat down in a chair, nearly knocking it over with the sack. No one thought to take it from her. They were riveted by her expression. She was quietly hyperventilating.

'He was there,' said Kip.

'Who?' asked Nancy, leaning over the table towards Kip.

'There's a man. There's a man down there. On the patio …'

'What man?'

'A man. I saw him last night. I can't explain it.'

'You've got a stalker?' (Nancy)

Kip nodded gravely, the sack shifting a bit on her shoulder.

'Don't let the fucker scare you. Chin up, ignore him.'

'No,' said Kip. 'Forget it, I'll –' She started to lift herself again from the chair, laundry sack heaving.

'I'm going to go look,' said Nancy, heading into the hallway towards her front room window.

'No!' said Kip.

Nancy stopped.

'I'll take care of him,' said Henry, heading out the door.

'Wait!' said Kip.

He waited.

They were both standing in their respective doorways, waiting for Kip to tell them what was up. But Kip realized she didn't want to tell them. Especially since she barely understood herself. She sat back down again.

Ten seconds went by. Twenty. She had to say something.

There was a young man, accessory as it happened, to the murder of Mani, out on the patio of the Temp. The silver-suited sullen son. He was sitting at a table with a cheap yellow flower in a glass. With her sales experience, Kip knew that yellow meant *friendship* or *the promise of a new beginning.* And sometimes *jealousy.*

Thirty seconds. She formed the vowels with her mouth to say something. But no sound came out. She was telling herself all the terrible things Nancy might do if she were to learn that this man – whose very existence was contrary to her vision for the city – was a sitting target under her window. *Like father like son.* Might she not drop something on his head, for example? Telling herself she could make it look like an accident? Wasn't there a broken AC unit in her room? Shit, she'd do it for sure, and it wouldn't look like an accident. So then Mani would be dead, Nancy arrested. If the Market was paradise, then they were all the children of paradise, doing naive, stupid things for which the world would sweep them away.

'I don't want you to look,' she said finally. 'I can't explain it, I just don't.'

And then she started to cry.

Nancy came away from the doorway. 'Okay,' she said. 'I won't look.' She crouched down beside her friend.

'I have to get out,' said Kip. 'You don't understand. That's all that has to happen.'

'You mean you have to get past the patio.'

They sat in silence for a full minute, during which time Henry got an idea and looked at the girls. Kip was looking at her shoes. Nancy was looking, concerned, into her face. He finally realized no one was going to notice unless he used his words.

As soon as they were gone, Nancy ran through the flat and looked out the window, down over the patio.

She was distracted for a moment by her annoyance at having learned recently that the clothing store next door had once been a dim sum place but had changed businesses some years ago because an old flu scare had kept patrons away from Chinese restaurants. Then she was distracted by the casual pace with which Henry was making his way out onto the road.

But then her eye was drawn to a figure just below the window. A young man dressed in casual attire with a silver suit jacket, sitting at a table.

Pat York.

She recognized him, though she didn't have quite as much dirt on him in the dossier as his dad. She knew he sat on the committee to replace downtown streetcars with trolley buses as part of the whole post-war-on-the-car thing. She knew he had a vested interest in digging new subways, since the economics of digging down meant the necessity for building up. She felt that was a hard equation, worthy of a graph. Most importantly, she knew he would knock down the Market. She perceived the pristine haircut, the reek of entitlement. Heir to a city-wrecker who would be a city-wrecker too. That was the cut of his jib.

And here was the old AC unit. It was sitting just under the window, gathering dust, begging to be put to practical use. She was slowly shaking her head down at him. Like a gorgon shifting her snaky locks. *Look up at me, you shifty prick. I'll turn you to stone. Plant your petrified torso as a gateway to the Market, let it be a warning.*

She made a decision. A radical impulse of preemptive war (*'I don't know what's come over me!'*). It took some heaving and hoing. But by the time she had gotten the big unit up into the open window, Pat was gone.

There's a whimsical notion, dreamt up a long time ago by a fellow named Ron Herron, called the Walking City.

People point to the pencil-shaped pillars of Toronto's OCAD building and say it's like the Walking City. But it's not. The Ontario College of Art and Design building is stationary. The Walking City

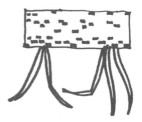 walks. OCAD sits there like a dead Martian war machine from a child's colouring book. The Walking City is very much alive, moving through the landscape and consuming resources and depositing waste as it passes by. The vision of it came out of the architecturally optimistic sixties, when resources were plentiful and the boneyard buildings made way for the sooty black towers.

The Walking City is not familiar to Henry, even though he embodies its essence as he heads down the alley and then up the avenue, cutting a massive and imposing figure in his black overcoat, flight case in tow, population two. Twice he has to bump up onto the sidewalk, blocking pedestrians, so that cars can pass on their one-way south. The laundry sack only adds to his bulk. Lumbering along like the city itself.

He left his instrument in Nancy's bedroom and worked Kip into the case in the shadow of the fire escape, just out of sight of the patio. They have agreed that he will get as far up Kensington as St. Andrew Street, and then pull up on the other side of the synagogue and let Kip out.

He rolls past some hackisack players in front of an abandoned store, including a girl with a long dreadlock ponytail who is trying to thwack the sack with her hair. It fascinates him momentarily, as many things do, slowing him down. But he's brought back to himself by two strolling businessmen, one of whom is gesturing to the Market all around, saying, 'Sure it will be chi chi, but a chi chi that you can love.' And the other: 'You're telling me to sponsor Pedestrian Sundays?' And the first: 'What's good for the hipster is bad for the merchant. It's a hard equation.'

And so we wind our way eventually to a worm's-eye view of Kip curled up inside the belly of a bass case, squashed like a bug between the pages of a book, thumping uncomfortably up Kensington on little wheels. Two hundred metres worth, and then she'll be home free. But it's not going to be easy. Given the places she's been in the last twenty-four hours, she's beginning to feel a little claustrophobic. She tries knocking down walls in her head to give her memory more space.

After the murder. Still in the house. A spiral staircase descending into darkness. Step step step. Down down down. Iron steps, like the fire escape where she lived only this set-up is round, not square, and cramped and turning in upon itself. Descending.

At one arm a young man, known to her, who didn't seem to understand the gravity of the situation.

At the other an elderly man *(You don't seem to understand the gravity of the situation),* a skilful and potent combination of gentleness with Kip *(I want to treat you as if you were my own daughter)* and intimidation *(We'll come after you if you tell anyone).*

She could see points of light below.

That the place was so strange did not help her get her bearings.

These same two men returned to the surface and dragged Mani thumping down the steps. They continued their debate, father and son, as they performed this unspeakable task.

'What do you think you're going to do? Pay her off? Why don't we just call the poli–'

'That new chief's an asshole.'

'Seriously? You're not going to involve the police because –'

'It's one of those things that make you think you've lived too long. And I will not allow anyone in the fucking press to say I was frightened enough to arm myself.'

'But you were frightened enough to arm yourself.'

'Shut up.'

'It was reasonable! He had a gun!'

'A pop gun!'

'It looked real. And now you're going to hide a dead body and give half my inheritance to a stranger on a point of pride?'

'Better her than your coke habit!'

'I don't have a coke habit!'

'Then why are you so jittery all the time?'

'From being your son?'

'I have a rock-solid constitution.'

'Dad, you just killed a man.'

'I'm going to seal the deal right now. She must have a bank account. I have my BlackBerry. Get her wallet.'

'She's not going to give me her wallet.'

'Ask nicely.'

Kip was left alone for a few minutes, listening. She was scared but had time to think. It was vague, more a matter of instinct than plotting. But she came to a decision.

And then they arrived with Mani, laying him out beside the view through the floor.

The points of light were embedded, illuminating a source of water running beneath. Below, Kip saw a large pipe made of glass, with a diameter of two or three feet, about one third full of sluggish water flowing through it: the storied creek, running through this hobby house before disappearing back into the gloom. Maybe someone would crawl through and help her, help Mani. One of those Vanishing Point guys who explore the city's sewers, staking out the buried creek. If Nancy were there and things were different, she'd be thrilled. She'd pinch herself. A private view of the Garrison. How wonderful.

But Nancy wasn't there and Mani was dead. And he needed a change of clothes.

Back to the bass case. Kip's mobile home.

She hears Henry stop and stop again, and wonders what his problem is. Makes her heart race and her muscles constrict. He starts up again even as her breath comes in short and the air evaporates around her. Bump bump. What was a serious distraction from the idea of air?

Mani.

But hasn't she betrayed Mani? That's losing her air again. Push that thought down, push it *down*.

Something nice about Mani then.

Mani as renovation project.

She's going to dress him up for where he's going. Clean out his gutters, paint his gables, clean his windows, plant his garden.

(No, don't think of the earth, burial, buried alive, lack of air, don't think of it!)

She sees Mani in a tuxedo. Smiling. A very clear picture. Except he's not quite himself. He's less than a foot tall and weaving a little in his shiny shoes, as if he can't fully stand up by himself. Mani is a toddler then.

Oh yeah. She forgot. She's pregnant. Unbelievably, this is calming her down. Making her breathing more steady. Why would the idea of being pregnant be calming her down?

And then, deep inside that bass case, it occurs to her.

It's all that's left of the guy.

Kip starts to wonder about how she's been thinking she will not keep the baby – the repercussions of that. She starts to think that maybe her thoughts on the matter can be perceived by the baby himself.

Maybe he thinks …

Is he in there: *You don't want me, guess I'll be on my little way then? Bye?*

But she's held on to the ultrasound appointment. Consolation there. Maybe the baby is aware of that too. The baby is part of her – her thoughts are his thoughts, aren't they? They are the same. Her convictions are his convictions. Ambitions, fears, loves.

So, then, be it established, if the baby knows everything that Kip knows, then the baby knows that Kip has kept her ultrasound appointment only because she is, essentially, indecisive and flaky. It wouldn't be enough to weigh against her heavier, gloomier, decidedly less flaky thoughts on the subject of ab–

On the subject of abo–

The syllables stand like a barbed wire fence between her and the shrinking zygote.

Aborboboobaborboobor ...

(Be it so noted, she has never had trouble thinking this word before.)

Or maybe the baby just thinks she will be too incompetent to let him come out of her. Like she'll fumble the ball or whatever. Like she won't be able to make it to the finish line. The 200-metre dash. Well, more like a marathon. Maybe that makes him feel trapped. Encased within a body that he'll never get out of, relying on the peregrinations of an indecisive human to guide him ...

If this is true, then Kip knows exactly how he feels.

Because it's how Kip herself is beginning to feel about Henry up there, out there, on the outside of this newly confining bass case. Not exactly Vitruvian architecture, this, not properly proportioned to the human body.

She feels all around her the grinding of the asphalt. Her left wrist, bent between her breasts, is starting to hurt. She tries to regularize her breathing. It occurs to her that there isn't enough air in here for two. What does carbon dioxide do to a b–b–? There isn't enough air in here for the b–b–b–

There isn't enough ...

AIR FOR THE B–B–B–

The agreement was 200 metres to the shadows just inside the parking garage on St. Andrew. They do not make it.

In fact, Henry is still within sight of the people at the Temp, at least those close to the street, since he's going up the middle, avoiding pedestrians. Vintage-clothing stores surround but do not obscure him, racks of jeans and cowboy shirts hanging outside. The case has begun to vibrate and emit muffled human sounds. Henry tries to pretend it's not happening, but this does not help. She's in there *mmf*ing and knocking with her head and her knees and even her feet. Henry wouldn't have thought it possible to make such a ruckus in such a small space. But she's all over it, and there are people all over the street. Cyclists and cars. Clothes shoppers. Henry rushing now to undo the latches before they snap off. It's a tough case, but not intended to withstand pressure from the inside. It's expensive too. He doesn't want to damage it. Maybe it's a little too late for that, but he's trying to reach around and give it some balance when Kip busts out, snapping the last latch off its screws and tumbling the whole thing over on its front. As it crashes to the ground, she narrowly avoids clocking her head against the pavement. And then springs up.

'Hey,' Henry says, to no one in particular. 'This isn't what it looks like.' He doesn't know if anyone heard him, though, because he can't take his eyes off Kip. He watches her open her mouth and waits for the flames to engulf him, but instead she only says, 'Take your sweet time, why don't you?'

And then she hauls the sack away and takes off up the street. She doesn't look back but can see how they were barely halfway to St. Andrew. Henry watches her go, imagining what she might be thinking, quite accurately, as it turns out.

Unbelievably, there are sirens, she thinks. Maybe they're not for Henry. She wonders what he'll say to the police when they arrive. He's calling after her, but she can't hear him anymore. No time. She runs past the Jamaican shop, up to the end of the street and rounds Baldwin, heading east and to the solace of the laundromat. She's halfway there before realizing she has a better idea.

And then there's

PAT,

who, despite his flaws (and his place in the dossier), is going to be in this story for the duration, so you're probably going to have to learn to get along with him, to identify with him on some level. Might be an uphill battle (who knows?), but here is as good a place to start as any. Here is where we must plant the post for Pat.

Walking east along Dundas Street, fairly quickly, just passing Spadina Avenue. Heart beating wildly because he's just had a scare.

Minding his own business, sitting on a patio, suddenly confronted with the spectre of the girl from last night, unmistakable, carrying a huge laundry sack, just for a moment, before she turned and fled back down the alley from which she came. And then, a few minutes later, a big, dubious-looking man, dragging a large double bass case, with the same laundry sack slung over his shoulder. Suspicious, no? But Pat could not put his finger on exactly why. And then, a moment later, the discreet view, reflected in the window of a parked car, of another girl, above him, struggling to move an old air conditioner onto the sill, giving him the distinct (albeit paranoid, no?) impression that she was planning to drop it on his head. Did all this really just happen, or was this the way the mind functioned when troubled by a guilty conscience?

Maybe this is the wrong place to start. Maybe we need to go back.

Before everything had turned sideways and decidedly surreal less than twelve hours ago, Pat had been trying to step up and *be a man*, support his father in some of his business dealings, seeking to prove himself a worthy heir.

He had noticed that the fire marshall had paid scant attention to the first volley of complaints regarding the Market's flaunted housing standards; there had perhaps been too many of them, or the city had perhaps smelled a rat, or someone somewhere was getting paid off. Or maybe they were just lazy. Still, it was galling. He'd noticed too (before the events of the previous night) his father's new preoccupation with security. This had troubled him more than anything else, made him a little crazy, he wasn't sure why, and caused him (he might argue), to overreact and behave in a manner that was outside his comfort zone.

So he'd conducted some quiet research and procured the services of two men who were familiar with his father. Having witnessed such deals before, greasing the wheels of progress, he'd given these men a small but tricky shopping list –

1) coils of knob and tube wiring,

2) several bags of marijuana,

3) an old heating lamp,

– and charged them with the task of breaking into an empty house – an abandoned house – at the cul-de-sac of a laneway in the Market. A simple task that would hurt no one. They were simply to coil the bum wiring along the base of the walls, plug in the heating lamp, pile the dried weed around it, take their leave and never look back, never contact him.

The house in question was right here, directly behind this bar called the Last Temptation.

It had now been more than a week since that conference had taken place, and Pat was dizzy with regret about it, even more so considering last night's events. He had seen a man die. He had witnessed his father behave like a thug in the guise of a philanthropist, and here he was, already following in the old man's footsteps, suddenly freaked out about where the path would lead. What if his business with the Kensington house caused yet another death? What if the Yorks were merely profligate slaughterers of their fellow citizens?

But he didn't know how to stop it, he had not established a follow-up contact with these shadowy characters – he didn't even *want* to have contact with these shadowy characters, he just wanted the whole thing to go away.

And yet something had drawn him here, some vague desire to correct a wrong before things got worse. But it wasn't going to be possible. And then he had seen what he had seen.

And now the vision of the black-rose girl, however fleeting, was upsetting him, like before, unaccountably, on the carpet of the Princess of Wales Theatre.

He was walking so fast on Dundas Street now that he had to step off the curb several times to get past the mulling crowds. At one point, his sudden swerve into the street caused a westbound cyclist to careen out into traffic, cursing Pat as he got clipped by the front edge of a car and flipped up onto the hood. Oh! Pat rushed on. The world was moving so fast, that should not have happened and he should not have contacted those thugs. He wished he'd given them a box with a light on it that said 'abort' that he could signal and then it would flash red over and over and over again.

Oh, what had he been thinking? He should never have let his father bully him into covering up a death that wasn't even a murder, just as if it were nothing, as if it were the kind of thing the old man did every day.

And on and on he went, past the Art Gallery of Ontario, and University Avenue, to the relative comfort and safety of Bay Street, where with a sigh he finally turned and headed south.

3

Kip's father was a man named Lionel Flynn who never had a penny to his name for most of his life. Like a kid, he lived hand to mouth until, late in the game, he sired Kip and put his precarious existence behind him. There was a woman involved too, of course, technically Kip's mother. But Lionel was always cagey about this part of the  story. He raised Kip as best he could, until she turned seventeen and then he threw her out because, he said, he didn't want her to pick up any of his loserly habits. He started missing her almost immediately, though, and regularly offered to have her move back in with him in his various itinerant digs. But Kip had discovered almost immediately that she had an entrepreneurial streak: she was a hawker, a peddler, could pick up and discard jobs in the retail sector as she needed them. If the fat man in the vintage clothing store said the jeans were too tight, she had a way of saying, 'Tight is good,' that made the man spend eighty dollars on them even though it was clear he would never wear them when they were safely in his home, not even once.

But this is not Kip's introduction. It's Lionel's. Kip had never been sure how old her father was. Though he looked like Methuselah, albeit without a beard, and he used to point to the subway station at Dundas and Bloor and say there'd been a church there where he'd served as an altar boy. 'It was so packed on Sundays,' he told her. 'Me and my buddy would have to sit behind the altar so the parishioners could sit on our bench. And the sermon was so long that we used to change into our street clothes and bike down to the ice cream shop on Howard Park, have an ice cream, ride back, change again and be all ready for the blessing of the sacrament. We were never caught.'

Perhaps, then, Lionel's desire to ride the TTC lines, where he said his spirit expanded to the limits of the transit car and filled him with quiet empathy for his fellow passengers, represented some kind of sublimated religious feeling, a public transit form of Manichean worship, wherein the gas-driven vehicles represented the evil force in the universe and the Dundas West subway station was the hub of religious experience. Now he would spend whole days travelling back and forth on the lines. It was like church for him.

Kip came by about once a month to visit her father, which was why he wasn't expecting her when she showed up that afternoon, buzzing off the bridge like a fly in a summer window. At the time this story takes place, he was living in a building perched at the edge of the Dundas Street Bridge, overlooking the railroad tracks, which looked to Kip like it was at the edge of the world though it was really only just beyond where College Street ended – where, if you looked back, you'd see that the CN Tower was finally not alone from this perspective: there was suddenly an old church spire beside it, nearly as tall.

There was an entrance right off the top of the bridge that led onto the second floor where Lionel kept his humble abode. The structure was all walls built around older walls a hundred years ago, one building completely enclosing the other.

Lionel was sitting and staring at one of the previously external walls, counting seven different varieties of brick, when Kip knocked at the door.

'What's that?' asked Lionel, tearing himself away from his studies, referring to the sack of clothes on her shoulder.

'Laundry,' said Kip.

'Mine's broken,' said Lionel. 'You have to use the laundromat.' And he followed her down the hallway to the stairs. He'd seen her in these moods before. Zipping here and everywhere.

'You're green.' He meant it literally.

'I haven't really been eating well.'

'You could move in here with me.'

'You don't cook either.'

'That's true …'

Kip stopped at the bottom of the stairs. 'But I might have to stay here for a couple of days,' she said, looking straight back up at him. He was startled to see her eyes tear up.

'Okay,' he said.

'Just a couple of days.'

'Whatever you want.'

She was looking around. 'Where's the laundry room?'

'You have to go outside.'

'You can't get to it from inside?'

'Not unless you blast a hole in that wall.'

Kip rolled her eyes. Lionel couldn't tell why she was hesitant to go outside on this beautiful spring day. They emerged onto Sorauren, below the bridge now, passed the wall and went into the laundromat where she dumped out the contents of the bag on a table.

'Are you hiding from that boyfriend?'

'Sort of.'

'But you're still doing his laundry.'

Kip stopped sorting and looked at him again, angry. He preferred it to the tears, it cheered him to know his girl didn't take any guff. 'Dad, just because I'm using your laundry room doesn't give you the right to look at my laundry. My laundry is private. It's private.'

'It's not a laundry room anyway. It's a laundromat.'

'All the more reason.'

'That's what I'm saying.'

'It's private.'

'I agree with you. It's private because it's public.'

'It's private no matter what.'

'Okay.'

Lionel shuffled and paced and Kip started the wash cycle. Then there was a length of time where they didn't say anything. It was a state they were both accustomed to and could have continued for the rest of the day. Finally, Kip sighed with frustration and asked if he was busy the next morning.

Lionel said he was working. He had a job at a small bookstore, also in Kensington Market, just across the street from the only car rental in town that didn't require a credit card. The job still felt new to him even though he'd worked there for two years, often walking down and meeting Kip for lunch at Akram's.

'Oh,' said Kip now. 'Forget it.' She was all bendy and elusive and vulnerable all of a sudden.

'Tell me,' said Lionel. 'What is it?'

'I have a – er – doctor's –'

'I'll take the day off. I'll call as soon as we get back up.'

It was another few minutes before Lionel managed to suss that she was pregnant and it was an ultrasound in the morning. And she needed someone to go with her. He felt suddenly like he was swimming through soup. Anger too. His neck was getting hot at the back.

'Where's the asshole then?' he asked.

'I can't talk about him right now,' said Kip.

'You can't talk about the irresponsible little prick?' asked Lionel, still trying to cut the edge in his voice, less aware of the words.

'No!' said Kip. 'I told you! One thing at a time!'

'Okay,' said Lionel. 'I'm a one-thing-at-a-time guy.'

So. It was covered. Lionel would go with her. The wash was on its first rinse cycle.

'How far along?' he asked.

'Six weeks maybe?'

'Isn't that early?'

'For what? Ultrasound? Erm. The doctor at the clinic put me down as an "at risk" pregnancy. I think he meant "at risk of termination."'

'I see,' said Lionel. 'I see.' Then, as neutral as possible, 'So then you think you might want to keep this baby.'

He felt a little awkward having such a conversation with his daughter. But he was trying to be brave.

'Well, it's complicated,' said Kip.

'What's complicated?'

'Well, erm … something happened … last night … to me … and to Mani.'

'Mani?'

'Yeah.'

'That's the asshole.'

'Don't call him that. We. We. Thing is, Mani's [dead] and, um.'

The spin cycle started as Kip tipped over into sobbing. A woman from the second floor came in and piled all her clothes into a machine while Kip sat there and dribbled. The woman seemed to be stalling, like she felt she was owed an explanation. But eventually she left. Kip was moving her wet clothes across the floor to the dryer. Lionel said it was safe but Kip kept mum as the clothes went around and around for forty-five minutes. When they were done, Lionel helped fold them. It was the first time he had folded clothes in his entire life. Of this he was certain, having much leisure to reflect on the matter as he folded. He found it remarkably soothing.

Finally they were back upstairs. Kip even asked him if the door was locked. Usually he left it ajar so the cats that wandered around the floors of the building could come in, but he went and closed it and turned the deadbolt. Out the windows, facing east, backhoes clawed at the earth across the bridge. There was a dump site there, fronted by a small shack that gave the lie to the miles of land it lorded over along the tracks.

Kip said she didn't know what to say or where to start. She'd felt strangely disassociated from the tears in the laundromat, like they'd been merely for display. There hadn't been any catharsis in them. This detachment from her own feelings was not something she'd ever felt before. It felt like fakery. She wondered if it was how she'd be for the rest of her life.

'Er. We robbed a house last night.'

'You robbed a house?'

'Or tried to. There was nothing in it.'

'There was –'

'It was a construction site. The door was open.'

'I see.'

'No, you don't.'

They heard a sound that startled Kip. It was a cat from the hallway inside the apartment. Lionel went and let him out.

Then Kip took the newspaper clipping out of her pocket. Carefully unfolded it and slid it across the table to Lionel.

'His house.' She pointed to the older man as Lionel's eyes widened. Couldn't quite bring herself to look at the image.

'Why his house?' he asked.

'It's a long story. But he had a gun. He came out of the floor and shot Mani.'

Lionel's eyes moved down to the picture. He flickered and froze.

'The shooter,' he asked. 'This is him?'

'Yeah,' said Kip.

'Cyrus York.'

'Do you know him?'

'Sort of,' he said. 'I've had some ... dealings with him myself. Actually. It's an odd coincidence.' He peered at her quizzically. 'Considering you were trying to rob him. I stole something from the man once. A long time ago. Um ...'

'What did you take?'

'I don't want you to think less of me,' said Lionel.

'I don't want you to think less of me either,' said Kip, and grabbed his hand.

'I could never think less of you.'

'What did you take?'

Lionel raised himself to his feet. Went and rummaged around in a kitchen drawer. Then disappeared into the bedroom and came out with a shoe box. Set it on the kitchen counter and rifled through it. Pulled out a gold watch on a chain, placed it in Kip's hand. It didn't look like anything special. In fact, Kip fancied she'd seen it before, when she was a child snooping through things. She turned it over to see if there was any inscription. None.

Was it bad karma from a stolen watch that led to a broken flower, a fit of pique, Mani's obsession and death?

No way.

'When did you steal it?'

Lionel had thought many times before about giving Kip this watch. He had two stories in his back pocket. One was the truth and the other was a lie that used elements of the truth.

'I worked a construction site once,' he said. 'Long time ago. I was young. Ish. The big downtown area. They were tearing a whole block down. Put up some black towers.'

'The Mies and that,' said Kip.

'Yeah.'

'I had no idea you –'

'No,' said Lionel. 'It was nothing. Unskilled labour. Clean-up crew. I had to make sure there wasn't any debris kicking around for someone to trip over. Anyway, I used to entertain those guys with card tricks and such. I was pretty good at that. Picked their pockets sometimes, just to freak them out. So, but, there was this one young guy, from the development company. He used to come to the site and strut around. Talk to the workers. He was at least ten years younger than me. But he already had leverage, or whatever you call that. Clearly had the common-man touch too. I always remember how he'd cover his brow with a hand and look way up high.'

Lionel was shaking his head.

'So … ?'

'So I picked his pocket,' said Lionel.

Kip held the watch up by its chain. 'This was Cyrus York's?'

'What I know about him,' said Lionel, crouched down now beside her in the big torn leather chair. 'From the news and that. It's a terrible thing what he's done to you. But he's a very private person. Very secretive. He's had his share of tragedies.'

'You're saying he won't come after me.'

'Whatever deal he made with you, I'd say he'll keep.'

After that, they spent a quiet evening. Lionel played five games of solitaire and worried, despite everything he had said, about Kip and about himself. No matter what happened, their relationship was going to change.

Kip looked up from her brooding at one point. 'Can I ask you – ?'

Lionel, from his cards.

'Why do you think I'm a good salesman?'

He told her she was an excellent salesman.

'Yes, but why?'

'I don't know,' he said.

'Is it because I know the value of something but I can't love it?'

'No.'

Slightly indignant. 'How would you know?'

'Because you're my daughter.'

'So you might be blind to it.'

'No, Kip. I think you can both love and be a good salesman. Seems to me that when you were small and we had visitors, and they started making noises about how it was time to go, you used to pull out everything you could find, one at a time, things that were special to you. A new doll or a new dress or a tin box or a secret drawer. You could stave off someone leaving for as much as fifteen minutes with that business. I always hooked your salesman ways with that.'

'But that's not selling,' said Kip, 'it's showing.'

'Doesn't look a lot different from where I'm sitting,' said Lionel.

Kip grunted to indicate the conversation was over. Lionel returned to his solitaire.

It was late now. Kip had to calm down. Tried to empty her mind. She called Nancy to let her know where she was. Nancy told her Henry had come back all freaked out. Kip said yeah she didn't treat his case very well. She hung up and opened the notebook she always had with her, started to doodle nervously. The bridge rumbled occasionally from streetcars going over and the sun went down. A commuter train swooped by underneath them on the tracks, heading north.

Kip covered a whole page, compulsively, with a heartbeat, the one she could feel below the pulse of her own. Two heartbeats for the price of one. The opening and closing of a valve. She could see it with her mind's eye. Opening and closing and opening. Like the bellows of a tiny accordion, moving in and out and playing just for her.

Next morning, Kip had her laundry bag with her as they stood at the streetcar stop on the bridge. Lionel was confused: her ultrasound appointment was not until eleven a.m., and here they were about to jump into 8:30 rush-hour traffic.

'I have an errand to run first,' said Kip.

'Okay.'

It was a slow, crowded ride. Kip spent the time drawing a picture of the tower and the church spire, as if they were her and Mani. When they transferred to the subway, the crowd got a little more skittish. Kip left Lionel sitting on the platform at St. Andrew station, worried that he might be skittish too (he wasn't) and walked up into the suity morning of University Avenue.

She was heading towards the so-called (by Nancy) sooty black Mies tower 5, which stood alone and separated from its polished compatriots on the south side of Wellington Street. But its position further south meant it didn't need to be as tall as the rest. It was not hit by their shadows.

Kip knew that Nancy hated these towers for displacing the old stones that were now sitting in the boneyard of the Guildwood Park. But Kip could not help but love this block of black behemoths, even now. They didn't make her think of Mani's killers, but rather of Mani happy.

The towers had been built for work, clad in copper windows and black-painted steel. But the spaces around them – over which they seemed to float on concrete pillars – were designed for the

leisure of the lunch hour. Kip and Mani had come here many times to lie in the grass among the sleepy-eyed cow statues. Time always felt more precious to them surrounded by office workers who snatched it greedily in little bunches. Even now, walking among them in the sunny spring morning, she felt the calm try to soothe her unwilling heart.

Her architectural reading had admonished her too, informing her that these towers were 'anti-Vitruvian,' not proportioned to the human body. But she also knew that builders had been steering away from the Vitruvian man (AKA Leonardo Da Vinci, rolling around inside his perpetual-motion circle) since long before the invention of the skyscraper. Some French dude in 1805 had even mocked the idea, saying a man's foot wasn't one-sixth of his own height anyway, so the hallowed Vitruvian proportions were already wrong. Things never stay the same, Kip thought. They're always changing. But she also felt that if Mani could fall asleep in the grass here, with his head on Kip's belly as she looked up at the black angles, then the buildings must be Vitruvian after all, in spirit if not in practice.

As it happened, there was a bit in that morning's paper on the subject of the new and the old, remembered and forgotten, unseen by Kip.

The article was a personal piece about J. C. York. In the interview, Cyrus expressed how, as far as he was concerned, rampant preservationists still had too much of a hold on the psyche of the city, keeping it from reaching the next plateau of greatness. Old edifices were not being permitted to fall down. 'My grandfather used to go fishing in his basement,' he said. 'That doesn't mean we should dig up the creeks again and let them flow over the downtown grid. Progress doesn't work that way. Nostalgia belongs in the mind, not out on the street.' He said he stood for a more daring vision of the city's high-density future, whereby all the warts in the landscape might be eradicated to make room for the boldness and economy of dizzying height. 'We climb mountains to touch the sky,' he said. 'Our buildings are still the smallest fraction of the sizes we see in nature. As a species, we've always been challenged by that, inspired by that. Why stop now? Mountains were made by glaciers and buildings are made by men who can harness the power of glaciers. I like to think of my projects as core samples of mountains, from top to bottom.'

Nancy, sitting in the 12 Kensington kitchen, clipped out the article and filed it away in the banker's box, under Y.

Kip was nervous about being stopped and questioned, so she dropped her laundry sack near the elevator and went straight to the security desk. Told the woman that she'd heard there was a great view of the waterfront from the top of the tower and asked if it was all right for her to go up to see it. The woman was very helpful, almost conspiratorial, and gave her directions. Not the top floor, she said. The second from the top. Advised her to ignore the stares of the waiters in the restaurant and just enjoy the view. They wouldn't try to stop her. Kip went back, picked up her sack and pressed the button for the elevator express to the top third of the building.

Once on, she hit 52 instead of 51. Came out facing an enormous sign with the logo for *J. C. York & Associates*. Below it was their newly rebranded logo: the simple image of a mountain in silhouette. Below that was a desk with a receptionist.

Kip approached the receptionist and said she was here to see Mr. York. Which one, the receptionist asked. The elder, said Kip, barely missing a beat and masking a strange full-body shiver that sat her trembling down into a chair to wait.

'Your name?' asked the receptionist.

'Kip Flynn.'

'Is Mr. York expecting – ?'

'I met him two nights ago. It's not urgent. He doesn't have to be afraid. I'm just dropping something off.'

'Uh huh?' said the receptionist, and picked up the phone. The boss often dealt with architects, a branch of humanity that, she had observed, was often eccentric and rarely coherent. He was also known to adopt causes that brought unpredictable callers to his door, like abused pets or baby seals. These are, of course, examples of the causes, not the callers, though once the receptionist had faced a man with a parrot on his shoulder and a goldfish in a bowl under his arm. 'Send him in,' the boss had called across the line, excited and impatient. She had therefore long abstained from judgment in the task of ushering courtiers into the old man's presence. He was a passionate hobbyist.

'Kip Flynn to see you, sir.'

A quick interrogative on that other end.

'She says she met you the other night.'

There was a pause. The receptionist looked over at Kip and pursed her lips. 'She says it's not urgent and you do not have to be afraid.'

From behind the big door, Kip thought she could hear a man coughing. It went on for a long time. The receptionist placed her hand over the ear of the phone and waited.

And then another door opened. Off to the side. Another office.

Pat the son appeared. He saw Kip and then it was his turn to be startled, backing out of the room again so fast she wasn't even sure she'd really seen him.

But she realized in an instant she'd gotten what she came for. Shown her face in these echelons. Or was she just chickening out? Decided not to push her luck. She hoisted the sack up onto the counter.

'Don't worry,' she said to the receptionist. 'It's all clean. He'll know what to do with it. Oh, wait. Have you got a piece of paper?'

The receptionist handed her a paper and pen. Kip wrote,

Clean clothes for Mani.

And then she stared at it, wondering what else she might say. She let out an involuntary sob. This wasn't the time to step out of her disoriented numbness. Mortified, she brought her hand up to her mouth as the receptionist flashed her a startled look.

'Sorry,' said Kip. 'Stupid hot dog.'

And then she looked at the sheet again and wrote, by way of further explanation,

Mani doesn't need a suit. He has a natural grace.

And then she wrote,

Unless you feel like getting him one.

And then, because she couldn't tear herself away from being one reading eye away from Mani,

He'll need the rest of it though. He's an alchemist,
he believes in the underworld.

Then she had another thought. Tore off a bit from the end of the sheet and wrote,

I love you, Mani.

And then, as the receptionist looked on, still holding the phone, Kip unzipped the bag, found a pair of jeans and shoved the second note into the front left pocket. Then she looked at the cover note one more time and laid it on top where it could be easily seen. Finally, she carefully zipped up the bag and stepped back, giving the receptionist a no-nonsense look.

The receptionist said, 'You're sure he'll know what to do with this?'

'Absolutely,' said Kip. And then she turned back to the elevator. Pressed the button and waited. She could still hear coughing. Despite the delay, she did not press the button again.

Again! There she was again! Still carrying the eternal sack of laundry! How was it even possible?

And all affecting actions aside (murder, cover-up, rose petals), why did the very sight of her make him so angry?

Desperate deep thinker that he was (shallowly deep? deeply shallow?), Pat York immediately thought of his mother.

It had always hurt him, his mother's death. He had inferred somewhere along the line that he had been a less favoured child than the one who had died. He never knew whether the sister was older than him, or younger, or what, just that she was favoured and she had been a girl. So girls, admittedly, had always enraged him. Plus they were irrational. You couldn't predict their behaviour. And if it was true for girls, it was true for women. His mother being the perfect example. Leaving him in the emergency waiting room at St. Joe's Hospital, getting up to the roof and jumping off. St. Joe's! The least she could have done was pick somewhere more civilized like Mount Sinai, with its soothing water sculpture. Unless the water sculpture wasn't there back then. The least she could have done was to leave him at a McDonald's with a happy meal or she could have left him at a doughnut shop or, god forbid, a daycare centre staffed by nice people who might have smiled at him. Why did she choose St. Joe's hospital? Why the emergency room? Was it her way of saying she was in a state of emergency? If so, then why didn't she give anyone time to do anything about it?

Pat didn't really dwell on the surprise of his mother's act so much as the idea that he had been unable to prevent her from doing it. The fact that he'd been far too young to make a difference was lost on him – after all, was it not the reality of his helpless self that should have been enough to prevent her doing what she did? Eh? Huh?

Whether he intended it or not, his pre-tragedy infancy was a heritage building set up on the stormy spit at the base of his brain stem, top of the spine, and there was a powerful lobby group in there, devoted to preserving it. In other words, he was stunted. He certainly *felt* stunted. Well, and *something* had given him the disposition towards little bouts of epilepsy.

The endless winding and unwinding of speculation regarding his mother's intentions had exhausted so much time in Pat's life. He strove, like a good York, to get past it, in libraries and schoolrooms and when waking from nightmares in pools of sweat. His father would never talk about it, preferring to put forward the brave face of self-repression. 'People do not pity the Yorks,' he said once to Pat, the boy having come home sniffling from an encounter with a schoolyard bully who had said inexplicable things about his family. 'Pay the boy off and put it behind you. It is for smaller men to dwell on the past. Just make sure he understands who is *gerrymandering* whom.'

Still coughing.

Pat'd had to go look up the word *gerrymandering*. Decided, at that point, given it was the only advice he'd ever received from his father, that he would indeed be a gerrymanderer, that he would not dwell on the past, that he would go into the family business of tearing down the old and building up the new.

There was a brief, if inevitable, teenage period of rebellion, when he began to collect and preserve old things – birds, toys, bicycles and other broken things, delicate things. Beautiful things. He once tried to build a replica of Da Vinci's flying machine. And he learned to nurse chicks that had fallen out of nests, with eyedroppers. He stayed with a pair of baby squirrels once, in the hollow of a tree that was in the process of being taken down, feeding them bits of bread sopping with milk. But the cow's milk killed the squirrels. In the end, he realized his only real model was his father. And, sadly, his father's interests lay elsewhere. Don't dwell on the past. Leave that to the experts. People do not pity the squirrels, I mean the Yorks, thought Pat.

This is who he was. Pat York. Son of Cyrus. He defined himself this way, deferring mystery, tragedy, femininity. Essentially half-content. No more, no less.

In the other room, his father had stopped coughing. The cough had not sounded so serious, necessarily, certainly not enough to warrant a spontaneous visit (which might connote an inappropriate tenderness). But he found the silence disturbing. He wondered whether he should check up.

Somehow, the first encounter with this girl, Kip Flynn, on the red carpet of the Princess of Wales had upset his acceptance of things. There was no other explanation for the rage that wracked his fine-boned frame. After all, what did he care about some broken petals of a black rose? He could have just gotten another one. The problem, he realized, thinking it over, was not the rose, but the girl. The zippy unpredictability by which she tried things out to get him to change his mind. What did she think he was? A regular customer? Oh, why don't you go jump off a roof, huh? That might pacify me!

Bitch.

He'd believed that such an unfocused arty type would have been gone by now, the lefty pinkos having long since moved (appropriately) to the West Coast where they'd be free to set up their ashrams on offshore islands and hide their cannabis farms up in the redwood canopies. He'd believed such types were easily dismissible. So why had she not been dismissed? Why had she been paid? Why was she popping up? Like the frigging nightmare jack-in-the-box pierced leather punk she was?

'Anything exciting happen?' Kip, back to the subway platform. 'Collisions? Brawls? Unicycles? Suicides?'

'Nope,' said Lionel. 'You?'

'Not really,' said Kip. 'Got rid of those clothes, though.'

'Salvation Army?'

'Basically.'

'I thought you'd be more sentimental.'

'And let that be a warning to you,' said Kip, as they stood for the car that would take them down around Union Station and back up to the Museum stop. She checked her new pocket watch. It was 9:55 in the morning.

The waiting room was full of women. Real live expectant mothers. With round bellies, little and big.

Perhaps it could be argued that Kip wasn't right in the head, that she was grieving. If she'd had a moment to stop and think, she might have turned her back on this quixotic enterprise. But Kip the entrepreneur was accustomed to making snap decisions and she was committed.

The woman behind the counter said, 'Can I help you?'

Lionel felt the overwhelming impulse to take charge. 'My daughter –'

But Kip interrupted. 'I'm Kip Flynn. I have an appointment for an ultrasound –'

'Have you got your card?' asked the girl.

Kip handed over her hospital insurance card.

'Be advised,' the woman said, 'that the technicians are not authorized to speak to you about your condition. That's up to your obstetrician.'

'Okay.'

And then the girl pointed to a sign on the countertop. 'You can ask your technician about this, though.' The sign said

Take home an image of your ultrasound. Twenty dollars.

'Okay,' said Kip. She didn't have a clear picture in her head of what an ultrasound might look like and whether she would want one. Maybe, though. Maybe.

'Have a seat.'

They sat. Kip looked around the room. There were paintings of elephants on the wall. Four women sat beneath them. Two of them were attended by men in business suits, the third by a more shuffly character. Not unlike Mani except he was still alive. He looked like he was about to run for the nearest fire exit but he was alive. Another man sat alone, presumably waiting for someone who'd gone inside. Kip glanced to her left. Her dad, sitting stoically beside her, gave her a moment's shock. She'd started to imagine Mani there. Picturing him sitting there and smiling like an idiot. Like she was an idiot.

They would have rolled out of bed this morning and he would have said, *You have that appointment.* She would have been unable to believe it. That he cared enough to remember it and remind her even.

Oh no, she thought now. Hold your horses. Let's be realistic. How would the night before really have gone if Mani had been still alive?

They would have been sitting (last night) in the kitchen. And Kip, unable to hold the secret anymore, would have said, 'I have something to tell you.'

And Mani would have said, 'What?'

'I'm pregnant,' Kip would have said.

And then Mani would have been silent for a long time. Kip would have felt a little bit of despair. And then an all-consuming desire to go to sleep. Mani would have said, 'Okay, I'm going then.' And Kip would not have known exactly what he meant: 'I'm going then.' Did the 'then' mean because she was sleeping or because she was pregnant? Did the 'going' mean for the evening or forever? But she would have been brave and said okay and asked no questions, making forgiving assumptions that such things were harder for Mani than most, estranged as he was from any family.

So then she would have climbed the wide stairs to her third-floor room under the roof. Crawled onto the futon on the floor where sleep would have claimed her.

Three hours later, in the middle of the night, she would have woken up, groggy and worried, even though it was pitch dark, that she'd slept too late in the morning and missed her appointment. She'd be staring at her clock, trying to make sense of it, and become gradually aware of a figure sitting in the collapsed armchair near the foot of her bed. Mani.

'What are you doing here?'

'I came back.'

He'd have sat and watched her sleep, protecting her from apartment-stormers, rats, electrical fires, monsters, mobsters, trying to will himself not to mind it. Her pregnancy. That's what would have happened.

Not that he would have encouraged her to keep the baby. No question about that, really. But he would have been concerned for Kip and her health. And that would have been enough. There was no question in her mind that Mani would still be alive right now if she'd had the nerve to spring the news on him a week ago. She would have given him something to think about to derail him from that runaway train of revenge.

But instead he was dead and she was sitting here with her father, intent on keeping the baby. Dead Mani = baby. Living Mani = no baby. It was a hard equation.

Kip's name was called just as a woman was coming out from the hallway. She was carrying a manila envelope with a photograph in it. Pulling it out to take a look. 'That's her,' she said, beaming towards her husband, who was springing up from his chair. Kip caught a glimpse of it. Gravelly and grainy, it looked like a bad black-and-white picture of the inside of a lampshade.

'Maybe I'll go for that,' she said to Lionel, who dug into his pocket, pulled out a twenty and crumpled it gruffly into her hand.

They were met at the door to the hallway by a tall Ukrainian woman in a lab coat who waved goodbye to the envelope woman and then looked askance at Lionel.

'Can he come in with me?' asked Kip. 'He's my father,'

The technician shook her head. 'Is no place for men. Women walking around half naked, you know?'

She had the authority of a doctor. (In fact she was a doctor, her tired eyes told Kip. She had practised in the Ukraine but left for a better life as a lowly technician in Canada, limned with bitterness.)

Lionel walked back to his chair and sat down, giving the thumbs-up to Kip as he looked with great interest at his shoes.

When Kip returned to the waiting room about twenty minutes later, she was escorted by the technician and two security officers. She told Lionel that everything was fine and then she fainted. After which the technician and the security officers explained, sympathetically and patiently, that his daughter had experienced an early miscarriage and had become deluded into thinking she was perhaps still carrying the child. Also that it would probably be necessary for her to seek psychiatric help to deal with her loss.

Lionel, it can be said, was not big on psychiatry. What's more, the sight of his daughter wet-faced and unconscious made something flip over inside him. Something deep and old. Losing a baby. 'This should not happen,' he thought to himself. 'Not to her.'

Deep inside her faint, and this newly bereft and barren feeling, Kip is, once again, thrown back again to the night and the place on Pendrith Street outside the house where J. Cyrus York has been transforming his basement. There is no baby to move her forward, so she has no choice – abetted by a lack of consciousness – but to go back.

She's outside in the dark and the air is cold. She's just been escorted there, by Cyrus York. He's asked if she needs a ride somewhere and she says her bike is there. He's gone back into the house. She looks down at her shoe. Sees an earthworm crawling on it.

Then she sees the worm pickers. Walking the front lawns of those streets north of Bloor. Their fingers in the earth. Prying open the doors of the earth.

It's such a strange vision, she thinks they're not real at first, but they're really there. Appearing around her on the lawns. The worm pickers are so small – smaller even than her – that she thinks they have ascended from the grass. People of the earth. Maybe they met Mani on his way to the Underworld. Then again, maybe not. Their faces are obscured by bright headlamps and the fact that they're looking down. Small buckets are strapped to their ankles, one on each side. Moving quietly over lawns, bent double, half her height in the half-light.

As she watches them, still wondering if what she sees is real, one of them faints, so quietly that the others haven't noticed. Kip approaches and sees her lying pale in the road, fallen off the curb, her eyes partly open. She looks like she's not breathing. The sight scares Kip into action, uttering the word that has been inside her since the blast of the gun. 'Help!' she calls. The worm pickers raise their heads and turned to look at her. Ten or fifteen bright lamps shining in her eyes, lighting her like Beauty onstage at the Princess of Wales Theatre.

They're gathering now, a small army that seems prepared to repel her. She calls out to them, in a loud whisper, gesticulating in an exaggerated downwards point. 'Your friend is sick! We have to call an ambulance!'

Two of them venture closer. They're Asian. Vietnamese, maybe. They're smiling broadly, a manner that is inexplicable to her. She speaks still more quietly. 'Your friend,' she says. 'Your friend,' and points down.

(Kip, lying on the floor of the hospital waiting room, her father holding her, bringing her back around.)

One of the pickers turns and gestures silently to his companions, who move silently to gather up their fallen friend, limp in their arms.

Then the man turns back to Kip. 'Thank you,' he says gently, in heavily accented English. 'You go now.'

The suddenness of her dismissal brings hot tears. 'No!' she says. 'We have to call an ambulance. They'll come look after her.'

' You are kind,' he says. 'But no.'

'But I just want to get her to the –' And then an incoherent G comes out instead of the H for hospital. And then another G, as if she's on the verge of throwing up the alphabet. Her throat is opening and then, to her great mortification, there are sobs. Oh god, she thinks. Not in front of the –

Another sob. And then another. Kip tries to finish her sentence. 'I just want to help her.'

The man is still smiling.

'She could be seriously hurt,' she pleads.

'I will tell her of your concern,' says the man.

'No,' says Kip. 'You don't understand. No. My concern doesn't matter.' And then adds, as if it grants authority, 'I'm pregnant, you know.'

The man looks at her for a moment, unblinking. She doesn't know whether he doesn't understand her or just doesn't know what to say.

'I'll go,' she says. 'I'll call.'

'You go,' says the man, nodding, pointing. 'You call.'

A pay phone must be found. She lacks a cell. Kip runs west to Ossington Avenue, finds one there, but it has been switched off by phone workers in order to discourage nocturnal drug deals. A small poster by the phone explains the strategy. Daytime conversations only. Kip runs another block south and finds one. Calls 911.

By the time she gets back to the place of the fallen worm picker, they're gone. Silence and stillness everywhere, like there's been no small headlamp army and no murder either. Just the sound of Kip out of breath. And then feeling dizzy and not knowing what has happened to her. Like she's been concussed. And then, in the distance, a siren. Rushing towards her, uselessly in the night.

There are some who might question the wisdom of Lionel's decision to take Kip home via streetcar. Certainly Kip herself, if she had been of sound mind, would have insisted on taking a cab. But Lionel felt the streetcar was sleek and safe, and there would be people to come to their aid if they ran into trouble. Much better than rolling the dice on the character of a single cab driver. The streetcar's salient (read: god-like) features also included gliding along at a reasonable distance from gas engines, which was good for Kip's health given her fragile condition, and the indisputable fact that it was a one-stop ride along College Street and over the bridge to his home.

They made it to the building on the bridge without incident, just before one o'clock. Kip wanted to sleep off the shock of her morning.

Lionel would have given her his own bed if not for the painful realization that the couch was cleaner, if not more comfortable. He decided he would head down to the bookstore. He figured he might need the money if it turned out Kip needed some looking after.

So once he heard her sleeping, he slipped out, pausing to consider whether he should leave the door ajar for the cats. Opting to lock it instead.

Lionel was a bit meandery by nature (like Kip when she was in shock but this is the way he was all the time), so instead of getting off at the fire station, which was closest to the bookstore, he disembarked at the top of Augusta and walked down into the Market, past the slightly seedy laundromat and the bicycle shop, Bread and Circus and the pies. Past three punks walking pit bulls. Past a grocer, out for a break, singing a song in Arabic.

He wandered down Augusta practically all the way to Dundas. There was a building burning at the bottom of the street. A bucket brigade was coming out of the laundromat and Lionel could hear the fire trucks coming. No, wait. The building wasn't on Augusta, it was on the other side. He walked down to Dundas and headed past all the Chinese hair salons over to Kensington. What if it was number twelve?

Now he was standing in front of the patio of the Last Temptation, looking up at Kip's apartment windows. Everything was quiet and safe. He could see the smoke rising from behind the building. There was a small house tucked in between the one street

and the other, accessible only by foot. It
was the one that was burning. Despite
the chill in the air, the tables of the
Temp were occupied by three or four
of what he'd come to think of as the
Fidels and the Chés of the Market, with
their cigars and their guitars – men who
were younger than him, self-appointed

guardians of the neighbourhood. Lionel had never done anything
like that, never pledged allegiance to anything larger than himself.
Born between the so-called world wars, right smack in the middle of
the depression, he held on tight to what he already had and figured
he'd never fight anything. Still all coiled potential is how he imagined
it. Wiry readiness. He noted that the great boomer guardians didn't
even know about the fire burning directly behind them.

He suddenly realized Nancy was in the window, waving at him.

'Hello! Mr. Flynn!'

'Oh! Hello!'

He had always liked Nancy. She generally treated him like an old
war hero, even though he'd done nothing to deserve it.

'Were you looking for Kip?' she called now. 'She's not here.'

'No! I was just on my way to work. But are you safe up there?
Shouldn't you maybe – ?'

'Nah,' she said. 'Looks like they've got it under control. Those
developers don't want to cause much damage with their sabotage.'

'That's what you think it is?'

Nancy shrugged. 'We are at war,' she said.

'As long as you're okay,' he said.

'Living the dream,' she said.

Lionel waved goodbye and went up the street. There were fire
trucks there now too, in case the fire spread onto Kensington. A little
spark, probably from some faulty wiring, despite what Nancy said,
and now the city was burning.

He passed within three feet of Pat, who was much more stealthy in his movements this time. Like a cat. Or a paranoid, freaked-out person, which better describes what he was. To wit:

It was the frigging little Market laneway house. Blowing up on this of all days. In the middle of the day, too. He'd only just started to tell himself that it would never happen, that the criminal elements he'd employed were by definition unreliable, that they'd taken the money and forgotten all about it, what a relief, they'd gone about some other more lucrative criminal enterprise; after all, they must have seen that Pat could not be serious, that he was scared, that he was just a source of free money and stupid ideas, not to be taken seriously, a stunted boy who could not help but think everyone around him was older, more grown-up, weightier, more experienced and deserving of moving through the world. And so now Pat was even more a lawbreaker than he'd been before. But he didn't want to be a lawbreaker, damnit. Aside from the ethical drawbacks, it brought so much stress! No wonder they called it a break. Broken things can be fixed, but they'll never again be like they were when they were new. Old stresses piled onto new stresses: deaths and cover-ups and blow-ups and maybe more deaths.

He'd been pushed up through the city towards this neighbourhood, couldn't help himself, felt compelled to see the damage he'd done, coiling 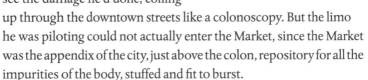 up through the downtown streets like a colonoscopy. But the limo he was piloting could not actually enter the Market, since the Market was the appendix of the city, just above the colon, repository for all the impurities of the body, stuffed and fit to burst.

Anyway, he could not ignore the story after hearing about it on the limo's radio. Fire in the Market. He'd been following his father's ambulance, so the decision had to be made to divert the driver over and have a little look-see. He'd gotten out at the corner of Dundas and Spadina and walked over and up. The very soul of discretion.

And then, just as if he had foreseen it: there was the crazy AC girl again! In her window! Like a spectre created from his own fight-and-flight brain, sent to punish him with her sneaky sentence of death. Sure, okay, she didn't see him, he'd pressed himself against the wall of the ugly-golf-shirt store, like a decal, but her very presence was like a nail bitten too short. Lucky for him that her roaming, all-seeing eye was focussed on one old man in the street. Pat pretended to shop, though he didn't know the first thing about how to do it and ended up regarding his own reflection in the store window as he moved close enough to listen to the end of the conversation, close enough to transform his anxiety into a kind of exultant indignation. Finally, *finally,* he realized, as the girl disappeared and the old man started walking up the street, he might be able to regain some balance. Zippy Kip Flynn had met his father. Now he had a chance to meet hers. Sure, J. C. York was likely getting pulled out of the back of the ambulance right at this moment. But Pat would get there, he just had an errand to run.

So, then: up through the Market, past coloured bolts of cloth, hand-painted signs, the door to a broken bank machine, ugly dogs, ugly people, incomprehensible fashions, criminally implicated businesses, stinking fish and garbage – urban dinosaurs, all soon to be gone, replaced by the finer things in life.

Two

NOT PRISON
BUT
A MEMORY

1

Kip woke up on Lionel's couch, having dreamt that Mani had left her. She checked the pocket watch, angling it to catch the light over the tracks outside: 4 a.m. She'd slept for fifteen hours. Should she not be working? Had she missed any appointments? Should she not be providing for the baby?

Oh yeah, there was no baby.

Still, she was worried about money. She was going to have to get up to something. Maybe return to the rooftop with its vat of tar. The black roses, the goth bars. She'd have to get started before her savings got too low – she needed cash to invest in fresh roses. Resolved to get up first thing and zip around the city for supplies.

And then she remembered. The bikes. Hers and Mani's locked together up near Pendrith Street. Corner of Christie. The image was bleak. Like the bikes themselves were lonely. She tried to recall the manner in which they were locked together. Was it her lock or did Mani use a lock too? Did Mani even have a lock? It was something she felt she should remember, but she didn't. With such small details already slipping, when was she going to lose his face? His eyes? Only a matter of time.

The thought inspired a vigilance of memory that brought her right to her feet.

And so she dressed in the dark and pulled on a wool hat for the spring cold. She tiptoed through the apartment and looked into her father's room, saw Lionel lying spread-eagled across the bed in his clothes.

'You're the champ,' she whispered.

Then she headed out into a night where there was no trace of dawn on the horizon and no evidence that it would ever come. She walked up Sterling. Past the looming shadows of the chocolate factory.

A starling was awake with her. Tree to tree, the bird followed Kip up through the old factory district, twittering past the silent pits and backhoes, and the tallest condoized industrial building in the city.

Then, far away to the east, Kip heard another starling answer the call. They started to go back and forth. The duet felt insistent, like they were worried the connection would be broken if one of them was going to have to travel through the tunnel of the wind. Maybe he would lose his way. So they stayed as they were, ramrod in their trees, calling back and forth with swelling throats. Kip kept walking and left the sound behind.

Up at Bloor Street, she jogged over and continued up Symington to Wallace Avenue. Zigzagged her way east along the short, quiet streets. When she crossed Dufferin Street she saw a car coming towards her from the north. Otherwise nothing. She overshot Pendrith Street. Came out to Christie above her destination and headed south.

The bikes were there at the corner. Locked to the signpost that said PENDRITH above. Kip's lock holding the front wheels and the frames. Mani's holding the back wheels.

Kip stood in the dark and stared at the bikes. Mani's was unlabelled and black with wide city wheels. Kip's was dorky – a powder blue girl's bike with big narrow wheels that let her go fast but were bad for catching streetcar tracks, which sent her flying.

A newspaper was blowing slowly towards her on the sidewalk. It seemed to be deliberately approaching her. She caught it in her fingers and picked it up. The headline read KENSINGTON MARKET TO BE TORN DOWN. It made her heart stop. It was from an inside fold, not even front-page news. Didn't make any sense. She'd only been away for a day. How was it even possible? She looked closer. Was that a picture of Nancy holding a placard?

No. It only looked like Nancy.

Then she noticed it was a British paper. *The Guardian Weekly.* Another Kensington Market, somewhere across the pond, was going to close down. Well, that was a relief. Nice to know there was another Nancy though, somewhere, taking up the cause.

Standing on empty Christie. Looked up at the sign again. Pendrith.

She decided to go look at the house. Wondering about Mani. *Where is Mani?*

She started heading down the street.

There was a – what was that? A white SUV parked at the curb. Only it was a limo. An SUV limo. Parked on Pendrith Street. She'd seen these cars before. Bullshitting their way along Queen Street on a Saturday night. Sometimes Nancy would whip off her shoes and go dance on top of one. Kip standing in the street and taking in her friend's brazenness with awe and fear, ready to run but unwilling to abandon her. All quiet below too, behind the tinted windows, until Nancy finally heard the sirens and they ran together. This one was far from its natural habitat. It was silent and still, but something told her it had only recently been running. She could sense the heat coming off it.

As she walked towards the vehicle, its front headlights came on, as if bidden by its own quiet mind. Startled her as they went dark again. Leaving splotchy stains inside her eye. She thought she might turn around, head back to Christie and walk south. But that, she knew, would give away what she was feeling. So she reached up and cocked her wool hat right down over her left eye. A tactic for dicey situations. Make yourself look slightly unstable mentally, and even marginal characters will leave you alone.

She walked past the front wheels and started to traverse the length of the vehicle. She was as silent as a cat and tried not to breathe or pick up speed.

And then, as she passed the front doors, one of the tinted windows began to roll down, revealing a curling forelock. Then a sleek, symmetrical scar. Puffy eyes. That was new. She didn't have time to ponder their meaning.

'May I ask you something?'

He was sitting in the front passenger seat. There was no one on the driver's side. Kip kept walking and tried to think of something nice. Despite being freaked out, she succeeded in conjuring Henry. Of all people! She'd parted poorly with him. Shouldn't treat people like that.

'Are you really going to pretend you can't hear me?'

Still she kept walking. She was passing the rear of the vehicle.

'Can you at least tell me what I'm supposed to do with all this garbage?' The tone was unstable, shifting between exasperation and self-pity.

Kip stopped. Turned to look. He was holding up the bag with Mani's laundry.

'It's not garbage,' she said. And then firmly, 'It's clean clothes for Mani.'

'I know,' said Pat. 'I read the note.'

He was mocking her.

'Most people get to be buried in decent clothes, you know,' she said, barely able to compose herself. 'A suit and a tie, maybe even a flower in their hand.'

'Like a rose, maybe?' said Pat. 'A black rose? That's maybe true in some cases, but not so much when they're buried in an old landfill somewhere, run by some corrupt old so-and-so with a long history of making things disappear.'

Kip was so shocked, she forgot to be afraid. What's more, the son had said this with a touch of loathing, as if he disapproved of it himself.

'He's in a place like that?' she asked.

'What else did you expect?'

'Someone will find him.'

'No,' said Pat. 'They won't. Unless of course they hear it from you.'

'I won't tell,' said Kip, remembering the old man's threats.

'Then no one will find him. People don't like to root around this particular landfill. It puts the cancer in your bones.'

'Anyway,' said Kip, trying to regain the upper hand, 'I didn't give those clothes to you. I gave them to your father.'

'My father's dead,' said Pat.

The sound of her own numb grief arriving from elsewhere gave her pause. For a moment it felt like she'd actually said these words herself, found herself imagining Lionel laid out in a brown suit. A sob came up. She bore down and swallowed it hard.

'Yes, that's right,' Pat went on. 'He was an old man. So when unpredictable things happen –'

Kip interrupted. 'You mean like killing someone?'

'I mean,' he continued, 'when a crazy fucking girl shows up at his office with laundry earmarked for someone he shot in self-defence, it puts a strain on the old ticker.'

'You're blaming me then?' She could hardly believe her ears.

'I am, actually,' said Pat.

'Fuck you,' said Kip.

She turned.

Pat went on. 'And this laundry bullshit is the kind of stunt that makes me question whether you're even taking any of this seriously.'

'I take the death of my friend very seriously,' said Kip, still turned away. 'Thank you so much.'

'Good then,' said Pat. 'So, that means you haven't told, for example, your insane flatmate.'

Looking back at him. 'What do you know about my flatmate?'

'I know she's insane.'

'I don't know what you're talking about.'

'I know the day before yesterday she tried to drop an air conditioner on my head.'

(So Nancy had gone to the window. Of course she had.)

Pat continued: 'She was reflected in the window of a car parked on the street. One of my thousands of urban supporters and allies.'

'Cars?'

'Yes. And then I looked directly up at her while she was preoccupied with trying to get the unit onto the windowsill.'

'Maybe she was installing it,' said Kip.

'A little early in the season, don't you think?'

'I didn't tell her anything.' Desperate now, not wanting to widen the circle of threat. 'You don't know her. She would do that to anyone who doesn't belong in the Market. She loves the Market. She's its great defender and you want to tear it down.'

'And I'm supposed to believe you didn't give her ammunition against me?'

'No,' said Kip. 'I mean yes. No, I didn't.'

'Well good, because you might be interested to know I went back there yesterday and saw her again. She was waving to an old man. I think it was your father.'

The circle of threat had just expanded to encompass the world.

'Why would you think it was my father?' she said.

'Oh … something about how your insane flatmate said, "Hello, Mr. Flynn," when he arrived and, "Goodbye, Mr. Flynn," when he left. Something like that. And then, you might be interested to hear, he walked up through the Market and into a quaint little bookstore where I presume he was working.'

'You followed him?'

'Not inside,' said Pat. 'He looks like an old man too. I don't know, it's just a guess, but I would venture that his heart would not respond well to unpredictable events either.'

'You're threatening my father?' said Kip.

'I'm threatening you, actually,' said Pat. 'You moron. I'm simply trying to confirm that you haven't told anybody so far about this situation, and to ensure you don't in future.'

'I haven't told anyone,' said Kip. 'I won't.'

She wondered whether the fact that she had told her father nearly everything was blinking like neon on her forehead.

But Pat relaxed a bit. He leaned his arm against the laundry bag as it hung half out the window. 'Look,' he said, 'I understand as much as you do that this is a complete mess.'

'What I don't understand,' said Kip, 'is why you people didn't just call the police?'

'That bullet,' said Pat, 'was never meant for a flower seller at the Princess of Wales.'

It almost sounded like an apology. Caught her off guard, a potential comeback suddenly stuck in her throat.

'Hold on,' he said now, registering her emotion. 'I'm just going to get out of the car.'

He shoved the laundry bag out the window. It flopped into the road like a beanbag chair as he opened the door and got out. She stood her ground. Glanced up. His silver jacket had gotten creased and he looked like he needed a bath in that way well-groomed people do when they have a hair out of place.

'Here's the thing,' he said, standing before her in the dark street, hands on hips, strangely cut down to size. 'I've got a lot of work to do. All my father's business falls to me. So I don't really have time for this. But I have no wish for his bad decision to be hanging over my head for the rest of my life. The truth is, it troubles me to allow him to squander a legacy that was meant for me, just because he had a moment of sentimental madness.'

'I have no idea,' said Kip, 'what you could possibly mean by *sentimental*.'

'By *sentimental*, I mean that he was a bit dotty and I suspect if you'd been a man he would have just shot you too.'

'So it's sentimental to kill one and not two?'

'It's sentimental,' said Pat, 'to kill the *man* and then give the *woman* an unbelievable amount of hush money. It's far more sentimental, when you think about it than, for example, the thought of a girl making a killer deal over her boyfriend's dead body.'

'That,' said Kip, 'was not my idea.'

'But you were eager to go along with it.'

'I don't want your money.'

'Then give it back,' said Pat.

Guh! Was that what this was about?

'How about I give that money back,' she said, 'if you call the police?'

'It's too late for that,' said Pat. 'Anyway, how is it even possible to report the death of a non-person? Your friend had no status, no SIN card, no birth certificate, nothing; he was clearly not supposed to be in this country, much less this city with its immigration freeze.'

But Kip wasn't listening; she was following her own path. 'You could just tell them it was all your father.' Thinking she could see a way out of her numb limbo. 'Maybe you didn't even witness it. I could testify –'

'I don't put a price on my loved ones,' said Pat. 'I don't sell people off a pushcart like they were flimsy black roses.'

'Those roses weren't flimsy,' said Kip, finally getting a topic that had no grey area. 'They were good.'

'The one you gave me was flimsy.'

'Well, I would have given you another one,' she said, furious, 'if you'd given me a half a second! Or I could have given you your money back and you could have gone and got one of the plastic ones you liked so much better.'

'Those were plastic?'

'Yes! They were plastic, you fucking moron!'

She felt an almost absurd level of satisfaction for calling him on his poor taste in merch, not to mention calling him a moron when he had called her a moron earlier. 'I don't really want your money,' she said. 'But I'm not giving it back to you. Maybe I'll take it all out and burn it!'

'I think you'll take it all out and spend it.'

'Are we done?' asked Kip.

'I guess so.' Pat shrugged.

Kip turned to go.

'Oh,' he called after her. 'You might want this.'

Against her better judgment, she turned to look. He was holding up something that glimmered in the streetlight, dangling from his finger: bicycle key, tied to a shoelace. Oh yes. Mani had been wearing it around his neck.

She wished she could let it go, but she couldn't.

Pat didn't move, so she began to close the gap between them. It was only ten or twelve steps. The key was dangling from his right hand. Something about that seemed significant but she could not say what it was. As she reached across to take it, he put his left hand on her arm, like he was going to detain her.

Kip felt a kindle of electric rage like she'd never felt in her life before.

The wish to detain *him*.

She'd never hit anyone before. But her fist came up from her side like a fin whale's breach and connected with the front of his mouth. She felt the lip split between her knuckle and his tooth. Violence. Her own mouth opened in awe at what she'd done. And her right fist was already curled, fingers up, at her side, to strike another blow.

Pat felt rage too, though he wasn't accustomed to violence either. Still, he was a little man and could move fast. He blocked her second blow as his other fist swung around, elbow out like the wing of a baby bird, and bashed her ear.

In a moment, they were flailing at each other.

It was more or less a fair fight.

'Hey, fucker,' she said, as the ringing in her ear subsided in the adrenalin rush, 'you killed my boyfriend.'

'You killed my father,' he said.

'Bullshit,' she said. 'That's such BULLSHIT! Your father died because it's hard on the heart to kill someone!'

'What would an arty huckster like you know about matters of the heart?'

He hit her in the face. She hit him in the face. They both gave up the difficult task of blocking. She pulled up her knee and tried to kick him in the stomach. She missed and hit the front of his thigh. It hurt him though, and he staggered towards her, losing balance. She had pitched forward too, the force of her own kick throwing her off balance. They nearly banged heads. At the last moment, he pulled up, fist hidden below his head, and clocked her in an uppercut to the chin.

The force of it knocked her back, onto the grass of one of the houses of Pendrith Street. She saw stars, many more than could be seen from the city.

Then he was on top of her and her voice was just about to come out in a scream. He saw it too, and clapped his hand over her mouth. So she bit his hand, the flesh below his baby finger. Her teeth broke the skin, and she held on as he made quiet, grunting pain sounds. She refused to let go, even as she got the unpleasant taste of blood in her mouth, even as he rained blows down on her head with his other hand, fists and slaps and pain given back in equal measure.

But something else was happening too.

They'd been at it for no more than thirty or forty seconds. Kip thought her peripheral vision was playing tricks on her, but she suddenly felt the presence of witnesses. Padding the periphery on quiet feet. Did the city have ghosts?

No. These feet were living, set apart, strapped with tin cans. And they were everywhere, all around her, on the grass.

The worm pickers made short work of pulling the man off the woman. There were too many of them to fight against. Several bright beams were illuminating their little ring of grass and curb and asphalt. Pat tried to shield his eyes, but his arms were being held.

'Hey man,' he said. 'She hit me first. Mind your own business.'

'Our business,' said a voice. 'We collect worms. You a worm.'

It was the man Kip had spoken to before.

As soon as Pat was off her, Kip was up in a flash and out in the street. Pat managed to pull his captors around with him as he turned to keep her in his sights.

'I want my fucking money back,' he said.

'What?' Kip said. 'So you can get away with murder?'

Held back by many arms, Pat mustered a new level of eloquence: 'You think that was murder? That was nothing, lady. I am the long arm of this city. I am the force that makes this city rise.'

'What the fuck does that mean?'

'It means that if I have to plough under a few assholes and plunge my rebars through your chest, and your boyfriend's, and your father's, and your roommate's −'

'Oh, now my roommate's?'

'The more the merrier, ladybird! The more the merrier!'

Ladybird?

Kip was being held back now too. Everyone was breathing heavily, damp from their exertions and the dew. Now she lunged forward from their grip and spit in Pat's face. And then she tried to pull back again. Pat leaned back against his scrum of captors and thrust out his foot, tripping her as she reeled away. Their two bodies came into contact again with such force that everyone got yanked out of their handholds. Kip twisted, in free fall, and dove headfirst to the asphalt, bounced up for a moment of dizziness, feeling the blood spit from her chin, and then went down again, blacking out.

She came to just outside Toronto Western Hospital, on the grass, soon after sun-up, warm spring morning, beside three orderlies on a smoke break. Mani's laundry bag was beside her. The orderlies were flipping a coin to decide who would be responsible for checking her in.

She came to again in a room. A male nurse shaking her awake. He was giving her a bottle to pee into, pointing to the bathroom.

She picked up the bottle and rolled out of bed. Nearly tripped on the laundry bag. She was dizzy and her body was very sore. Her face in the mirror was a shock. Anti-gravity hair and a double gash on her chin that had the texture of asphalt.

She woke again, back in the bed, to another doctor telling her he was going to put three stitches into her chin. The freezing needle brought her right back to her senses, pushing the mudslide back out through the broken window, its sharpness making her think of the kind of people who excavated rivers and built cities, killed lovers and disposed of their bodies.

The stitching was swift.

'Any idea who brought you here?' the doctor asked.

She shook her head. Felt something move around her neck. Reached up and felt a key tied to a string. No idea. She'd missed it during her trip to the bathroom, distracted by the gorgon in the mirror, had to wait until the doctor was done. Then she squinted down towards it, pushing her tender chin into her neck.

It was Mani's bicycle key, tied to a shoelace.

Worm pickers. Strange allies.

At one point, she heard a TV playing. She looked up and saw that there was one in her room. Another bed with an old woman in it, groaning quietly to herself. The TV was playing a documentary about the Galapagos. That's what I'll do, Kip thought. I'll escape to the Galapagos and carve a door into the back of a turtle. Lie low for a while. Maybe Mani's already there. Maybe he just forgot to tell me.

And then her reverie was interrupted by a spectre in the hallway. Pat York. Hitting her like another freezing needle in her chin, really a shadow flickering past the door.

He had not seen her. Kip felt fear as deep as the sub-basement. Perhaps it was her frailty, the concussion, but she was thinking this man was trying to *own* her.

Maybe she hadn't just 'sold' Mani, as this man asserted. Maybe she'd also sold herself.

She was up in her hospital clothes and over to the doorway without even knowing she'd done it. Away from all thought, her spine peered around the corner. Pat had reached the end of the hall and was turning around. Kip's lizard brain was all readiness, news from her eyes bypassing everything to get to it, sparking like bad wiring. He had a bouquet of flowers. She was feeling dizzy. If a forest of flowers were covering the earth, she could hide there, everywhere, just by ducking and crawling.

But the flowers didn't cover the earth. There were just a few, plucked and dying in his fist.

He grew.

Now her brain was all jaw, hanging open, like a backhoe in the off hours. She failed to step back into her room.

Pat turned and saw her. Raised an arm. Cain. Called out. 'Hey!'

The end of Kip's hospital stay.

Later, when the nurse came into the room, he found the bed empty and a couple of dozen roses beside it. The ninety-year-old woman from the next bed was sitting in a chair. She looked up and startled the nurse with a sweet smile. 'Roses,' she said, nodding and pointing. 'Beautiful.'

The nurse went over to the main desk and asked what they'd done with the girl in room 314.

'We didn't move her anywhere,' said the head nurse. 'She should still be in there.'

'Oh,' said the floor nurse. 'It's just, there's a bouquet of roses in there. They don't seem to be for her.'

'Why not?'

'Because we never contacted anyone for her.'

'Maybe she contacted someone herself.'

'But she was concussed. Plus she's got no cell and there's no phone in the room. And she's been asleep for most of the –'

'Maybe she contacted someone before.'

'Before she was concussed?'

'Well, someone must have brought her here.'

'She got dumped on the front lawn.'

'That's true. What does the note say?'

'No note.'

'Well, if it's true she's gone,' said the head nurse, 'it's hallelujah time. We need the bed.'

Kip could barely walk at first. Dizzy. The air around her was full of specks and atoms. She'd grabbed the bag and her clothes, but her dis-orientation had sent her through a door in the hospital that wasn't the exit. It was a storeroom for clothes, she'd stood and stared at the shelves for a minute and then she'd dropped everything and changed into a doctor's green scrubs. There were shoes there too. She put them on. Normally, she would never have presented herself with this kind of bland uniformity, it would have caused a shock to her system. But now all she was doing was externalizing it. Anyway, she'd be more anonymous this way.

Outside the hospital, she headed south, crossing Dundas Street, laundry bag hoisted over her shoulder. Through the speckled atoms, she was planning an exit strategy on the fly. Implementing it already.

By the time she hit the next block, going south, her hips and her head were used to the movement, and she no longer had the feeling that something was going to get shaken out of her. She was feeling positively feral. Continued to speed up until she was running. Heading south towards Queen Street, and further south over the tracks, past the highways, towards the beaches and the marshes and the islands.

2

Like some of her activist compatriots, Nancy felt both love and hate for her deep-cover job as a buttoned-up downtown tour guide on a faux British bus. Surrounded by tower cranes, portables and luffers and new condo buildings caked with glittering shit, she sought to keep the edge of her passion keen by riding daily through the carnage with a courtier's smile. Fresh losses were still in her mind: the new building on Front Street where another eighteenth-century ship had been uncovered during excavation, like the one cited in a popular old novel from which Nancy had derived no consolation. Or the hotel condominium whose parking lot dig had exposed five Georgian houses from the early nineteenth century, built by a butcher. In both cases, a month or two had been provided

to archaeologists before the cranes were planted, crushing these delicate artifacts with their monster footprints, developers saying *I'm sorry but, look, if you want to see history you might consider taking a vacation in London …*

It bothered her, too, that Kip – despite ushering her into the activist environment in which she had grown and thrived in the past couple of years – would not support the cause in any more than a half-hearted way. On their trip to the semi-reconstructed ruins of Guildwood Park, she'd explained to Kip that it required little people like them to speak up or else nothing would be done. Kip was a perfect example, Nancy said, since she was a psychogeographer of the first order.

'I don't know what that is,' Kip had said.

'Just the other night, you got me to do a waltz with you in the drying cement of that sidewalk. And then you carved the dotted lines between the steps so other people would be able to follow them.'

'They covered that over the next day,' said Kip.

'But you tried,' said Nancy. 'Your aim was to draw people off the beaten track, get them to waltz on the sidewalks.'

'It was more for a laugh,' said Kip. 'Not a statement.'

'Buildings aren't like clothes,' said Nancy. 'You can't open vintage stores when all the fashions change.'

'People do what they want to do,' said Kip.

Now Kip was at the side of the road, looking like the only row house left on a knocked-down street, imprints from the fallen buildings still clinging to her sides. She was dressed in weird green clothes. And Crocs! And there was something wrong with her chin. She didn't look like herself. And she was toting her big laundry bag full of clothes. Nancy would only ever dress in such a hideously comfortable way if she knew she was going on a long bus ride, but this was even more extreme: she'd never seen Kip out of uniform. Could she be going on a trip? Nancy got the driver to open the doors and Kip climbed on, sat down in Nancy's single seat at the front of the bus, dropping the sack at her feet. She had stitches in her chin.

'Ladies and gentlemen,' said Nancy, suppressing her curiosity and speaking into the microphone. 'Who can tell me the name of the building to our left?'

Most of them were staring at the newcomer. Still, one or two put up their hands. Nancy pointed and got an answer.

'Courthouse, very good. Ten points. Old City Hall. Great example of the nineteenth-century Romanesque Revival.' She glanced down briefly at Kip, who kept looking sidelong out the window, one way and then the other, as if she was looking for someone.

Nancy continued her spiel. 'Made the news in the twenties when the jaw fell off a gargoyle, crashed through the roof and nearly killed an elected representative of our fair city. The building had replaced another city hall and was itself replaced by another before that one was replaced with the fake futuristic shark tank we're passing now, which itself replaced a huge, vibrant neighbourhood that politicians who called themselves *of the people* declared a slum: St. John's Ward.

Ahem. Ten points to anyone who can guess with any accuracy what style of building will replace this one.'

She realized the comment was more pointed than usual, guessed she was trying to impress Kip.

She paused, waiting for takers. There were none, so she went on. 'We'll be heading south in a moment. Thomas, your driver, will fill you in on some of the sights.'

She handed the mic to the driver and then squeezed in beside Kip, who had been looking at her shoes.

'Right here, on your left,' said Thomas, 'we have a beautiful example of the vintage Morrow tower crane, standing for nearly eight months now.'

Kip felt her friend slide in beside her but could not look into her face. She wished, not for the first time in these last few days, that she could be a cyborg instead of a human. Or a dancing building like the one she'd seen in the newspaper. A dancing building didn't have to be afraid, love, grieve or destroy friendships out of fear. A dancing building didn't even have to fear the wrecking ball, since it was a full-fledged tourist attraction.

'Are you okay?' asked Nancy. 'What happened to your chin?'

'Coming out of the bass case,' Kip lied.

Nancy, relieved: 'Oh yeah, that's right. I thought that might have been a bad idea.'

Kip got straight down to the unpleasant business of bridge-burning.

'Did you give Mani a gun?' she asked.

'I ... ' said Nancy. 'What do you mean, did I – ?'

'It's a pretty simple question.'

Nancy stuttered. 'Guns are hard to get.'

'Did you?'

'Um,' said Nancy. 'I – I ... You were going into a very dangerous –'

'So you did.' Kip was nodding, bleakly, mouth hanging open, lower lip drooping like a fish's. 'You got him a gun.'

Nancy was blushing, two sides of her personality coming into collision. 'It was just a pop gun.'

'But it looked real, didn't it.'

'Well, the Mies tower looks like the Seagram Building, but it's not, is it.'

Kip looked back down at her shoes in disgust.

Nancy felt sorry. 'Why?' she asked. 'What happened?'

'Nothing,' said Kip, shrugging and laughing a bit. 'Nothing happened. They were very nice is what happened. They were understanding.'

Nancy was trying to think. There was too much information coming at her. She was glued at the shoulder to her friend in the little seat but they were divided by a pit – two buildings on the bereft block, not just one – speaking in low tones, with their heads down, as Thomas the driver spoke something into the microphone about the view of the stadium.

'You,' she stuttered, 'you got caught?'

'Yeah, they caught us,' said Kip. 'And Mani had a gun.'

'Well, if they caught you, then they found out it was a pop gun.'

'I'm moving out,' said Kip, moving to the next level.

'You're –' Now Nancy wasn't sure she'd heard right. 'You're –'

'Yeah. It's too dangerous up on the third floor, um, firetrap, and it's all going to get expropriated soon anyway. For building projects or whatever. I don't want to live there anymore.'

She paused, still looking at her shoes.

'Look,' said Nancy, after spluttering a bit. 'I'm really sorry about the gun. Maybe it was a stupid idea, like, an overreaction kind of thing. I shouldn't have got involved.'

'No, you shouldn't have.'

'But Mani was keen, so –'

'He's not keen anymore,' said Kip.

'But is he okay, is he –?'

'He's fine,' said Kip. 'He's fine.'

Nancy said, 'Okay, so, but I'm wondering if we could just talk about this when we get ho–'

'I'm not coming home,' said Kip. And then she headed into the planned statement. 'You should know, though, that the main reason is because I'm going to have a baby and I don't want you and this city or anyone in it to be a bad influence on my baby. We're going to move to the country. Mani and me. Leaving today.'

Nancy didn't hear for a moment. Her eyes nearly turned into whirling rainbows. Then:

'I'm starting to think you're not okay.'

'I am okay.'

'But your chin. Could you be concussed, or – ?'

'No,' said Kip. 'That's nothing. I've never been more clear.'

'Maybe I …' Then Nancy forgot what she was going to say for a sec. 'Maybe you're just panicking or something. You say you're going to have a baby? That's great, but that's no reason to … You're going to hate it out there. Have you ever even been outside the city?'

'No,' said Kip, 'but –'

'You're going to hate it. There's nothing there. Nothing and no one! You'll go totally broke too. I mean, who's going to want to buy your snot hankies or your –'

Kip interrupted her. 'I don't give a shit about my snot hankies.' She paused. 'I'm going to start making baby things.'

'For who?' Nancy asked, too loud, causing everyone on the bus to swing their noses around from the windows and look at her. 'The trees?'

'Baby people move out there,' said Kip. 'Into houses. Big houses that are cheap.'

'Out into the vast emptiness of the country? All that nothingness and ennui and right-wing ideology?'

'It's just a mirror to say that,' said Kip. 'It's not real.'

Thomas was turning onto Front Street now. If she didn't get back to the microphone pretty soon he was going to be pissed and she was going to be out of a job.

For her part, Kip was proving she had always listened when Nancy held forth about the kind of person she hated the most. The city fleer, the abandoner – the person like the people Nancy grew up with, who bred. Kip was using all that information against her.

'I'll have neighbours,' she said. 'I'm sure it will be news to them that they're not there. I'm sure they'll have good values.'

Good values. The *coup de grâce*. Nancy would either have to burst out laughing or go all in.

'Well, good luck with the good values,' she said. 'I wish you luck in your flight from urban life. I see you've already got your gardening shoes. Good luck too, holding on to Mani. The first winter will probably bury you both. They'll find you in the spring, rotting by the woodpile.'

'I will hold on to Mani,' said Kip, with low force now. 'Neither you nor this city are going to swallow him up.'

'Okay, so let me get this straight then,' said Nancy. 'You're not even coming home.'

'I've already got my bus ticket,' said Kip. 'Meeting him at the station.'

'And you're all packed too, I see.'

The ubiquitous laundry sack.

'I am.'

'Fucking Mani,' said Nancy. 'What a fucking wuss. So what am I supposed to do with all your shit?'

'You can do whatever you please,' said Kip, trying not to think of her books and her clothes and her dog-eared letters from Mani, 'with all that shit.'

'Thomas,' said Nancy, standing up and swinging around the pole in the floor so she was facing the driver. 'Could you let my friend out please? She's got a bus to catch.'

She took the microphone and did not look at Kip again. Kip got off the bus, already beginning to shake. Nancy didn't notice. She was striving to pull herself together, tears rolling down her face, gearing up for the flatiron building, the train station, the invisible fucking nineteenth-century ship.

'So,' she said into the microphone, slipping into a fake Southern drawl, 'where do y'all come from? New York State? Buffalo? Well, yer a real patient, polite bunch of people.'

Kip ran. Fear is a great motivator. A friendship destroyed, the loss of a home, destruction of memory: she was doing away with all her shelters just when she needed them. Whereas Henry's bass case had given her the feeling of being more confined than she'd ever felt in her life, here in the street she felt cracked open. She was going to have to get used to it. Maybe it was a good feeling. At least it lined up with her invisible grieving. Maybe that would finally spill out, putting an end to the numbness. She was embracing her own obliteration; maybe it would bring her closer to the dead.

She suddenly remembered reading about an architectural notion called 'negative space.' Essentially, the space between buildings, it's the area of the world you travel through when you're on your way some-where. Everything that isn't architecture. If the horizontal were ver-tical, then you'd be falling through it, under the influence of gravity, and you might hit a ledge or two on the way down, maybe get a little banged up, but you wouldn't stop until you landed at your destination.

Your destination, naturally, is known as 'positive space': your home, the office, the library or the movie theatre, the bloody pulp of your body on the asphalt, or the bar where you're meeting your friends.

Kip knew, for the unforeseeable future, that negative space was the space she would be occupying. She took a moment to try and feel what it was like. Came to a stop just past the corner of Front Street and something.

She felt the people keep moving around her, felt them establish themselves in opposition to her, as if she'd become just another ledge in their free fall. Felt how difficult it was to stop when everyone else was going. Felt the left side of her head start to buzz, for a moment or two. Felt her vision blur.

She thought, *My body is shutting down?*

She thought, *I'm just going to wait this out.*

For her fellow travellers it was as if she had suddenly defied gravity, halted in mid-air. The laundry sack made her an even greater impediment than what she would otherwise have been. Someone, feeling inconvenienced, mumbled, 'You people are selfish.' Kip had

the presence of mind to wonder what he meant by 'you people':
Statues? Medical patients? Delusionals? Architects? Hucksters?
Grievers? Fuzzy thinkers? Flynns?

She thought, *I have to keep moving.*

And then she did, falling again through the negative space.
Swung down further south to Queen's Quay. Eventually she looked
up. Saw seagulls, herons, mallards, geese, monarchs, sailboats,
canoes, cattails, swans, a single filthy cormorant with its wobbly tail,
up and down; they were all swooping through negative space too.
What was up there? The sky. Nothing so hard about living in the sky.
Kip could do it too, as long as she kept moving.

A small-engine airplane was hovering up there too. Who was the
pilot in there? Now she had the sense of someone's eye on her. Being
watched from above.

She threw the bag clear and hurled herself into the reeds.
Wondered if anyone saw. Anyway, there was no one around down
here. She decided to stay put for a while.

3

Did you know that the CN Tower follows the precepts of the Golden Section? Perhaps you don't know what that is. It's an ancient system of proportions. A ratio of thirteen to eight, combining the principles of a circle to a symmetrical triangle within a square. Often, it's applied to a rectangular building where the height is eight and the breadth is thirteen. But in the case of the tower, it's divided in a straight line: thirteen from the base up to the observation deck, eight from

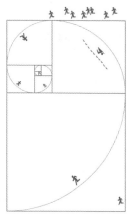

the viewing deck up to the top point. When you render it geometrically, it becomes an ever-widening spiral like the one pictured on this page, albeit usually without the little Kip figure fleeing from the centre to the periphery. Bisected squares of eight as portions of rectangles of thirteen. It's depicted this way to show how architecture elides with the spirals of nature, and thus with nature itself. It's how Kip perceived her own thoughts, made up on one spiralling Golden Section after another, for some time. To wit:

Over the next few months – the negative-space phase of Kip's existence – only two things of note took place.

The first was finding a public washroom with an outlet so she could shave off her dreads with electric clippers she'd stolen from the inside ledge of a barbershop. The proprietor of the shop saw her make the grab but decided not to chase her down even though he'd had the clippers since the sixties – powder blue and designed like a Eldorado Cadillac – because, well, for one thing he was old, but also he had just made the decision to sell the shop and knew in his heart that within two months it would be transformed into a neo meat-and-potatoes restaurant with passersby exclaiming enthusiastically, *'I can't even remember what was here before!'*

In short, the barber would spend late spring and summer trying to grieve the loss of something he couldn't even visit, just like Kip.

The second was choosing a place for hiding out, something properly suitable for all the weeping that would soon come, humming low in the cool mud like a toad.

She'd ruled out several options before making the decision. Including supplementary notes she was hardly aware of making in her head:

– *The Don Valley. People live in there, outdoor communities. Heard tell of a tall woman who ran a gang out of there in the 1800s. Been going on ever since. Must bring a peace offering.*

– *Bathurst Street Bridge. Underneath. Maybe too close to the Old Fort. Built to repel Americans. Might repel me too. Probably still guarded.*

– *Gardiner Expressway. Underneath. Heard tell though of a man who lived down there drowned from the rain rushing down and in, from the slopes. Watch out for flash floods then, if.*

– *Go west. Another city. You'll never survive the winter here. Get over this before winter then. Don't go west. People go too slow there. You'd go mad. You are mad.*

– *St. James Cathedral. King St. Park rotunda. No good? Too much out in the open? No windows? No doors? Reminds me too, reminds me … how … once I read … can't remember where, but I read how in a city in England, London maybe, in the old days, a long time ago the police would remove the doors and windows from any house of dubious reputation. So … the whole city is my house of dubious …*

What she chose instead of the above options was a drainpipe in the Humber River located just south of the remains of a bridge that had been washed away by a hurricane in the fifties, along with several houses. She ensconced herself about ten metres back from the entrance of the drainpipe (or, more properly, its exit), which was covered with a loose grill and emptied its trickling contents onto the (generally dry) flood plain on the west bank of the river. Nancy would have told her the spot was too close to what she called the maw of the mayor – all the major highways that bring the suburban commuter in from the west.

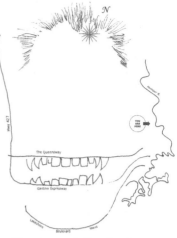

THE MAW OF THE MAYOR

But the location suited her and she stuck.

One day she found a red vinyl tent at the end of someone's driveway. 'I need a home,' it said. Not out loud, though it might as well have, Kip was so surprised to get it. The tent was torn along a couple of seams, but was designed to be a tensile structure. So it was pretty easy to put its sail-like parts together. She had carefully divided it into three discrete and self-contained pieces, devoting a whole sunburnt day to the task.

One piece she used to create an overhanging membrane along the top of her pipe. Something to catch the light from the setting sun with its red balloon texture and protect her from dripping condensation.

She set the second tent piece between her nest and the entrance – a barrier for privacy and protection from the wind. During one torrential rainstorm that came and nearly swept her into the river, she held on to this second piece like a sail, thought to herself, 'One day I'll master the ocean.'

The third piece she placed beneath her, sans poles, to protect against seeping moisture from heaps of dead leaves she'd piled there for a bed. The drainpipe was mostly dry, save for a trickle that came right down the centre. It sifted through her leafy mattress and continued on its way. An imperfect solution, it also soaked and eroded (and rotted) the mass of leaves, so she had to top up the pile regularly.

She ventured into nearby neighbourhoods to raid the city compost bins at the sides of houses. Their clips and latches thwarted

raccoon fingers but not Kip's. And the open bags inside offered a wealth of the previous evening's rejected meals: not salty enough, not fatty enough, not meaty enough, etc.

In other words: And then four and a half months went by.

By late August, the water level in her drainpipe was low, so she didn't have to somersault in from above, like a gibbon in a tree, to avoid the rushing river. She could walk down to the entrance, bend over and walk in, like civilized people. There were signs that other people had passed through there. 'David died on this very spot' read one graffito that she took seriously, bringing sprigs of grass and wild flowers daily, although it had been inscribed two years earlier as a joke.

And Mani's face. The grotesquery of his irritation in the half-light turning to stillness and stone. When she was vague, she saw only that and didn't know what it was. When she was clear, she tried to get past his anger, but it worked like a sentry at the gate of her memories.

Anyway, she was rarely clear.

Until the first really cold night came. Turned out to be an anomaly in the seasons, the coldest night in the pages of this book. Kip had nothing to protect herself from it. She tried to stuff herself into the laundry bag with the clothes, but it wasn't good enough. And then some water trickled through the pipe and dampened her. If she refused to leave, a voice inside declared, another night like this would kill her. Or maybe this one, all by itself.

She slept in her wet clothes and she nearly died.

In her dream, she did die, in fact.

She died and saw Mani.

Sees him. He's smiling. Is this happening now? Or is it a memory? She thought, If you're dead, how can you have a memory?

Or, she wondered, is death nothing but memory? Is death nothing but time? And time is relative, so is death a moment of life that lasts forever then?

Well, let's just see:

Here's Mani, first helping her cut jack-o'-lanterns out of the back of a van on Queen Street. They've been turning them out hand over fist. Thwicker thwack. *Come buy come buy.*

'Ladies and gentlemen, have you got your jack-o'-lantern yet? Ma'am? Don't be intimidated by all those faceless pumpkins on the street corners. Impress your neighbours! They come in cackling and evil or scared and sad, I mean the jacks, not your neighbours, heeha! Take your pick. Oh, hi Mani (*smooch*), hold this one for me. It's getting awfully late! Ten dollars! Oops! Five dollars! Three fifty, two fifty, one fifty, bingo! November first. What are we going to do with all these pumpkins? Hey sir, you look like you need a drink; well, guess what I have here, port-a-bar, back seat of a car, right here, right now, I can fix you a Black Russian, fix you a White Russian, and a whole buncha non-commie drinks too, heeha, serve it up on a pumpkin plate!'

Grabbing Mani, he her, kissing and falling down.

So it is memory then, zipping along, making a beeline to the present, and the immediate future, where Kip freezes to death in a drainpipe.

It pauses at the moment where she sees Mani in the sub-basement. But instead of lying there dead, he's lying there with his eyes open, talking to her.

'You take that money, Kip, you take that money.'

'But it's blood money, Mani!'

'You take that fucking money! Take it and look after yourself!'

'What about revenge?' asked Kip.

'What about it?' says the dead Mani. 'The dead don't ask for revenge. How could they? Their travels are too far.'

'I don't believe you,' says Kip.

'I'll show you,' says Mani.

Now they're standing at the corner of Pendrith and Christie. Their bikes are there. Kip pulls the shoestring off from around her neck and unlocks them. They're a bit rusty, the tires are flat and the wheels are bent, but Mani's brought lube oil and a pump and the bent wheels turn out to mean nothing at all.

Now they're riding. They head over to Spadina and then down through the Market, where the block-long edifice of a condo on Baldwin features storefronts selling cheap jewellery, sunglasses, hats, ice cream, clothes, headscarves, incense.

They swoop down Kensington, past Kip's building. There are all these pieces of blackened drywall piled at the curb. Someone has been cleaning up after a fire, but the second-floor apartment is shining as ever.

They round Dundas, heading west. West is where you go when you're dead but still have some living to do. Eventually they hit the railroad tracks. Mani stops short of the bridge and swerves down into a landfill site on the east side. He wants to say goodbye to a body buried here. Kip looks up from the sight and has a clear view of Lionel's window.

'This is where you're buried?' she asks.

'Totally,' he says. 'Is the creep factor not good enough for you?'

So the city is full of death, but death, from her current perspective, is nothing but the recollection of life. Death is no harder than memory, memory poured into the structures and foundations of the city, the city for travelling through, like memory.

So they cross the bridge and swoop up along the old First Nations trail, head underground into the subway tunnels and pass Lionel – Lionel! – sitting patiently at the Dundas West station. They glide to a stop. Lionel is wearing vestments, as if he's a priest. No, he can't be a priest. He's a ten-year-old boy. An altar boy. Kip stops to say hello. She's wondering why she's dreaming about her father as a young boy. She must miss him too. But he's all right, isn't he? He was all right the last time she saw him, sprawled and sleeping on the bed. *You're the champ.*

'Sermon time,' says Lionel now, conspiratorially. 'I can go for a milkshake but I don't want to lose track of time.'

Kip digs into her pocket, hands over the watch.

'Thanks,' says Lionel. 'Nice watch, I'll get it back to you.'

'Don't worry about it,' says Kip. 'It's yours.' And they head on. Lionel gets on his little bike and heads in the opposite direction.

And so they go, Kip and Mani, towards the north, where she's going to send him off. They go deeper into the earth, past buried creeks and beyond and below, past the subterranean lake and then up into the countryside of turning leaves, past the hills of the escarpment and out and over the lake and the bay ... and the other bay ...

Up into the the green, and the gold, and the brown, and the stone, and the light.

And the cold.

Now Mani the alchemist is crouched beside her in the drainpipe, and his mouth is close to her ear, whispering, his breath, real breath, making little clouds, his voice blending with the sound of the river outside.

'Did you take the money?' he asks.

Kip is breathing deep like the dreamer she is, but also from the skin-prickle feeling of being close to him. Her eyes are clothes, water-logged and sinking, the pleasure is five fathoms deep.

'I did take the money,' she says. 'But I don't remember why.'

'Because I told you to,' he says.

'No, you didn't,' she says. 'That wasn't why. But I'm going to regret it for the rest of my life.'

'That's not going to be very long,' says Mani. 'Since you're here in a tomb.'

'I'm not in a tomb.'

'This drainpipe looks like a tomb to me. You're freezing to death in here.'

'No I'm not.'

'Yes you are. And if it's true you're looking for revenge, then now is the time to wake up and go do it.'

'Why?'

'Because three reasons. One is look at me.'

She opens her heavy eyes and looks at him.

He's wearing a suit. A clean suit. How did that happen?

'See?' he says. 'I'm okay. Well and truly mourned. Two is you're cold. That's ideal.'

'Why ideal?'

'Because haven't you heard? Revenge is a dish best served cold.'

'I haven't heard,' she says.

'Well that's what they say,' he says.

'I'm new to the concept,' she says.

'You're not well suited to it,' he says. 'You tried to talk me out of it.'

'Don't try to talk me out of it!' she says, without antithesis.

'I'm not trying to talk you out of anything,' he says. 'I'm telling you to go do it. Mostly because of reason number three.'

'What's reason number three?'

'Is if you don't wake up right now, this minute,' says Mani, 'you're going to freeze to death. And then you'll be dead. And I don't want you to be dead. I want you to be alive and high-sticking it. I want you to be finding the next big thing. After the late, great black roses. So get up, now, and go and get your cold revenge.'

'But Mani, I —'

'I'm going to count backwards from three.'

'Why can't I just stay with you?'

'Three.'

'It's nice here. We have all these vistas.'

'Two.'

'I have you. We're together.'

'One.'

Kip woke up. It was dark. She couldn't move her legs. It was an hour or so before dawn. She stirred painfully in the dark and then managed to sort of shimmy like an old woman backwards towards the entrance of the pipe, dragging the laundry sack along behind her. It took a long time. Eventually burst out, in a manner of speaking, into the first signs of light, the glimmer of the river, a cloudless sky, a few leaves changing colour. A faraway doppler effect.

The day was warm again. And sunny. Sunday. She could tell instinctively because there wasn't so much street sound, the hum of traffic on the Gardiner much reduced. Even the birds didn't seem to come around so much on Sundays – Kip used to think, in lighter days, that they all liked to fly around empty buildings on Sundays, returning to their trees during the week.

She was exhausted, wet, shivery, hungry. But the sensation was starting to come back into her legs and the sun was going to dry out her clothes.

She stood and she wept.

Then she slipped the Crocs onto her feet and stumbled up into the mansions of a neighbourhood and then beyond them into the drab fifties apartment blocks of another higher-density one with people out walking dogs, before she figured out she was on the opposite side of the Humber River to what she had thought. Stonegate neighbourhood instead of High Park. West side instead of east side. Wide water dividing her from her home. How had that happened? She had to wander back down to the lakefront and cross the footbridge with the joggers, cyclists and dog-walkers gazing at the ducks paddling through sludge. There were sails out in the bay and an airplane high overhead. She looked up at it.

Then she walked down the path towards the city, eventually crossed over the highways on another footbridge into a neighbourhood unfamiliar because she was entering it from the wrong side.

It was finally clear to her why she had taken the money.

She found a bank machine on Roncesvalles, pulled out her much-abused wallet, extracted a plastic card, slid it in, pressed the buttons of her PIN and discovered she had fifteen million dollars in her savings account, with more to come in monthly installments for the rest of her life.

It was hers. She accepted it.

Because she was going to be Batman and the Terminator, Hulk, Wolverine and Godzilla, all rolled up into one.

4

But, fortunately or unfortunately, depending on how you look at it, things were not quite as Kip had left them when she entered her drainpipe. From spring to fall, the world was not the same anymore. Mani had said that revenge was a dish best served cold. But it can be difficult to serve any dish at all when the patrons have switched tables, the tables have been moved and the whole restaurant has been torn down and replaced with a yoga studio.

To wit:

Kip's enemies were no longer her enemies, her friends were no longer her friends, and her family was no longer anything at all, since her father was dead.

Things always change. They never stay the same.

Here's how it happened.

First: Pat York (whom we left in a compromised position, you may recall, in the clutches of a small army of worm pickers who did not wish him well).

He'd closed his eyes and counted down from three, expecting a bullet in the brain. Instead, though, *A message for you from Joseph Luong: The house you blew up yesterday was for friends to live in. Immigrants to sponsor.* It's true he'd been worried about fatalities. Had there been any? His imminent own would answer that question.

But then they dumped him down a hill in Christie Pits, sending him rolling into a pool of water that had gathered in the grass at the bottom, soaking his silver suit. So, they were sparing him to lie there in misery and think about what a poor son he was to a disappointed father. A dead father. A father as dead as he'd ever been distant. In truth, their relationship had not changed much. To be as silent as the grave was something that merely had an explanation now.

But the son could not even take a proper and competent revenge against the woman who had harried the old man to his grave.

After that, he slept very poorly through the dawn hours, crashing by the trickle in the sub-basement on Pendrith Street and dreaming erratically of his father saying, 'Just make sure he understands who is gerrymandering whom.' Then he arose late morning with the earth in darkness and decided, in hot, moustache-twirling revengitis, to ascend to street level and stake out the bookstore where Kip's elderly father worked. He only had the vaguest idea what he might do. But, oh, he would do something.

Completely exhausted and disgusted with himself, he headed over to Kensington but felt too conspicuous to enter the store. So he ditched the limo and walked down to one of those vintage stores deep in the Market – in a building the city was already in the process of expropriating for his development benefit. He purchased a loud shirt and a pair of vintage glasses that still had their original lenses in them. His hair was a little longer than usual and he knew from experience that even close associates would fail to recognize him when he altered the least little thing about himself. He was malleable that way. Clothes made the man. Suddenly he looked like what he really was, a boy in his mid- to late twenties.

He headed back up to the bookstore and stepped inside.

Lionel was there, behind the counter to the right of the door and a few feet away. There was another doorway behind the old man that led both to a back room and down some stairs. Pat headed up one of the aisles, realizing this was more a used-book store than a new one. The shelves were higher here. He lingered, paced, glared at Lionel, looked up, looked down at his feet, looked back up.

'Can I help you?'

It was the old man speaking. Pat nearly jumped out of his shoes.

'I'm trying to reach a book,' he said, using the annoyance he really felt about his own cowardice and stupidity, pretending he thought such high stacks were the summit of bad taste.

On the top shelf there was a series of first editions. As the old man walked over, Pat tried to imagine which one seemed most likely to appeal to a small man in vintage glasses and Hawaiianesque shirt. The prescription of the lenses blinded him a little. The only title he could fully make out had the word 'Toronto' in it.

Lionel was beside him now. Taller than Pat, he raised his arm to point. 'Which one?'

'That one.'

'Oh yeah,' said Lionel. 'I know that one. *Toronto of Old*. Its chapters are nicely divided. Here, I'll show you.'

Lionel reached up. The book was at his fingertips. It was a tender operation as he worked it out from between the dusty tomes that surrounded it. It seemed so much work. Why didn't he just get a stool? Pat was about to tell him to forget it when the old man's hand jerked down suddenly, as if by reflex. And then he fell to the floor. The book tumbled after and would have hit him in the head had Pat not batted it out of the way.

Bugger.

Pat had a lunch meeting with a rep from the Catholic Church about selling an old community hall. Still, he had failed to shave and was dressed like a Bermudan apothecary. What was he doing here?

The old man was lying half on his back, legs crumpled beneath his torso in what was clearly an uncomfortable position, head tipped back with a bewildered and apologetic expression on his face.

Pat had been frozen for almost a minute, staring distastefully, as if Lionel were a puddle in his path. Finally he looked to the open door behind the counter to see if anyone was there. 'Hello?' He felt an impulse to turn and go, but then his eye was drawn again to the problem of the crumpled legs. Really, it was too much, such a contortion had to be corrected, for whatever reason. It would only take a sec and no one else was there. Jesus fucking, fucking Christ.

Against his better judgment, he crouched and touched the old man's knee.

'Would you like me to – uh –?'

He made the gesture for *adjustment* a little too vehemently, causing his fake eyeglasses to tumble to the floor. Now he was looking down at Lionel with an exposed face. Well, at least the myopia was cured. The old man was giving him a wide-eyed look, opening and closing his mouth.

'Just try to relax,' said Pat. A meaningless directive. And then, making another wildly impulsive decision, he shifted around to the old man's shoulders, tucked his hands under his arms and pulled him up, thinking he could prop him against the spines of the bottom shelf.

It didn't work. Mortified, Pat suddenly found himself cradling the man in his lap, like the fucking *Pietà* or something.

He thought of his own father, from whom he had maintained a respectful distance as he died, as had been appropriate. Then he tried to think of something to say here, now.

After an eternity, a prematurely grey-haired woman finally appeared from the storeroom in the back.

'What *took* you so long?' Pat barked.

'Oh my god!' she said. 'I was down in the basement.'

'Please,' he said. 'Call 911.'

The woman rushed around the long hardwood counter and picked up the phone. The old man, relaxing a bit into Pat's lap, opened his eyes, almost lucid.

'What happened?' he asked.

'You were getting me a book,' said Pat, feeling an impulse, unfamiliar, to mask his impatience. 'You fell.'

'Oh.' And then: 'What was the book?'

'Uh. *Toronto of Old.*'

'I see,' said Lionel, wheezing a bit. 'Yes, I remember. I've read that book. It's a perk of the job, all these books, all this reading.'

'Maybe you shouldn't talk,' said Pat. And then, 'There's an ambulance coming,' looking up at the woman talking on the phone. 'You're going to be okay.'

And he thought, What an absurd thing to say. I don't know how he's going to be.

Lionel was shaking his head.

'What's wrong?' asked Pat.

'I'm just worried,' he said. 'She's all I've got and I don't know where she is.'

A non sequitur, thought Pat. Involving his daughter. Except, he considered, it wasn't really a non sequitur. If the man loved his daughter, the thought of her would naturally be just a breath away, wouldn't it? Not a non sequitur at all then, you stupid, insensitive, barely human prick. 'Non sequitur' better describes the things *you* might choose to say: *Lie still*, or *Don't worry*.

'You could call her,' he ventured. 'Does she have a cellphone?'

'No,' said Lionel, gesturing. 'She had a few bad days. She was at my place, but now I don't know where she is.'

'Would you like me to try to get hold of her?'

'I don't want to worry her,' said Lionel.

The old man's hand had not quite completed its gesture; it was flapping around like a moth against a lampshade. Pat reached across and grabbed it. It went slack and fell into his grip. He thought he might let go and then did not.

And then he thought, *Wait a second. This man might actually be dying.* He looked again towards the exit, then to the woman, still on the phone. It had been forever. Was she on hold? With 911? She seemed the type to tolerate something outrageous like that. Accustomed to dismissal from people in positions of authority. Inviting it even. People like Pat. She was beneath contempt.

'Your hand is warm,' said Lionel. 'My hands are always so cold.'

Warm hands. Huh. Funny. Really? Hands that were warm. Was that a virtue? Warm hands, warm heart? Or was it warm hands, cold heart? Oh well, what did it matter if this man was appreciating Pat's warm hands, he obviously wasn't judging them. He obviously didn't have time to consider the implications for the character of the man who was providing his hands with warmth, even as he lay on the floor with his own cold hands. Pat should just enjoy the compliment, if that's what it was. Yes, that's what it was. Was it? It was! Of course it was. No one had ever told him that before. Warm hands. No indication about the heart other than the *sharing* of warm hands. Warm hands! He felt a strange little throb of pride.

And then he found himself contemplating these two people he'd met. Father and daughter. A good father to a good daughter. He had perhaps sought to punish her for the selfish actions of his own father.

No, that wasn't true. Let's not get sentimental! She should not have taken that money!

Which was not to say his father was not a bastard. Very much the opposite of this man here, it seemed. Or, it wasn't so much that he was a bastard. He was just repressed. And eccentric. Paying more attention to ostentatious hobbies than his little family. Lacking self-awareness.

And then it occurred to Pat, on the floor of that bookstore cradling another old man in his arms, that perhaps he lacked self-awareness too. The very model of the father. Spitting image, probably. The inconsiderate, eccentric old bastard. No wonder she got suicidal. No wonder she succeeded. No wonder.

Lionel spoke again, startling him.

'Thank you,' he said.

What could he possibly mean by *that*?

'For what?' asked Pat.

'Staying with me. You must have business to get to.'

'Oh no,' said Pat. 'Not really.' Thinking of the bishop.

Lionel said. 'I'm losing myself a bit. I keep thinking your hands are hers.'

He meant Kip Flynn's. There was no other explanation.

The prematurely grey-haired woman came over and knelt beside the old man, taking his other hand. She was finally off the phone, the masochistic bitch. Pat felt a small prick of resentment, shocking himself a bit. Was he really so needy? Was he really so contemptuous? Was he really so misogynist? Pull yourself together, man.

'Do you hear the siren?' asked the woman. And then: 'Hang in there, Lionel.'

So much despair in her voice, Pat had to suppress the urge to tell her to get a grip. Displays of affection do have their downsides, you know. Emotional repression is good for certain situations – emergency situations for example.

Just not a whole life maybe.

Lionel spoke again. 'There's a book over there on the floor. This gentleman was interested.'

'That's all right,' said Pat.

'*Toronto of Old*,' said Lionel. 'I hope I haven't damaged it.'

'Don't worry yourself,' said the woman. 'We'll take care of it.'

'What a thing to do to a patron!' said Lionel, laughing.

'Don't even worry about it,' said Pat. And then realized he meant it. Where had the rage gone away to? The impatience, even? He couldn't locate any of it.

And if that wasn't enough, when the ambulance came, Pat found himself insisting that he ride along.

'Are you a relative?' asked the paramedic, inevitably.

'No, but –'

'I'm afraid it's not possible.'

Rage again. There it was. For a moment, Pat thought he might have a seizure. Maybe a seizure was a good idea. At least it would earn him his ride along. He could do it too, a huff and a puff, he knew he could. He considered it, but in considering it, he calmed, and the moment passed. Then he thought, *But what if he dies in the ambulance? What if he doesn't speak to his daughter? What if he dies alone?* Not even J. C. York had died alone. Pat had been on hand, bravely standing just over there.

He looked up at the paramedic, who had been regarding him closely. 'All right,' she said. 'You can come.'

No clue what had happened there. No clue at all.

If you had been looking at Pat in this moment (like the paramedic was), you would have been able to see with perfect clarity how he was the sort of person who wears a mask. You might have considered, like the paramedic, how this is very common practice among adults and certain children. They arrange their expressions to form the mode that gives them courage to face the world. A frown, a smile, a smirk. You might have thought, like the paramedic, that it can take years to create, but if truth is beauty, in the end it's not that hard to conceal.

The mask is cladding. An attempt to turn people into architecture. But it can't stay in place forever. No architecture ever does. Nature takes its toll. In a moment, presumably one of consequence, the mask transforms, without a single line displaced, to become the opposite of what it was.

And so, when pinch-faced Pat tended to Lionel somewhat fastidiously, the paramedic saw how his face suddenly didn't seem so pinched after all. It seemed rather attentive and considerate, the tiny scar more of an interrogative than an exclamation. It didn't require a close-up to see, like a president's tears. The paramedic saw it. And she marked the battle that saw him want to fight and then lay the fight aside in consideration of higher priorities. She saw how unfamiliar these emotions were to him, though perfectly natural, stirred. Like an old zoetrope, twirling lamp, heating into life.

Later, in the hospital, Pat found himself experiencing further unfamiliar feelings. His father had already been cremated (as stipulated in his living will: the man had a horror of turning into refuse and wanted to be gone). Pat had overseen a few preparations for that funeral, and now he was padding the white halls tending to the needs of the bookstore man. He even bought flowers, just for something to do. Wasn't that what people were supposed to do? He thought maybe the old guy would appreciate them.

And then, out of the blue, there was the girl. Kip. The daughter. He saw her – she had a gash in her chin, stitched up, he'd put it there – and thought, *There she is.* He thought, *Oh my god, she doesn't know.* He thought, *Someone has to tell her,* and then he thought, *Oh good god, it has to be me.*

He raised his hand and called, 'Hey!'

He went as fast as he could. Hospitals require care and discretion. He tried to catch up to her. Failed.

He felt compelled to analyze, to reassert control.

Well, for one thing, it was occurring to him that he really had scared this person. Like *really.* He had sort of thought of her as an adversary, equally matched. But maybe he had been more or less an all-powerful city-wrecking godzilla-type bully. And perhaps she had not deserved it. Sure, she had taken the money, but honestly it had been more money than he knew what to do with. And it might have even represented, for her, the principle of the thing. A deal is a deal. Not to mention she was in shock! Maybe still in shock, maybe she's been moving through a fog since the moment his father pulled that damn trigger! Which meant she'd been in shock when he'd punched her face. Which would suggest the fight, which he'd thought of as evenly matched, wasn't evenly matched at all.

Now her father was dying, at least maybe, and she was here, right here, in the same hospital, and the only person who could put them together was Pat. But she had run and now she was gone. But really, how far could she get?

As far as the moon, as it turned out.

He should not have run, he should not have called, he should have quietly alerted a nurse. He should have, he should not have, he should not have, he should have. He should have. He should not have.

In short it wasn't, uh, it wasn't actually *fair*, what he had done.

Even for him, had it not been more about how easily and callously his own father had divided his inheritance away? As easily as slicing a priceless painted canvas with a knife? It was only money in the sense that money represented love and affection and its easy division, its lack. And there was nothing this girl could have done to make up for that lack or change its reality in any way. He had chosen the wrong target. And in so doing, he had divided two people who loved each other.

Well now. Come on. Consider again. Was it really so harsh as all that?

Yes it was.

That's what he'd done.

Later, at home, he lay in his bed and flipped through the pages of the offending book, *Toronto of Old*, which, ludicrously, the bookstore owner had insisted he take – $140 pencilled faintly on the first page inside the cover. Here was Pat, a fucking millionaire, just about to inherit a house on the Bridle Path. He'd put a man in the hospital: all alone. He'd scared that man's daughter away. And the struggling bookstore had given him, in reward for this behaviour, a $140 book.

Not fair. Not just. Not equitable.

Still, he could see what Lionel had meant about the chapter divisions. Headings like,

– *Palace Street to the Market Place,*

– *from Brock Street to the Old French fort,*

– *King Street: from John Street to Yonge Street,*

– *from Yonge Street to Church Street,*

– *digression southwest at Church Street,*

– *Market lane,*

– *the valley of the Don,*

– *the harbour, its Marina,*

– *from the Garrison back to the place of beginning …*

He found himself picturing Kip Flynn running through all these streets. Up and down and always away from him.

It gave him no pleasure. Gave him no pleasure at all.

And so, then. Enemies were no longer enemies. How were friends no longer friends? How was family no longer in proximity?

There were actually two bookstore ladies. Pat had been so preoccupied that he failed to notice the second one, buzzing around behind the counter and trying to give Lionel space for air. Their names were Jennifer and Danielle and they had opened the bookstore in the Market a few years earlier after (they found out later) an independent bookstore had been kicked out of the very same spot by a greedy landlord who wanted more money but eventually got significantly less from these two transplanted Montrealers. Now they were upset because they didn't know how to get hold of Lionel's daughter. But they did know the big bass player: Henry. And they knew Henry knew everyone in the Market. It was because they were great fans of live music. They knew Henry was playing that night at Graffiti's on Baldwin Street. So they bided their time, anxiously, and then they went to see him.

When the two prematurely grey-haired women came by, out of the blue, and interrupted his gig with news of Lionel's hospitalization, Henry just happened to be backing, for the third or fourth time, an egotistical front man who could not prevent himself, at the most inopportune moments, from berating his bandmates. 'Your playing is shit!' he shouted, barely caring if the eight people in the audience heard him or not. Henry was growing tired of it. The leading man was a talented boy, it was true, who sang like the frog in the Bugs Bunny cartoons, so sometimes Henry allowed himself to forget he was an asshole. But even a singing frog could be an asshole, was his conclusion.

Therefore, when the bookstore ladies showed up with their worried faces and bad news, Henry stepped down off the small stage to give an ear to what they had to say. And then he packed up his hardshell case, preparing to take his leave.

'Where do you think you're going?'

The frontman could not believe his eyes. Having been apprised of Henry's intentions, he ribbited to the crowd that his former bassist would never 'plink plunk in this town again.' It gave Henry an unpleasant feeling of déjà vu for future fuck-ups, but he blew it off and gave assurances to the worried librarian-types that the froggy dude was just blowing off some foggy dew and really there was nothing to worry about. Wishing perhaps that someone would say something like that to him.

And then Henry swung down Kensington to find Kip. But Kip was not at home. Just Nancy. So he brought Nancy to the hospital.

'Is Kip already there?' Nancy asked, with a neutral expression.

'Nobody knows where Kip is,' said Henry.

'I know where Kip is,' said Nancy. 'And that's beyond help.'

Visiting hours were essentially over but Pat had arranged, anonymously, for Lionel to have a private room. The nurses weren't sure he was going to make it through the night. So they made an exception for the pair. When Henry and Nancy arrived, the old man was lying with his head elevated, eyes closed and mouth open, hooked up to a heart monitor and an oxygen tank. He looked like he was dead. But he wasn't.

In fact, he was awake, somewhat slowed down, but still lively.

Nancy tried to resist mentioning Kip, but finally couldn't help herself.

'So she won't come?'

Lionel looked up at her. 'If you know where she is,' he said, 'I'd sure like to know too.'

Nancy hesitated for a moment. Considered making a cutting remark but instead she shook her head. 'I don't know where Kip is.'

Lionel looked away. 'I don't know either,' he said.

He looked like he was about to drop dead right there. It upset Nancy so much she had to go take a walk.

'Anything you need there, Mr. Flynn?' asked Henry, once she'd left.

'No,' said Lionel, reassured. 'But call me Lionel. I'm a dying man.'

'Okay,' said Henry.

Lionel was sizing up the compassionate stance of the big man in the chair beside the bed. He cleared his throat and raised his head, conspiratorially.

'What?' said Henry.

And then over the course of the next forty-five minutes, while Nancy was wandering halls with weird unplacable guilt, Lionel told Henry all about his life.

'I was raised by women,' he said. 'That's why I'm so feminine, you know.'

This made Henry laugh. He thought the man was joking. But he wasn't. Perhaps from another generation's point of view, the grizzled Lionel was androgynous.

He went on. 'It's because my father died in a plane crash when I was three. It was a small light aircraft. He flew recreationally, if you can wrap your head around that. And he crashed into the side of a mountain around the same time that Amelia Earhart disappeared.'

(Henry, thinking: *This dude is old.*)

'So maybe,' Lionel went on, 'I missed a certain fatherly guiding hand. I don't know. Everyone else cultivates that supposedly adult behaviour that just looks fake to me. It just looks fake. Me, I haven't changed, far as I can tell, since I was five years old. Now I'm old. So. I know, I know. What can I do? I'm just an asshole, I guess.

'My wife was pretty, like that girlfriend of yours,' he said at one point. Henry was unaware how unprecedented the subject of Kip's mother was. 'I married pretty late. She was younger than me, it's true. I just loved her. Didn't realize she would change my life so much.'

And then, after a brief pause, Lionel told a story that Henry would never forget, though he lacked the first clue as to what he was supposed to do with it.

It began like this.

'My wife died in childbirth. At home. Our new little baby died too. Little girl.'

After Lionel told that story, there seemed to be a weight that lifted off his chest that allowed him to sit up in the bed and tell a few tales of his time with Kip. The good days they had.

The last thing he said was, 'Do you think she can ever be happy?'

And then, a few minutes later, he died. As Nancy was winding her way back up the hall.

Henry and Nancy walked home in the early light of the morning, University Avenue aglow with evidence of passing rain. They were quiet for a while.

Henry said, 'Hey, when you see Kip next, could you pass something on to her for me?'

'Sure,' said Nancy, lying. 'She'll be home later, I'm sure, probably.'

'It's not a little thing,' said Henry. 'It's a big thing.'

Lionel's wife had died in childbirth. And so did the child. It had happened at home, very suddenly and without benefit of a midwife, at 11 o'clock at night. Insane with shock and grief, Lionel had taken the dead baby and burned it in the basement furnace of the Parkdale building where they lived. And then he walked down into St. Joe's Hospital – some fateful force making him invisible – slipped unseen into the maternity ward and stole a baby. As it happens, one of a pair of twins. He told himself it was a good choice, the parents would miss the missing child less this way. He'd once worked here as a janitor. He knew his way around.

A pocket watch was lying between the preemies, on top of the glass, as if it had been left there by a proud and lingering father, also aging, also with a younger wife, who knew he had business elsewhere and finally departed with such haste that he left it behind. Lionel had taken the timepiece with the baby, he'd never really known why. Some kind of insurance perhaps, or maybe just a reminder that this new relationship would not last forever.

As for the baby …

'I brought it to her,' he told Henry, speaking of his wife. 'I laid it in her arms. She had been dead three hours. I thought a living baby would bring her back to life. I really did. And little Kip really didn't seem to mind. She was always tough. She always tried to do what was right, even if it was hopeless.'

Eventually, he called 911. The police came, and the ambulance, and everyone saw the tragedy that had unfolded. The scenario didn't look like anything other than what it was – a mother had died delivering a baby and the father had refused to believe it for many hours. It cast no aspersion on his perceived capacity to raise the child as a single parent. On the contrary. Here was a man who loved.

Lionel also told Henry that he knew what her original name was: Patricia York. At that time, he'd seen the father only once, many years before, while working clean-up crew on the building site for the Mies tower.

There had been pleas in the press, but Lionel could not bring himself to make contact. In his mind, this child had tried to save his wife. He felt he could never be parted from her.

Things got difficult a couple of years later, though, when it became clear that the original mother, as Lionel referred to her, began to have troubles that could not be kept out of the press. She was institutionalized. Lionel had gone several times to the drawer that contained the pocket watch before telling himself, 'What's done cannot be undone.'

Eventually, inevitably it seemed now, she had died by her own hand.

Then, eventually, the story had disappeared into the void of news, forgotten by everyone except, of course, the pair of fathers. Cyrus was the sort of man to never share such a story with his son. Better to forget it. Better to let him think what Cyrus probably preferred to believe: a baby died. Maybe she was older than him. Yeah, by a minute or two.

Not that Lionel had shared the story with his daughter either. It was a repressive impulse the two men shared despite their separate castes. Living in a city where you learn to smile openly, the better to hide your feelings.

And then came the day Kip appeared at his house with her story about meeting Cyrus York under the worst circumstances.

Here Lionel told Henry about the death of Mani, the deal with the Yorks, whose particulars he was unaware of but which likely involved cash, Cyrus's modus operandi. And he even told Henry about the miscarriage ...

Lionel had planned to seek out Cyrus York this week and reveal the truth to him. But then the man's death was reported. And Kip up and disappeared from his house. The strange coincidence had confused Lionel deeply, frightened him into cowardice and silence, leading him to wonder whether the original father had somehow been reunited with the original daughter. Had Kip gone to him with that pocket watch? Perhaps while Lionel had waited on a subway bench not far from the Mies? Had the man divined its meaning? And was this not why Lionel had given it to her in the first place? Because it's a relief, isn't it? When the truth is out?

But he didn't even know if the truth was out.

And it scared him that she might have finally been told of the sin Lionel had committed without the context that he felt made it understandable. Was this why she had disappeared? Had she gone to her real father? Had he recognized her and taken her into his more highly perched nest?

All this was confessed by Lionel on his deathbed, as Nancy trolled the hallways. And Henry was telling it all to her now. Assuming Nancy would pass it on to Kip. But she wouldn't. It would never happen. The only way Kip would finally learn of it all would be from Henry's lips. And, as usual, given his luck, he had a bit of a row to hoe before that happened, our Henry.

For Nancy, it was a crossroads. Either she had to blame herself for her complicity in the escalation that led to the death of Mani (it was just a fucking pop gun!) or she had to question Kip's motives for covering it up. She chose the latter, aligning it with all the corrupting mechanisms that greased the wheels of this fucking city with its fucking city council whose members had either caved to the will of a suburban mayor or else had been dragged off to the madhouse in a fit of chair-twirling pique.

Kip had been paid off. That was Nancy's suspicion and her surprise. Kip had been paid off.

To Nancy, the payoff/birthright was proof positive – right down to the DNA – that her old friend Kip had gone to the other side, because that was where she belonged: her pedigree in fulfillment of her birthright. Not an authentic city rat but an authentic city ruler. The enemy.

And, come on, if there was one thing she hated more than anything else in the world, it was a fairy tale romance populated by rich people. What a *typical* thing to happen in the new bared-teeth city. Poor little girls getting rich. No way, man. No fucking way.

So, in the days following the visit to the hospital, Nancy became unhealthily preoccupied with Kip Flynn and Pat York, separated at birth, playing out a brother-sister twist on the Beauty and the Beast story, complete with roses and an appalling flight from her home in the Market, even as the billboards were starting to go up –

SIGN UP FOR A WORLD ABOVE KENSINGTON

– providing something for Nancy to stare at as she shuffled back and forth from the curb in front of the Temp with Kip's boxes of landfill-destined junk. You want to join the carbon copiers? You want to align yourself with someone who ploughs over history? Let me show you how it feels. As she dropped the last box on the curb.

Some swift tagging wit had already marked the rest of the boxes with high-rise windows. It lightened Nancy's mood for a moment. Maybe these Market condos could one day be carted away as easily as all this junk.

But in the end, Nancy was so disgusted by the idea of living in an apartment that reminded her of her failure with the Market and her erstwhile fairy tale friend, that she finally moved out, telling the Ghost it was his roost now to rule.

'The Market is the city's beating heart,' she said, 'and they're going to substitute it with a pig heart.'

'I heard those things really work,' said the Ghost.

'That's not the point,' said Nancy. 'Jeez. People like you made Van Gogh cut off his ear.'

'I heard Van Gogh didn't cut off his ear in the end,' said the Ghost. 'The latest on that is it was a cover-up after a duel with Gaugin.'

'Oh my god,' said Nancy. 'Fuck off with the information! Or I'll cut off your fucking ear!'

And then she was gone, thumping indignantly down the fire escape.

Nancy was intimately familiar with the history of the city. She knew it had once been called the meeting place, and so that's what it still was. The meeting place. Where else but in the meeting place would you meet the polar opposite of what you are? Isn't that what Kip Flynn was? For days she kept thinking she heard her name called by Kip in the street, seeing her among the crowds. But she wasn't there.

Usually, when Nancy rode the subway – a mode of transport she used to love but had come to hate along with urban digging in all its forms – she had the rather superstitious habit of counting all the cars in the unit and then running like hell to sit in the middle one. But her preoccupation with Kip's betrayal had put her off her game.

One day, just a few weeks after the revelations, when things were still rife but maybe about to calm down just a bit – though there were still so many questions and she was still distracted enough that she still wasn't choosing the middle car and had even failed to apply her usual contemplation as to whether she should transfer at the St. George station, getting it over with in a mad rush of the crowd, or wait for Spadina station with its leisurely walk to the farther transfer point. She was still preoccupied when the train stalled – she was suddenly not even sure whether she'd transferred yet or not. Was she travelling east or south?

And then, as she turned to see the other car come speeding around the bend, the name that was lit up on the front of that train was

KIP FLYNN

But then, during the sleep that followed, the sign she saw morphed again, transformed into other signs. Down in there with the flight and the fight, Nancy's lizard brain was searching for somewhere to lay the blame for all this – not just what had happened to her, but also what had happened to her city …

… eliding that search with her sense of who she was, as if she herself were the city …

… as her quotidian activist mind, occasionally flickering on and off above, lit up the orange lizard sky with words like 'infrastructure' and …

NEGL

The feeling of personal betrayal grafted onto these signs, shuffled through their abstractions and sought an outlet with a new, more powerful name to replace the old:

YORK

– the city developer: responsible, if not for deliberate sabotage, then certainly for the mindset that allowed aging infrastructure to go the way of Pompeii. So a bridge falls? We can build a new one. A ferry topples? We'll build a bridge instead. The bridge falls? Hallelujah, we've achieved stability.

The new name still carried the old cradled within it, though, curled up like a secret in her ear. They were all Yorks.

Such were the flickerings of Nancy's subterranean sleep, deepening her commitment to the cause, embedding it like a rebar in her crumbling doric spine.

'I don't know what's come over me,' she said to the fireman who found her among the carnage. 'And I don't want you to think this is my fault, but –'

'This is not your fault,' said the fireman, tears running down his face.

'But,' said Nancy, 'does this mean they might reconsider digging new subways?'

She emerged from the long ordeal that followed looking exactly the same ... if somewhat fleeter of foot, more mercurial, more like fire – more, um, translucent, one might say ... Unless she concentrated very hard, in which case she could be as earthy and solid as a wall.

She had been baptized by subway.

And for her enemies and frenemies, there would be hell to pay.

She would be revenged on the whole pack of them.

Nancy poured herself into all the structures and foundations of the city, made it hers; for travelling through, *everywhere*, like memory. Barely corporeal. Pure spirit. Not precisely among the living. But aching for their engagement and acting upon them nonetheless.

To wit: she didn't need the tour-bus job anymore. Not that she could have accomplished it anyway, but we don't have to tell her that. To her, it had always felt like token protest, like the inspiration towards revenge rather than its instigation. These days, though, she was so much more potent. She wanted to be right inside those buildings. And she didn't need inspiration anymore. She was herself inspiration. Vengeance felt like the forge of life itself, its essence even, both contradicting and affirming all her convictions. Architecture, for example, acts as a kind of revenge against nature and memory, she thought. This used to be a rolling swampy meeting place at the shore of a lake. From that point of view, everything that has come after is an affront. An affront to the marsh. And, what's more, all human energy and work and culture comes from this same force of revenge. Doesn't it? Front lawns are planted in revenge against the memory of bone-breaking labour, clearing rocks and trees from the land, aren't they? Earth-corrupting golf courses have risen in revenge against their displacement from the bumpy, chilly highlands. *And so,* thought Nancy, *the rest of us have to be punished by all the water-wasting greenery.* Pipes set in walls against the waste that comes burbling out of the human body. Bathroom sinks against the stink of standing water with its mosquitos and concealed diseases. Electric lights against ghosts, furnaces against winter, AC against summer, asphalt streets against winding paths that lead to cliffs and tumble over them. Buried rivers and city grids arising against the horrors of asymmetry, whereby you can take a single step and twist your ankle. Fast food: revenge against the taste of dirt and gristle. Famished meat. Urns and caskets against earthworms or even death itself.

One revenge deserves another.

Nancy, in short, felt reborn from the depths of the subway as the bearer of the city's buried memories. Like she would rouse all the buried ghosts from the depths and send them into battle against these creatures of the light.

And the name that burned as bright as the morning star in Nancy's constellation of lights to be put out was

Not to mention his fucking fairy-tale, city-fleeing sister.

But how would she do it? It was something to think about, as she returned to her new place in the west end, which was, she had to admit, getting dustier and dustier as the landlord tried to figure out what he was supposed to do with the belongings of the woman who'd lived there. Nancy's parents had not even entered the place, had not even bothered to find out about *any* of the places she'd lived since leaving home. Such was their revenge on the life she'd lived away from their patient cultivation. Their only wish was to bring her back to the room they'd preserved for her, and planted her broken body in the soil of her childhood bed, leaving all her adult possessions to be dealt with by strangers, since, after all, the adult Nancy had been a stranger to them too.

But she wasn't a stranger to herself. She was her own best company now, and knew herself better than she ever had. And she was patient. Revenge takes patience. It's a life's work. Not crude like a bullet. It was not invented in modern times, when people desire to produce the largest result at the least cost. It requires extravagance. It requires an impractical imagination, unfettered by constraints of the world. It requires a disposition that is fixed, and won't ever change.

And that is how friends became enemies and enemies became friends.

So now, one may ask, where do we go from here?

Back to Kip.

And her feet of clay.

Three

NOT A BEAST

1

It was September. Kip had taken a few days to catch her breath and clean herself up, buy some clothes that would allow her to move unnoticed, or rather noticed – the perfect combination of unnoticed and noticed – through the echelons of power. Her hair had grown in lighter than her dreads had ever indicated, and she'd had it shaped into a Jean Seberg cut. The studs in her lip and nose were long gone, and the holes had scarred over to nothing.

She'd also discovered that her father – Lionel Joseph Flynn – had died. She went to his apartment in the building on the bridge and was bluntly informed of the fact by a neighbour in the laundromat, a lady who seemed to be clucking behind her hand, wondering half aloud how a daughter could so neglect a father as to fail to notice his death. But Kip didn't feel any anger towards her. There was no room. The news turned her back to stone for several more days and gave her the detachment she needed to purchase the French movie star's clean-lines wardrobe.

And then she fell apart, a few more days, in the Park Hyatt Hotel at Bloor and Avenue Road; from there she stared down at the museum and it stared back.

Now she was standing in front of 12 Kensington in the swiftly transforming Market. There was a front entrance now. The door to the bar had been moved to the right and there was a new door beside it, with a window through which she could see stairs going up, presumably into the middle of what had once been Nancy's bedroom. There was a doorbell too. But she was not going to use it.

And the door to the bar didn't lead into a bar anymore. It led into a high-fashion clothing store. Since 12 Kensington had once been the epicentre of the city's most intense scrum of vintage and small-time designer stores, this was about as shocking a change as the Market could provide. She wondered where Nancy was, with her special talent for undermining the signage on such places with a well-placed tag. Gap TOOTH, Aveda BLOCKERS, Vice REGAL, American Apparel CHILD MOLESTERS.

Still, she took it as a small miracle that the building was there at all, considering the construction all around.

And another shock: the entrance to the alley, by which Kip and Nancy had once upon a time gained access to their fire escape, was fronted by a big black iron gate. The cracked asphalt beyond it was as littered as ever with butts, cups and broken glass. But at least the gate was open. No need for scaling this afternoon. Still, she stood there a bit stunned by all the change until a cyclist leapt onto the sidewalk to avoid a car and breezed by her back, making her jump.

And then there was a small bouquet of field flowers lying on the third step of the fire escape. She paused partway up to remove her shoes, a bit too fancy. She knew (from watching others try long ago) that she wasn't going to master the gaps, and headed the rest of the way in bare feet. At the top, she knocked on the door. Felt for the key, which was not there. Still, someone came. An old flatmate. Not Nancy but, unbelievably, the Ghost.

'Hey – uh, hey!' he said, opening the door. 'I know you.'

'Yeah ... '

'That's so funny that you came up the fire escape!'

It should be noted that the Ghost had never seen himself as a minor character in this story, his function merely to save Kip and Nancy $400 a month in rent. He perceived himself rather as an old friend who'd always cherished the good old times sharing this flat with the other two, and had tolerated all the changes for the sake of nostalgia. He knew nostalgia was an unhealthy condition but could barely help himself. Anyway, he'd heard that it was only great men who were not sentimental and he'd long ago come to the conclusion he was not a great man. So why not be sentimental? Why not indulge in a little nostalgia? This was what it was like to be the Ghost, undergoing continual negotiations with the historians who would not be writing about him some day.

No more fiancée, Kip could tell right away as she stepped into the shaded and messy kitchen. It was neat and clean but something about it said bachelor. A state-of-the-art espresso maker took up most of the counter, leaving little room for the preparation of food.

'What's with the gate?' she asked.

'Yeah, isn't it awful? They put that up for the house in back. Do you remember that house? Vietnamese family lived in there?'

She remembered the house.

'Well, they moved out and then it stood empty for a while. I thought all that happened before you left, actually.'

'It did,' said Kip.

'Well, apparently someone started stashing drugs in there. Stealing electricity too, I heard. Eventually something caught fire and the whole place just blew up one day.'

'Uh huh,' she said. The Ghost had a special talent for making even the most potent information underwhelming. 'Is that why there are flowers out there?'

'What flowers?' He explained that he rarely noticed flora or fauna of any kind beyond the mice that still still scurried through the place and made him yelp.

'And what about the gate?' asked Kip.

'Well,' said the Ghost, 'someone bought the land three or four months ago and put in four condos. It's walk-in access only, same as before, down the alley. Some of the new owners like the padlock, others throw it away. Everyone keeps giving me new keys.'

She looked through the office off the kitchen and out the back window overlooking the Temp's old skylight. It used to be a battered cottage back there. Now the building ascended above her eye-line, an unfolded tesseract, à la Dali, with ochre stucco.

'Uh huh,' she said. 'That's ... '

'... not as bad as the other stuff that's happening,' said the Ghost, risking an aesthetic opinion.

She admitted it was not. There was something about it that felt at ease with the Market. A tesseract, after all, folded into the fourth dimension. Or was it the fifth? The fourth was time, wasn't it? A dimension that had been compressing and expanding like an accordion for many months now. At least for Kip.

Anyway, there was always more to the Market than ever met the eye.

The kitchen chairs were the same as before. Sixties chrome and vinyl. She sat down in one.

'The gate, though,' she said.

'No, the gate's a bad sign,' said the Ghost. 'Totally. I missed most of the action, went away for the summer!' He was pleased that he had scored an agreement and was glad to tell her about the expansive events of his life, evidence that he'd changed, he'd grown, he'd matured, he was able now to offer considered –

'Where is Nancy?' she asked.

'She moved out,' he said. 'It's just me now, uh, here. I think she mailed me a forwarding address. Although I went away to Europe, I think I did manage to keep it carefully filed –'

'How long ago?'

'Oh, I took off in May and just got ba–'

Kip bit her lip and spoke through it. 'How long since Nancy moved out?'

'Oh! Sorry! Just after the big split.'

'What big split?'

'Between you and her. 'That must have been some big-ass fight you two had. It's none of my business, but –'

'That's right,' said Kip. 'It is none of your business.'

'Yeah,' the Ghost went on, undeterred. 'She wouldn't talk about it either. She threw all your possessions out onto the sidewalk. Then she moved out too.'

That hurt. Everything Kip had from Mani. Photographs, letters, all gone in one smug anecdote, offered up by a ghost.

Her own fault though, no? Too much fuzzy thinking. A poorly planned revenge. Her own little *Hamlet*.

'Where did she go?'

'West, I think.'

'Out of the city?'

'West in the city.'

'Okay,' she said. 'So where's Henry?'

'W – um …'

Suddenly the Ghost was hesitating. 'You don't know? he said.

'If I knew,' said Kip, 'I wouldn't be asking.'

'He's in, uh, in prison.'

'Prison?'

'Yeah. I guess he got mixed up with some sorta femme fatale, ended up in prison because of it. Happened just before I left.'

Femme fatale. Sure, Henry was maybe the type for that. But prison?

The Ghost clammed up though. Was looking at the floor. It seemed he knew more about Henry than he was saying, but he wasn't going to tell it despite all her threats. Was he being loyal? She felt she should respect this despite the inconvenience, as it may have been the only positive quality he possessed.

'Can I take a look around?' she asked.

'Be my guest,' said the Ghost, taking great interest in the counter-top.

In the hallway, she came to the final shock in this momentous visit.

The third floor was gone. There were steps that still went up to a small platform, a mere fragment of what used to be Kip's whole storey. But the area where she had once kept her bed? Where she had curled up with Mani? Gone.

'It makes for a high ceiling,' called the Ghost from the kitchen. 'Do you like it?'

'No.'

'Oh. That's okay. Change is hard. I didn't do it though. Just so you know. But I was allowed to keep the lease after renovations.

'Who's the owner?' she asked.

'Uh, it was a fellow from the development company. They expropriated the whole neighbourhood and then this guy came in and snapped up this place. Said he wanted to make sure this one stayed standing. Guess he liked it.'

The Ghost had been cleaning his coffee implements in the sink, head way down. Now he finally turned to see if she was still there. She was. Right in the doorway. Still staring at him. Her jaw was set like it might snap in half.

'I'm moving in,' she said.

'Sorry?'

'You can stay or go, as you please. I don't care. But I'm going to move in up there.'

She pointed behind her head, into the hallway and up towards what was left of the third floor.

'That's my storage area,' the Ghost said, weakly.

'I'll get you a locker,' she said. 'I'll move it for you.'

'But … there's no privacy up there.'

'I'll put up a curtain,' she said. 'Don't worry.'

'Okay,' said the Ghost.

They say you can never go home again? But you can. You just have to live with a ghost.

As for Henry: though temporarily forgotten, he is by no means gone forever from this story. So it might be a good idea to pry open the tight lips of the Ghost and get him to spill the details of what happened, if not for Kip then at least for you, dear devoted reader. Don't be shy then. You've seen how harmless he is. Come up the fire escape. Thunk thunk thunk. The door handle has finally been replaced so it won't come off in your hand. Anyway, it's already open so you don't even have to worry. Come in, sit down at the deco table. Have some bodum coffee, for old time's sake or a fancy-schmantsy espresso or maybe a glass of wine. Sit and hear the story of Henry.

Sometime back around the middle of May, as it turns out, Henry was hit over the head by a man in the rear hallway of a bar, after a gig, with a Grolsch bottle, and given a serious concussion. By the time he came to, more or less, it was several hours later and he was way out in the west end, Humber Loop, standing beside a ditch, holding a cell-phone in his hand. There was a man's body in the ditch, lying beside Henry's open flight case, both looking much abused.

After standing for several moments in the throes of shock and stupor, Henry made the decision to call 911, whereupon he was obliged to piece the facts together for the dispatcher. He'd come here by streetcar. The body must have been in the case. *A walking city, bereft of memory, housing the dead.* Where was his instrument? Must be back at the bar. Still. No idea why he'd killed a man. No idea how. Was he being set up? No. It was all true. He vaguely remembered it. The coroner said later he'd broken the man's trachea with his fingertips. Did he recognize the man? No. Well, yes. Well ... no, but he had a pretty good idea who he was: Henry had been hanging out with a crazy sexy woman. A recent development. There was another man in the picture somewhere. Turned out the other man didn't appreciate being just part of the landscape. He'd attacked him in the back hallway of a bar, after a gig. Henry had stuffed the body into his case out of some instinct to conceal his action.

Henry was in big trouble. But once he came clean, he discovered that it was considered by the authorities to be a clear case of self-defence. The lawyer even called it a 'complete defence.' There was conclusive evidence that he was suffering from a concussion that had been induced by the deceased party.

The major problem turned out to be the flight to the Humber Loop: the fact of Henry, concussion or no, having committed an indignity to a body. That caught him six months inside.

This mitigated prison sentence was the best bit of luck Henry had experienced in a long time. Essentially, his character could be distilled down to this: he was afraid that bad things would happen, even and perhaps especially as a consequence of doing a good deed. And, generally, bad things did happen to Henry. As such, the world was becoming more and more of a haze for him.

Now he'd killed a man, which was bad. But he'd been given a six-month sentence, which was good. But he'd still killed a man, which was bad.

In other words: no luxury of a Manichean universe for Henry. The good and the bad were all mixed up together inside him, guided by an addled brain that would go through the shivers and sweats of withdrawal a few times before the end of this story.

A little bit of research gave Kip the only possible route to Pat York. The problem with it was that it was on a vertical rather than a horizontal plane. She knew she had to get up to his office and she knew security protocols had been ramped up since her last visit. So it was going to take some real scheming and a not inconsiderable amount of luck.

First things first. She was going to need a gun. No, two guns. Well, no, in point of fact, given the plan unfolding in her head, one of them could be a pop gun, as long as it looked real. But the second had to be lethal.

In the old days, such a purchase was a task she might have gone to Henry for. Now she had to do it on her own.

She decided to walk through Parkdale in the west end and see if an opportunity would present itself. Parkdale was a vibrant place:

food-, flâneur- and family-oriented. But did people not get shot there from time to time? She found no evidence. Traffic slowed to a snail because pedestrians jammed the crosswalks. Its density didn't indicate violence so much as it predicted the city's more populous future. Maybe there were guns to be had somewhere here, but she either didn't have the radar or she was putting out the wrong signals. All day she walked the neighbourhood. No go.

Next day, she tried Etobicoke, dreaded suburb, site of the mayor's ranch-style home, haven for long-gun rebels, stomping ground for bored and ruthless teens. At least that's what she'd heard. A desperate, backward place where a pedestrian with a twenty-dollar bill could wander forever, unable to get transportation or sustenance.

But the storied suburban hellishness did not present its face to her. There were merchants aplenty, peddling their wares from the low-rise strip malls. Okra. Falafel. Veggie patties and veggies unadorned. Italian eateries with a West African flair. Culture.

No guns.

Three more days went by. Jane Finch. Regent Park. Jarvis Street – had it not been named for a man who fought a duel in 1817? No guns.

On the fourth day, though, at the end of the day, she was making her way along College Street, not long after dark, about to dip down into the top of the Market, en route home, hoping the Ghost (who was always there) would not be there to sharpen the edge of her impatience. She was approaching the lights at the top of Augusta, north side of the street, where the sidewalk was wide.

Across the street, top of the Market, where Zak's Convenience Store used to be, there was a hole in the ground three storeys deep, fenced in and running east almost all the way to Spadina Avenue and south to Oxford Street. What had been there? A bunch of computer-supply stores up front, old family homes behind. A Buddhist temple maybe? Oh, and of course all the shops on the east side of Augusta, the seedy laundromat, the bicycle shop, Bread and Circus, pies. All gone. A tower crane presided, imperiously, rendering the area newly desolate.

The north side of College Street, though, was the same as ever. There was a pharmacy that she and Mani, last year, had seen a rat enter, bounding through a door propped open by a janitor's mop. His hind legs could barely touch the ground. For days Mani had imitated that bouncy gate, puffing his cheeks and raising his elbows as if they had a girth to clear, and then he'd go *bloingy-bloingy-bloing*ing along, all the way down the street ahead of her …

And Kip would laugh. She was laughing now.

The city was full of such geographical pinpricks of memory. One leading to the next, to the next. Now she let Mani's rat dance play out in the back of her mind. The day would come when all these buildings would be brought down and take all memories with them. Faded words on sheets of paper in the rain.

The pharmacy had turned her head, and, all unawares, she was fast approaching a tight circular scrum of men who had gathered on the pavement. She came abreast of the circle as someone on the periphery made a swift movement that caught her eye. She turned her head just as a small man in the centre was struck.

Some kind of frontier justice was going down. The blow startled her to the present. Rebooted a sense of fair play in the blink of her eye. She turned her eyes but not her head. The man in the centre wasn't small after all. He was down on his knees, and there was a vendetta happening right out in the open. Kip's mouth fell open, but she did not gasp. Felt instead, against her better judgment, a flash of rage.

Swift thoughts ran through her mind as the hand in the scrum was raised to strike another blow. She felt, distinctly, the return to her mind of Kip the motor-mouth salesman. She tried to suppress it; put her head down, a civilian motoring past, see no evil hear no evil speak no evil, touching the circumference of the circle on the way past, and she quickened her step. But as she passed the closest point, she allowed her heel to turn in a crack in the sidewalk. And so she fell, sideways, to the left, tumbling directly through a gap between two bodies, piercing the circumference of the circle into the striking place, the centre.

This is where I will find guns, she thought.

2

In the centre of the circle, things were not much different than how Kip had imagined them. Dust had been raised and the man in the middle had marks on his face – he'd suffered more than a single blow. She also realized, in this moment, there'd been a murmuring conference that she was interrupting. The centre man was being subjected to a patient lecture as part of his punishment. The timeless wisdom of the violent being shared. And so Kip was not a welcome distraction as she planted her face in the grit and began to execute a spazzy roll, shouting the whole time. 'Excuse me! I'm so sorry!'

Protests were rising quietly among the silhouettes around her. She thought she saw a weapon disappear into a little bag, the swift glint of steel in the streetlights. As she finished her roll, having scratched her cheek fetchingly, coming up on one scuffed knee, she was still repeating apologies in her most clued-out tone. She wasn't quite dressed properly for this. With the old Kip, they would have known right away what kind of woman they were dealing with; now it wouldn't be so clear.

Someone grabbed her arm, intent on jettisoning her from the circle, no harm done in getting back to the lesson. She had only a second to speak.

'Maybe you can help me,' she said calmly in the direction of the silhouette holding the little bag. 'I need to buy two handguns.'

No change of expression. The rough grip was still pulling her in the wrong direction as she sped up her words. 'I'll pay two thousand a piece for them. You people can help me, yes?'

As soon as she named her price, several eyebrows went up so high as to nearly depart the shaded faces.

The man who held the bag that concealed the firearm spoke up.

'No,' he said, 'we don't have.'

'But you can take me to someone who does, yes?'

Seek the answer yes. Or some engagement at least. The trick of the salesman.

They looked Chinese. Or Vietnamese? Like the family who'd lived in the house behind 12 Kensington in the days before death and unfolding tesseracts.

'Busy now,' he said, almost politely. 'You go.'

'One-time offer,' she said, trying to will blood to flow through the grip on her forearm. 'Who's your boss? He won't want you to pass it up.'

The man with whom she had briefly shared the centre had not moved from his place. He was on his knees, head down, but his fingers, which had been gripping the back of his own neck, were down now, supporting his weight on the sidewalk, a sprinter at the start line. She tried not to look at him. But then he spoke up, quiet and unexpected: some low canto to the one who held the small bag, who looked for a moment like he might strike him again. But then a look of doubt entered his expression. The man on the ground spoke again. The tone was an appeal to reason. Common sense. Advice from a subordinate who had once been superior. Respectful, slightly impatient. Smart.

Then he fell silent as the standing ones conferred. She cast a glance his way, negotiating with herself about the zero-sum morality of taking a life in exchange for saving one.

They reached a decision. One of them would leave the scrum and take Kip with him down into Chinatown. But she didn't have one single agenda.

'No,' she said.

No?

'I don't trust where one alone might take me.'

'*Chee seen*,' said the man with the bag. 'Your trust. *Chee seen.*'

She pointed to each of them individually. 'I will pay your boss one hundred dollars for each one who comes with me.' There were eight of them standing in the circle. She got to the ninth, on the ground, and pointed at him. Her finger stayed there. She wondered whether they could see her true intent. On the other hand, the guns were her true intent. Presumably they could see that too.

Which is how she ended up overshooting the Market that evening and walking south on Spadina, still encircled, somewhat less geometrically, by eight thugs and their intended victim. He was directly behind her. It was not clear how long she had deferred his punishment. But she had deferred it. *I saved a life. So …*

Fingering the bicycle key around her neck.

They took her to a bar on Spadina with a painted sign and a dark, red vinyl interior, slightly run down. The Red Door. White bartender, Viet bussers and kitchen staff, a mix of servers. It looked like the Temp from the old days, enlarged and improved. Even the food on the tables was giving her déjà vu. Chicken on rice, hot chilies.

To the back, past the kitchen, a dingy office whose only decorations were a laminated recent newspaper article, brand-new, on the wall and a dusty black rose in a beer bottle that Kip failed to notice. There was a wiry man, in his fifties maybe, maybe older, perpetually youthful despite little scars on his forehead and cheek. A mop of black hair. He looked familiar. A no-bullshit character. About the same height as Kip. Didn't look troubled by the entrance of the nine, mostly because he was finishing a phone call.

'What am I supposed to do with that?' he was asking. *'Ngaw bei nei chui jeung.* You got for me ten useless pieces of shit construction machinery pieces? What am I going to do with that? I only just got rid of storage bins I had to store. First storing storage bins, now this. You think I'm Sanford and Son? *Chee seen!* Fix it.'

He hung up. Looked at Kip. 'People in the world,' he said. 'They're all bad. *Teen haa woo aa.'*

Then he took in the whole gang around her and his mood changed. 'Who is this girl who has hijacked my guys?' he asked, amused. He was addressing the man with the bag, who responded in the other language. Not Vietnamese, but Cantonese. He was a whole head taller than his boss. Kip noticed they both wore tan leather vests. One of the vintage stores in the Market used to have them hanging always on a rack outside. The boss reached up and tapped him on the cheek with the flat of his fingers. A son perhaps? Nephew?

Finally he dismissed them and they all filed out. Kip grabbed the sleeve of the last, the man from the centre. Holding him there, careful not to touch his person, just the fabric. Turned to the boss, who rolled his eyes.

'It's a private matter for them,' he said, distancing himself from what was being done in his name. 'I'd rather not get involved.'

She still held.

'You have no idea what he's done,' said the boss. 'But you don't care, you don't care.'

'I'll give you ten thousand dollars if you spare him,' she said.

'Maybe I'll just take your money and do as I please,' said the boss.

'I'll want monthly reports.'

'Maybe I send you Photoshop.'

He laughed. And then he approached her. His expression changed.

'*Nei*,' he said. 'I know you.'

She was still holding the sleeve. The man's head down.

'Okay,' said the boss. 'I'll tell you what he did. This man here took all the clothes we collected for Chinese widows and orphans. Yes he did. He stole them from their storage bins and diverted them to a bunch of people without taking any pay for them.'

'You mean he diverted them to widows and orphans?'

'Exactly,' said the boss, looking like he might smack the man about the head. 'Ten shipping containers. Six months' worth of business.'

'I don't understand.'

'No,' said the boss. 'I can see that. Everyone trying to turn me into a giver these days. Writing confusing flattery!' He gestured to the laminate clipping on the wall. It was a picture of him, recent, above an article that appeared to be about philanthropy. '*Chee seen*,' he said. 'Maybe I'm sick of it! But I hear you have other business. *Jek so*. Let's talk about that.'

But Kip was still mulling over the widows and orphans.

'It was meant to be a scam, you idiot,' he said. 'This man turned it into a legitimate charitable enterprise.'

'On your behalf?'

'Well, of course. Everything is done on my behalf.'

'So you don't want to be a philanthropist?'

He shrugged. 'It's very good for money laundering. But it doesn't just take away the problem. It also takes away the money.'

'And it makes you look good,' she said.

'I never cared about what people thought of me before. Why should I care now?'

Her turn to shrug.

'But I know you,' he said.

'You said that already,' she said.

She was still holding the man, his head still down. The boss walked past them, through the door. 'Richard!' he called.

The tall man with the bag reappeared, clutching a pint of draft. They had a brief conversation. The younger man said something in a complaining voice and the boss admonished him. Then he smiled and said something else and they both laughed. Finally, the sleeve was released and the man slipped away without looking back.

'Happy?' said the boss. She didn't respond. He rolled his eyes. 'You want a drink?'

'Sure.'

They walked out past the kitchen to the bar. He found a booth attended by some of the men. They cleared out with their pints and the boss gestured for her to sit while he went to the bar.

She slid in. He returned with two pints of dark ale.

'You don't recognize me?' he asked.

'No,' she said.

'No, huh? Funny, I look the same, it's you who look different.' Then: 'Where do you live?' he asked, blunt.

'Um, I used to live in the Market,' she said, hesitating. 'And I guess I live there again.'

'Thought so, thought so,' he said. 'You lived in my building.' A broad smile cracked his face, rendering him suddenly eleven.

'Twelve Kensington?'

'My building before,' he said. 'And the bar. Mine too.'

She remembered him now. Joseph Luong. He had owned the Temp. She'd no idea the whole building was his, but then again he was the sort of man who held his cards close to his chest.

'You were my landlord?' she said. 'We mostly dealt with Suzie.'

Suzie was the bartender, a beautiful Chinese woman that Joseph always seemed to be courting despite a wife somewhere.

He nodded. 'You remember Suzie?'

'She was really nice.'

'Suzie.' He shrugged. 'House she and her father grew up in, Shanghai, got torn down. One day her sister walk outside, see a white tag on the wall. *Chai.* Here it means tea. There, it means gone. I felt sorry for her.' He shrugged again, as if it were an unpleasant fact of life. 'Sold the whole building to her. Gave her a deal too. No idea she would turn around, make such a killing with the land deal.'

'Gentrification,' said Kip.

'You got out just in time,' said Joseph. She was surprised by his angle: gentrification as a bad thing. Rising property values might not be so great for the Vietnamese, ethnic Chinese gangster set.

'I'm back,' she said. 'Going to try and degentrify it.'

'Good luck with that,' he said, raising his chin and slashing across it with the edge of his hand. Cutthroat.

'What do you mean?' she asked.

'I also owned the building in the back,' said Joseph. One day it blew up. You hear about that?'

'Drugs stashed in there, I heard,' she said, 'stealing electricity, bad wiring –'

'First of all,' said Joseph, showing some exasperation, 'you don't need to steal electricity to store drugs. You steal electricity to grow the drugs, see? But yeah, I read that story too. And the wiring was all good. I used to have friends living in there. I take care of my friends!' He was indignant. 'Bad wiring,' he spat. 'That knob and tube they found in there, it was all just fake. A plant. But after it all exploded, there was too much light shining on me. You know? I had to pay a lot of money to make that shit go away. Man like me can't afford to be vindictive and certainly not sentimental. In the end,' he shrugged, 'I had to sell. Suzie jumped on that bandwagon too.'

'Who bought it?' she asked.

'Oh,' said Joseph. 'One of those guys. Those Market-killing guys. *Teen haa woo aa.*'

'People are bad,' said Kip, remembering.

'All over the place,' said Joseph.

He got chatty after discovering their common currency. It turned out he had his hand in many businesses, the least of which came as a great surprise to Kip: a worm-picking enterprise, a battalion of nocturnal prowlers who strapped buckets to their ankles, wore powerful headlamps and harvested urban lawns for shipping out to lakeside towns in cottage country.

'You,' she said, mouth open. 'You're in charge of those, um – ?'

'Good job for recent immigrants,' he said. 'I am for sure a philanthropist of the recent immigrant. As I was once one myself.' After a pause, he added, 'They can also keep an eye on things for me now and then.'

'What kind of things?' asked Kip.

'Anything that takes my interest,' said Joseph. 'Houses for sale, renovation projects.'

So the worm pickers had been spies? So it had been no coincidence, them crawling around the York house on Pendrith Street in the spring? Unbelievable. They were keeping an eye on things for Mr. Joseph Luong, Kensington Market landowner, entrepreneur, reluctant philanthropist, gangster and wooer of untouchable bartenders.

Joseph had been a bona fide boat person, from a rich family in Vietnam who had lost everything. So he was older than he looked. Another country's greatest generation. He'd been to university over there, had studied Latin and Greek. His favourite author was Nikos Kazantzakis. Had she read the work from this genius?

She realized suddenly what the Temp had really been called.

'*The Last Temptation of Christ,*' she said.

'That's right, that's right,' said Joseph, smiling. 'Genius book. How to live, fixed between the passion of the body and the will of the spirit. Gravity pushes you down to the earth, spirit pulls you up to the sun.'

'Sounds like the philosophy of philanthropy,' said Kip.

'Spare me,' said Joseph.

'Okay, okay.'

'It's no mystery,' he said. 'Merely the interesting philosophy of European Catholics behaving like Hao. Nice for me, who should be a Hao but got raised Catholic Hoa.'

'What's Hao?' asked Kip.

'It's a branch of Buddhism.'

'And what's a Hoa?'

'What I am,' said Joseph. 'Born in Vietnam of Chinese origin.'

'Hao and Hoa,' said Kip.

'Hoa,' said Joseph, correcting her. 'Not Hao. That's me.'

He paused for a moment. Seemed dejected.

'I love the Market,' he went on. 'That apartment above the bar, it was my home once.'

'Really?' she said. 'You lived at 12?'

'I loved that place,' he said. 'Fire escape, old door. Third floor, under the roof; hidden balcony out the back window. I loved it!'

'Me too,' she said. 'People keep leaving flowers on the fire escape. Do you know why?'

'No idea,' said Joseph. 'But for me,' he went on, 'I am a businessman, yes? But that doesn't mean I can't love the Market. It was my first home here. It welcomed me. Epic place. How could I not love the Market?'

'I need a gun,' she said.

But before we get to the guns: the origin of Joseph Luong's recent philanthropic confusion and woe. This could be traced, believe it or not, to a midsummer encounter with none other than Kip's old friend, Nancy, who, in her barely corporeal way, had attempted to recruit him to the cause.

While lying on a slab somewhere for several hours, Nancy had experimented with consciousness by concentrating on a television documentary that was playing somewhere in the building about organized crime in the city – how some of the old small-time hoods were rubbing up against housing developers. Many hints about vendettas happening right in the Market. Even a mention of the fire at 12½ Kensington. Except they called it 12 Kensington. Some things are just too subtle for the media, she thought. They just can't handle it.

She found herself thinking of her old landlord. Joseph Luong. It seemed pretty clear that he was involved in the underground economy. That made him an automatic ally to an undergrounder. Perhaps he could be brought onside in her barely formulated little revenge scheme against the developers. Did it not make sense? Landlords and tenants banding together against those who would dig up their burrows and knock down their buildings?

So: Nancy took the wind. She found a brochure on a park bench in front of the sooty black towers downtown. It was a celebration of Pat's new condo development on the Humber River. With the help of the wind, she peeled the brochure up from the bench and blew it along King Street, from the corner of Bay all the way past University (where it was run over eight times in the intersection) to Spadina, then managed (with some difficulty) to get it to turn the corner and blow north. Though the brochure was sturdily designed, it was not made to win the war against the road. *Roads are built for buses, cars and trucks, not for brochures*, she thought. *Brochures are more delicate, like bicycles. My heart bleeds for them but their destruction is their own fault at the end of the day.* Still, when the brochure she'd commandeered finally arrived at the entrance to the Red Door and was picked up by Joseph Luong (who was no great fan of littering in Chinatown), it was still legible enough to read. And then, when Joseph Luong read it, he felt the glimmer of an idea about how he might thwart such a high-class dwelling project by his Market nemesis. He liked this glimmer of an idea so much that he took it for his own, which misapprehension he could be forgiven for, despite the fact that it did not resemble any of his other schemes. Not in any way. Still, how could he know that it had actually been whispered in his ear by the mercurial, barely corporeal Nancy, with some assistance from the wind?

The idea was to target Pat York's proudest new condo development: a state-of-the-art building going up on the west bank of the mighty Humber River, surrounded by parkland that had itself once been a residential neighbourhood washed away by Hurricane Hazel. He would turn it into a spontaneous makeshift, corrugated shantytown. Chaos. Delight.

Joseph would endeavour to surround this new condo with a series of homeless shelters made from shipping containers. It was a perfect idea; he'd acquired hundreds of these eyesores five years earlier in a salvaged-scrap deal with a bankrupt fellow former boat person. He'd been spending a fortune on their storage (the storage of storage bins). Now he was going to kill two birds with one stone. Or, more specifically, he was going to kill one condo, house a hundred birds and rectify his storage problem.

Joseph was confident his action would stain Pat's project with the taint of chaos, despair, preemptive nimbyism. It didn't occur to him that he was doing anything charitable, so focused was he on thwarting his great Market nemesis.

Unfortunately, the shelters, once installed, didn't have quite the effect on Pat's reputation or sales that Joseph (or Nancy) had hoped. Quite the opposite. They turned out to be functional and surprisingly attractive, adapted by their squatters in myriad styles. And so, in an increasingly hyper-driven housing market, they merely shifted the media spotlight onto the development itself. Pat noticed immediately, whereupon he lobbied to have the area rezoned, making the shelters legal, and then renamed his Humberside condo the Sally Ann.

Inevitably, hundreds of denizens of the creative class left their condo queues in the vicinity of the Drake, clamouring to purchase arty new 'shelters' in the York building, directly above the alleged squalor. 'After all,' one anonymous buyer exclaimed to the press, 'my new home is just about the same shape and size as one of those things. But I get a view!'

In other words, Pat York won the day. And that might have been enough to engender an escalation of the war between the two. But the next thing that happened utterly disarmed Joseph Luong.

At a crucial moment in the month-long affair, someone in the press suddenly noticed all the evidence of Joseph's obsession with the mid-twentieth-century Greek writer Nikos Kazantzakis, as indicated by the Kensington resto bar he'd once named the Last Temptation, along with another Market watering hole called Zorba's and a short-lived coffee shop on Queen Street called The Fratricides.

Relying on good old-fashioned shoe-leather sleuthing, the journalist created an expansive and not unflattering profile of Joseph for the front page of the newspaper, mistaking his thorn in York's side for a clumsy attempt at honest-to-goodness philanthropy and, in the process, inevitably (if somewhat predictably) comparing him to Zorba the Greek.

The day the article appeared, Joseph got a morning phone call from a one-time Hoa rival, Francis, a man brought low by new developments along the city's waterfront that had been responsible for the dredging up of a cement-filled oil drum containing some telltale remains.

Joseph could hardly believe it when he realized his former rival was calling to extend humble congratulations in an effort to accept the law of karma and embrace his Hao roots (as distinguished from his Hoa roots, also present).

That fate had chosen such a path for Francis while at the same time crowning Joseph the new King of Kensington was a source of deep reflection, affording the new king an opportunity to consider the fork that suddenly appeared before him in the road.

He wasn't completely changed, mind you, as evidenced by his desire to punish the underling who had diverted the clothing to widows and orphans, not to mention his willingness to get the guns to Kip. But Kip's questions intrigued and troubled him too. It was all very *interesting* – very, very *interesting,* indeed. Not a day went by that he didn't pronounce the word *philanthropy* at least one time.

Needless to say, Nancy was not happy – the failure of her scheming, the success of Pat's Sally Ann, the new drift of Joseph Luong's thinking. No, she was not happy at all …

3

Kip left the Red Door with her heart a little fuller. Full flutter. One gun: check. (And a pop gun was en route from Australia, almost swifter than the moon's sphere.)

Now came the easy part. It was all business.

Pat York occupied his father's old corner office with south- and east-facing windows near the top of the black Mies tower 5.

Windows. They're always a building's weakest point. And word had always been that Mies windows were flimsier than most. There was a famous story about a lawyer who threw himself against one once, at a party, while boasting of their impermeability to some students or interns or, anyway, the young. The glass shattered. He fell a long way.

So, for Kip, then, it was a simple matter of

1) finding the company in charge of the cleaning of the Mies windows, presumably one of the five top hits on Google,

and

2) masquerading as the super's secretary (Janice), and convincing the cleaners to rejig their schedule due to the imminent, short-notice visit of an architect from the very firm that had designed the building (Janice: 'We must have that polish! We must have that shine!').

In short, nothing that was not in the purview of a person who knew how to talk people into buying things they didn't necessarily want to buy and doing things they didn't necessarily want to do.

Kip was prepared to manipulate a pair of seasoned window cleaners. As it turned out, though, the only way the cleaning company could accommodate *Janice* on the day in question was by providing a pair of neophytes. Cleaners on training wheels, as it were, who could be serendipitous playthings in her long, Jean Seberg fingers. She had not planned for this – she thought she'd be dealing with hardened professionals. Maybe now, since they were going to be beginnings, she wouldn't have to play hardball, maybe a bribe would be enough, and the more frightening plan she'd been devising could be reserved for Plan B. In any event, the plan seemed to be unfolding as if the fates themselves were in favour of it, as if Justice had removed her blindfold and was conducting the orchestra from a plinth.

Then she rented an office across from the black Mies tower – in the hideous BMO building, the makers of which had prided themselves on towering over Mies, even when their white cladding pieces started sliding off and hurtling towards the street. Kip was happy to sit down in this (by definition) vengeful building, eyesore to all on the east side of the black towers, to spy on the eastern windows of Pat York, who barely left his office at all during the day. He seemed to be hooked to his computer, conducting meetings via Skype. Her nemesis turned out to be an eccentric loner. Who'd a thought.

The day of zero hour, fairly early in the morning, Kip walked east and south from the Market, past Chinatown and past the refurbished AGO (courtesy of Frank Gehry, the architect who had turned down Pat's father, who had made the Dancing Building dance and whose design for this art gallery now reminded her of the afternoon in the 12 Kensington kitchen when, with a living Mani by her side, she'd first heard the name of York), down through Grange Park and zeroed in on the tall buildings downtown. She was feeling some anxiety about Nancy. Didn't know why. It occurred to her that she herself might die today and might never see her old friend again. Never get a chance to explain what happened. She'd been so hard on her about the toy gun. But she'd just gotten guns for herself, by any means possible. So it was Mani, not Nancy, who'd acquired the gun last time; therefore Mani, not Nancy, she should have been angry with.

As she walked, the anticipation of glass shattering – flying back into her own face, some of it falling towards the street below – set her teeth on edge. No, the force would propel it all inward.

Sky was clear, though. Sunny September day. Not a cloud to be seen. On her way, she bought a pack of cigarettes, even though she didn't smoke. A Zippo lighter too, which would be able to work among the wind tunnels of downtown buildings. She got the clerk to fill it up with fluid. Unwrapped the cigarettes.

There was one aspect to all this that was making her uncomfortable. Not so much the firing of the gun and the shattering of the window. No, the part that was bothering her was the seduction of the window cleaner. The possible necessity for coercive sex. Plan B. She could not quite wrap her head around it. She walked by ads in bus kiosks wherein the women were essentially doing what she was going to have to do. Making their lips go a certain way and their eyes go a certain way, as if to say, to all the passersby, all I want is you. Languid. Inviting butterflies to hurl fragile bodies against their surfaces.

Anyway, it would only come into play if Plan A didn't work. Sex, in case the bribe didn't work. She only had two cleaners. Two options. Two men (or, rather, two boys: neophytes, boys in men's bodies): one who would look more likely to want money, one who would look more likely to want sex. This was the only decision she would have to make. One choice that would govern both Plan A and, if that failed, B.

She pulled out a cigarette and put the tip in her mouth. Sweet Caporal. Tried out the Zippo. It worked. Tried to breathe in with the smoke the feeling, pre-Mani, of being at ease cohabiting with assholes.

All around her there were cranes, quiet monsters, things being erected everywhere, even around the Mies tower, where space was at a premium. Buildings between buildings and on top of buildings, buildings where parking lots used to be, where roofs of other buildings used to be. Still, there didn't seem to be any workers around today. The only ones, sure enough, were the pair of presumably neophyte window cleaners way up high, clinging to the cladding of the

Mies. There, as promised to *Janice* the receptionist. Fate had dealt Kip a pair of jacks. All she needed now were some aces. Access.

Over the course of the next couple of hours she stood in the shadows and watched the cleaners work their way around the building. They were at the south end of the west face when she arrived, just pulling themselves up to rejig their rig and slide down the west side of the south face. Up and down twice more until they got to the extreme east side. She watched them pull themselves down past Pat York's window, with his view of the morning sun, and lower and lower to her point of contact.

Then she walked out into the gleaming sun and waved suggestively, recklessly. One of the cleaners had a pair of binoculars. The type to better appreciate his surroundings. He looked through them. She beckoned. They came down. It took them a long time, getting up to the roof and then footing it down through the building. She wasn't in any hurry. She knew what she was doing, willing it to work. She knew they would come and eventually they did.

The taller one arrived first. At about thirty paces she had him pegged as the one who would be all about the cash, which was convenient – person one arriving on his longer legs to initiate Plan A. She offered him some money to take her up on the cleaning rig. He shook his head with a furrowed brow just as the second man was approaching. It was clear from the brow that the taller one wanted the money, but there was going to be too many strings attached. So she changed her strategy on the fly and offered him the same amount to take a long break while she turned her attention to the smaller one. This he found acceptable. So. Paving the way for Plan B.

But was Kip ready for Plan B? She could barely even remember what it was to have sex with anyone. She'd closed her warmth to the world several months ago. That was about to change. Right now. Plan B. What was it again? The sweet deal for Shorty.

To whom she turned and addressed as follows: 'Hey there, have you ever, uh, [fucked a nice girl] way up there in that thing?'

'I beg your pardon?'

Oops. She tried to resist the impulse to clear her throat – a decidedly non-alluring option – then looked around and did not speak again.

'Uh, no,' he said.

'I'm surprised,' she said, blushing and warming to her task, 'because that's a prime piece of real estate and it's all yours for the day.'

'Just the morning, actually.'

'Okay, just the morning,' she said, affecting a pout she used to use with the asshole who had immediately preceded Mani as a boyfriend. 'I'll tell you just the spot,' she added. And then paused to see if he might guess. But he was gazing at her with his mouth open, so she looked up and pointed. 'See there, just above the fifty-second floor?'

'I see it.'

'There are no windows there. It's private, wouldn't you say?'

'I don't get it,' he said. 'Did somebody send you?'

'Let's just say I'm here to celebrate your first big job.'

'Oh man. You mean … Tozer … ?'

'They like to make the first job an experience for you big boys,' she said, taking her time with the words like she was in an old movie.

'What about Jason then?'

'His turn will come. It's yours now. Don't tell him, though. Best it's a surprise.'

The partner Jason came back from smoking his cigarette. The smaller one gave him a begging look without realizing it, and then Kip told him the deal required an early lunch. He was on his way into the Mies building, presumably to eat there, but she said, 'No,' and pointed for him to go to some other building, on some other street. He went.

The remaining window cleaner was a small, muscular, round-headed man named Wilson, who turned out to have a black belt in karate, but that didn't mean she couldn't handle him. She barely noticed her surroundings as they went up through the building and out onto the roof. She allowed a fear of heights to overtake her as they climbed into the rig and he pulled them down. He told her to put her arms around him if she was scared. She rewarded his instinct for gentleness. She may have been behaving like a femme fatale, but that didn't mean she didn't have standards.

It was a little colder up the south face than she'd expected, and she felt the goose bumps rise on her legs, like a small army of rebels.

He was good and kind and gentle. In the moment of no return, she felt a flash of wishing him dead, but pushed it down into a feeling of heat within and cold without.

Anyway, one single death would be plenty.

A life for a life.

'Are you okay?' he asked. Her eyes were wet. Blurring a bit.

She said, 'Tell you the truth, I'm new at this. I thought it would be a good idea to make a bit of cash. Now I'm not so sure.'

'Do you want me to stop?'

'No, no, it's beautiful up here.'

'Your eyes are so wide.'

'I'm just a clumsy girl.'

The window cleaner suddenly got very earnest.

'I'll take care of you,' he said. Was the man more likely to want sex than money also more likely to be kind?

'No,' she said. 'It's my job to take care of you.'

She rolled him over and planted him. She felt the wind whirlpooling in her ears. She felt compassion. More tears. The next task was pushed far back in her mind, though she knew already she would try to spare this man. She thought *The cut worm forgives the plough* and wondered where that came from. A book of poetry or something, long left by her bedside, by Mani. Abandoned by Kip. Dumped in a cardboard box on the sidewalk by Nancy.

More tears. More.

Everything that lives is holy.

When they were done, the window cleaner was happy, He even told her a little about himself. How he did not visit prostitutes nor did he pursue casual sex in bars. He'd heard once you could pick up girls at a used bookstore in Little Italy. So he'd headed over there one time, ended up buying a whole bunch of pulpy murder mysteries that he was still struggling to get through. He'd made the decision to embark on a new job that was going to be exhausting and was going to prevent him from making the wood sculptures that he wanted to make. He'd been depressed about it. But here he was, on his first unsupervised outing, visited by an angel from heaven who would inspire him forever.

'Glad to help,' she said.

They were entwined, lying lengthwise in the narrow trough.

It was summoning time.

She said, 'Can I look in a window?'

Wilson the cleaner said, 'What window?'

She said, 'Just below.'

He tidied himself up a bit and then brought them down. It was about 11:30 in the morning.

For a moment, as they passed the top of the window, she thought it was tinted and she would not even be able to see inside from so close up. But the tint merely gave everything she saw a bronze hue, the feeling of permanence: living statues.

Like Pat, for instance. There he was, in bronze, a monument to her own memory. As if she'd never left. He was pacing back and forth between the desk and another window at the other corner side. Perusing some papers.

Although she had formed some affection for her window cleaner, she had no choice but to change the story of this late morning. She reached into her handbag, pulled out the two guns, held one on the cleaner and the other to the window.

'Sit,' she said.

'Wh –'

'Sit.'

He sat. Then she realized she had the wrong gun in the wrong hand. Had to switch them so the toy gun was pointing at the cleaner and Joseph Luong's gun was pointed at the window. The cleaner didn't seem to notice the significance of the act.

Pat had not seen her yet. The cleaner's face bore a mixture of fear, betrayal, disappointment, anger. Everything was moving as if she were in a bronze-tinted dream, as if she were falling, through negative space again, wondering whether she would ever land, the cleaner sitting placidly, wordlessly, waiting for her to make the decision that was going to destroy his life.

Passing close to the window, Pat was clutching three sheets of a quarterly report. His face had fallen. He'd failed something, somehow. Zigs were zagging, all of a sudden. A dreaded financial jabberwocky was rearing its manxome head.

She prepared herself to squeeze. Wilson the window cleaner waited.

Could she do it? Inflict such violence?

Oh my god, she thought. *Maybe I can't.*

And then Pat turned from the other window and looked at her. They locked eyes for a minute. He was very close to the glass. Stared at her, uncomprehending, blinking. Then, unbelievably, he smiled. A little warm smile of recognition. And then, just in case she didn't understand he was really communicating with her, he lifted the sheet he was holding and turned it to face her. Mouthed some words. They looked like 'I'm so fucked.' The zigzags were going down down down. And then, with a rueful smile, he mouthed something else. Uh oo ee.

Just shoot me.

In forgiving Kip Flynn, Pat never quite forgave himself, but he found within himself the need to take care and be kind, at least within his own standards, so that he would be ready, one day, to tell her about the gift her father had given him.

So in his work, the last few months, Pat displayed good taste and got a lot done in a very short time. Things were suddenly financially tricky, but he seemed to be staying ahead of the troubles. He was even getting some smattering of popularity with the public. The Sally Ann had come along at a perfect time, just when he was thinking he should do more real philanthropic work. It was inconvenient that his ally in that business was actually a nemesis, but he wasn't interested in fighting anymore. He even went up to the riverside and oversaw some work to insulate the shelters against colder weather. And he began to prioritize projects that emphasized reclamation rather than razing. Too late for the Market, of course, and he wasn't about to stop being a high roller, but he went so far as to step away from several early-stage projects so he could embark on a popular and ambitious scheme to modernize the Royal York Hotel, adding twenty-five sleek new storeys to the 1929 building, meant to augment and celebrate its original style. Hugely popular to the majority. Enraging to a select few.

He defined himself, too, with a hobby that was the opposite of his father's. Whereas the old man dug below the city, Pat would rise above it.

He cultivated a stunning rooftop garden on top of the Mies tower. He even had a sizable oak tree transported there at great expense, complete with a healthy root system that had to penetrate several floors, filling up closets and storerooms and hallways with earth.

More and more, he would take his work and head up there, where his time in the sun felt like leisure, no matter what he was up to. And so he became half content again. As he'd been for many years before the incident on the red carpet of the Princess of Wales Theatre, during intermission for *Beauty and the Beast*.

Half content.

Until the day when, standing in the middle of his fifty-second-floor office, he turned towards the window of his office and saw that face again.

Kip, at the window, was still aiming. It wasn't over yet, though the window cleaner was sensing her hesitancy – *I'm a trader not a taker I'm a merchant and a pacifist* (citing Jane Jacobs's *Systems of Survival*) – and was starting to voice his objection. 'You're so fucked up,' he very quietly ventured.

And then, on the other side of the bronze, Pat mouthed the words I – O – O – E. It took her a minute to decipher. I – oh – oh – ee.

I'm ... so ... so ... rry.

Then he did something frankly shocking: he dropped his three pages and loosened his tie.

Oh oh oh ai ah ay. *Don't throw your life away.*

Kip thought: *Is this some kind of new manipulative corporate bullshit?*

It was all happening so fast that the three pages, drifting separately, had only just come to a stop on the bronze carpet.

And then, as if things weren't quite strange enough, behind the window, Pat had a seizure. First one since he was six years old (unless you count the *petit mal* on the red carpet of the Princess of Wales).

He fell against the pane with a thump. The windowpane buckled from the blow. Startled, Kip recalled again the reports of the man who came through. Pat struggled now to fall away from the window but tripped and fell against it again, even harder. The frame stayed in place, though, the glass didn't shatter.

If the bastard broke through, they'd be killers, both of them, of some innocent pedestrians, way down below.

Pat fell against the pane again, one arm flailing.

Thump.

This time he stumbled back and she saw his face. Bronze features full of shock, apology, hope, regret. His eyes rolling up into his head. Shades of his rage on the red carpet. But this time it was more compulsive. Helpless. Didn't seem so much like he was behind glass as beneath it, wriggling like a butterfly on the pin.

Thump.

She buckled this time, with the window. She either had to pull the damn trigger now, or let it all go.

Now the window cleaner was getting restless, making a hesitant half move. 'Stay there!' she shouted and he settled again.

And then, 'Pull us up.'

The cleaner hesitated, getting mixed messages.

'Do it!' she yelled, still staring through the window at Pat, who looked out the window at her, frozen now with the five fingertips of his left hand touching the glass. He had a ridiculous expression on his face. He was calming down. Was approving of this new development. Yes of course you approve, you fucker. Somehow you've stopped me from putting a bullet in your eye.

It just wasn't as easy as she'd thought it would be.

'Can't you go any faster?' she asked, and though she could not back up her command with levelled eyes, the cleaner pulled them up, and up, and out of Pat's sight.

'You're fucked up,' he said, as they clamoured out onto the roof.

She was preparing for despair, adjusting her clothes for civilized life. 'I'm sorry,' she said to the cleaner, 'but such an easy mark should not be so quick with the insults. I won't tell anyone if you don't. Anyway, it was a toy gun on you. The other one was real. But you know what, too? You gave me the nicest few minutes I've had in a really long time. And I believed while they were happening that they were going to be my last. So you can hate me, you can think I'm fucked up. But I will always remember you. So goodbye.'

She barely registered the green beauty of the roof, as she rushed over it, with its bushes and hedgerows and hillocks, as well as, in the centre, the living white oak.

And then she went down through the building, ready to walk into a scrum of waiting policeman if the world so willed it.

If Pat so wills it.

So had all this been for nothing? He knew she was back. What would she do? She just lost her best and only chance at vengeance.

Turns out she had not wanted vengeance. What did she want?

She went down the elevator. Blocks of floors. The doors opened into the lobby. There were no policemen by the elevator banks and none around the corner. None by the security desk where she had once confided how she wanted to see the view. And so she kept walking and came out of the building, passed the cows where she'd once lolled with Mani and walked north without impediment, up Bay Street.

And then she swung to the east eventually, finding herself outside a refurbished little church. She went and sat inside.

What was she going to do now?

4

Late the next morning, still in her bed behind her curtain, Kip pulled out her cell and made a call.

'May I speak to Pat York please? It's about his windows.'

Then she checked through the curtain to see if the Ghost was gone. Called, hoarsely. No answer. What did he do for a living anyway? Some kind of computer job.

'Hello?' The voice on the other end of the phone, very small.

'Hello,' she said. 'You can have your money back. I can't pay you the portion I've spent so you're just going to have to let that part go, but –'

'I don't want my money back,' said the voice. 'I'm going to bring you up to speed as quick as I can. First of all, you don't have to worry about that window cleaner. He was upset, but he's been paid. The main thing I have to tell you, though, is, last spring I went to the bookstore to have it out with your father, or to find you, or to do something. I wanted to do something really bad, I didn't even know –'

Kip's breath caught in her throat and then she pressed 'end' on the phone. Lay frozen in her bed for a while. Had she allowed Pat York to kill her father? She had to find out. Punched the number again.

'Hello, can I speak to Pat York? It's about his … uh …'

Pat, back on the line, went straight on.

'Your father had a heart attack while getting me a book. It was a coincidence. I wasn't threatening him, he didn't even know who I was – he just collapsed in my arms. I helped the manager get him to the hospital. They let me ride in the ambulance. You were there too.'

'What?' Kip found herself asking, confused, inadvertently engaged. 'I was what?'

'In the hospital, I mean to say. You were in the hospital. You had stitches in your chin. I tried to get to you so I could tell you he was there. But you ran away. Naturally, you were scared of me. Naturally! If things weren't going so fast, I could have alerted a nurse to tell you, but I was frustrated and confused and I think it was too late anyway.

The first time I saw you, you saw me, and then you were gone. It was all just so inevitable. I'm sorry. I came back to visit him the next day but he had died in the night. I'm very sorry for your loss.'

He paused to let her take it all in. After a few moments of silence, he asked, 'Are you still there?'

'Yes,' she said.

'May I go on?'

'There's more?'

'Just some small details.'

'Okay.'

'I made sure he had a funeral and I bought a plot for him up in the St. James Cemetery on Parliament Street. You can go see him there. I took the liberty of choosing a stone and I commissioned a statue of an angel holding a baroque trumpet. It's very nice. People will pause and look at it. I don't know but I do feel it's what the man deserved. I'm aware it's no real consolation. But I've said my piece and now I'm done.'

'So ... ' said Kip. 'You got to talk to ... ' And she felt the sob rise.

'Your father spoke about you,' said Pat. 'He said he wished he knew where you were but on the other hand he didn't want to –'

'That's your fault,' she said.

'Yes it is,' he said.

'You prevented me from seeing him!' she shouted. Her voice was shaking. Where was this rage when she was holding the gun at the window? 'Jesus Christ, he's fucking dead! And I never saw him and it's your fault!'

She was sobbing now, on the phone, and she didn't care what he thought about it, whether it gave him any satisfaction. It was just the way it was.

'I'm sorry,' said the voice. 'I'm so –'

'It's your fault!' she said. 'In three days, you took my whole life from me. Everything!'

'I know,' said the voice.

'But I just don't fucking have it in me!' she went on. 'This fucking vengeance bullshit! That's why I took your stupid money you know, just so you know. So I could bring the wrath of god down on your head. That's why, you stupid fucking tool! But I couldn't do it and I don't know why it's so easy for some people but it just isn't easy for me! The feeling just keeps sliding out of me, no matter how hard I – I don't know what's wrong with me!'

'You're a good person,' he said. 'Like your father.'

'No!' she shouted. 'I'm not a good person like my father! I'm a fuck-up like my father!'

'You're not a – he's –'

'Let me finish! The only person who saved me from my own capacity to be a fuck-up was Mani!'

And then she stopped for a second, wondering if she was really going to proceed, and then she said, 'I'm going to tell you about how I met Mani, I met him while I was working, I always only meet people while I'm working –' (Pat, thinking: *That's how she met me*) '– and I'm just going to tell you that story so that you'll know, so that you'll really know what I'm missing, since you want to be sorry for what you've done to me.'

'Okay,' said Pat, almost too quietly to be heard.

'I'm going to tell you that story and then I'm going to be all done, I'll be finished. Are you still there?'

'Still here,' said Pat.

Kip was wary and halting at first. But she'd told this story before, in happier times, in good company, and a bit of that comfort was built into the story now, like stained glass above a broken door.

She told how she used to fire breathe, in the old days, as a way of attracting a crowd so she could peddle her wares.

'I never used ethanol,' she said. 'I used paraffin. It's easiest on the mouth though not as spectacular as kerosene. Fewer cancers. So, yeah, I did that for several months with the last lousy boyfriend I ever had, last in an epic string. People used to tell me I was trying to punish my father but, seriously, oh my god, I would punch them in the face for saying that.

'Anyway, at first the last lousy boyfriend was pressuring me to be a fire eater and twirler instead of a fire breather, but I really wanted to breathe. I was good at it too, so I finally gave in. We used to busk at the bottom of the Market and made some pretty good coin. Over in that little park, bottom of Augusta.'

'Bellevue Park,' said Pat.

'Yeah, Bellevue. Normally that area is pretty dead of an evening, but we managed to draw a crowd.

'Okay, so, anyhow, the guy: his name was Gunthar. I don't think it was his real name but I never learned his real name. He went by Gunthar. He liked to use ethanol for his tricks, since it made him a bit heady and fundamentally he liked to be out of control. We used to do this trick where I would blow out across an area where he was doing back flips while blindfolded. He was that kind of guy. Except the blindfold was fake, he was that kind of guy too, trying to look more impressive than he really was. The blindfold had these narrow eye slits in it. Are you following?'

'I think so,' said Pat, gratefully.

'So, but, there was this one night when Gunthar knocked the blindfold off kilter with his forearm while he was pulling back for his first flip, so that all of a sudden it really was blinding him. But here's the thing: instead of pulling up and letting me know he'd gone blind, he just kept going. There was a big audience. Biggest we'd ever had. So. I couldn't tell he'd become impaired. I had no idea. All I could see was that he was heading in the wrong direction. He was only off by a little bit, but it was taking him straight towards a wall of people. Have you ever been hit by a six-foot redhead back-flipping asshole?'

'No,' said Pat, truthfully.

'No,' said Kip. 'You'll want to avoid it.' She laughed for a sec, which shocked him and then a sob came up and then she paused and went on. 'So I spat out my paraffin and yelled at the people to get out of the way. Which was the right thing to do since moments later Gunthar came to a stop right in the spot where they all used to be standing. He was really pissed, though. Because as far as he was concerned he'd done what he was supposed to do, but I hadn't. He shouted something about how I'd blown the act and I said I had to warn the crowd, and he said someone else could have warned the crowd and I said no way. Now he was enraged that I was contradicting him, especially in front of all these people. And he was a little bit drunk from the ethanol, which can get absorbed through the membranes in your cheeks.'

'You shouldn't excuse him' said Pat, firmly.

'No, I shouldn't. That's what everyone always says. That's what makes me a fuck-up, too much empathy, lucky for you.'

'Lucky for me,' said Pat (humbly, gratefully, truthfully, firmly). 'What did he do?'

'He walked over and picked up my can of paraffin and threw it at me. I jumped out of the way but it got in my hair. I had long hair then.'

Pat imagined the girl with long hair. Wished he'd known her then. Wished he'd learned how to breathe fire too. Wished he'd led a whole other life. There was still time. He was still a young man, just wearing an old-man suit.

Kip went on. 'Then Gunthar lit his torch and took a swig from the bottle and blew it my way. All over me. Naturally, my hair caught fire. But I was dealing with the shock that he would actually do that. So I guess I just stood there looking at him while my hair burned. I don't really remember. Meanwhile, half the audience thought it was all part of the act. Like an updated Punch and Judy show, you know? People can be such assholes, I tend to forget that despite the evidence. But Mani was there too. Beautiful, total stranger Mani. He was there. There were some guys beside him who had come over from the patio at Amadeu's. They were drinking their cheap draft straight from pitchers, the thieving cretins, pointing at me and laughing, apparently. But Mani was – Mani …'

She stopped for a moment. Her voice was stuck. Pat waited.

She went on. 'Yeah, so, I'm going on. Mani was comprised of a physical kind of grace, no matter what you might have thought of him.'

'I didn't know him,' said Pat.

'No, you didn't. His cast of mind was anti-mob and he moved like an angel. The night your dad shot him he was just off his game.'

Pat swallowed hard.

'He grabbed two pitchers by the lip, one with each hand, and pulled the handles right out of the fists of the boys, hurling himself in the open circle so the beer wouldn't spill. And it didn't. That's how fast Mani could move. He was little, like me, but he could really move. So he was already in the circle when my hair went up, apparently, and he threw the contents of the jugs at me. Paraffin is oily, though, so my hair was still burning, and now Gunthar was turning on Mani. Mani didn't give a shit, though. Not about the battle part of things. He was all about –' she hesitated again. 'He pulled out this big folding knife he uses for eating, clipped it open, reached in and grabbed a handful of my burning hair, apparently, I don't actually remember, and he sliced it away. Just like that.

'Then he threw the hair to the ground, still burning, pulled me into his chest and rubbed the top of my head against his shirt and his face. It was a hot night and he'd been sweating up a storm. That's the part that I remember. Everything before was rescue, he would have done it for anyone. But that part was something different. That was a little more, um … He pulled off his T-shirt and covered me up since I'd stripped down to my bra for the show. And then he picked me up and ran. Gunthar had already whacked him across the back a couple of times with his fire stick, but Mani just ignored him and kept going. His hands had second-degree burns from my burning hair, and his back had bruises and burns, and his face and his chest were burnt and bruised too, but he didn't even look back when some of the assholes clued in that the whole thing wasn't an act after all and finally grabbed Gunthar and his stupid fire stick. Mani just carried me, running the four blocks over to the Western Hospital emergency. And then he went through the whole registration process with me. And then he carried me home again after the treatment for minor burns. I wasn't even as badly burned as he was! I told him he didn't have to carry me but he pointed out that I'd been doing the act with bare feet and my shoes were long gone, and that there was broken glass all over the streets, scattered there by drivers who sought to thwart the cyclists of the city – which, by the way, is the moment when I totally fell in love with him.

'So he took me home and put me in my bed and sat with me while I went through a strange post-toxic asshole-withdrawal fever. Or maybe it came from being burned. But Mani never got that fever. He sat in this big collapsed armchair at the foot of my bed. The only time he left in three days was to go get me food. Some cheap Japanese goop that he made into soup. What's that stuff called? You get it in plastic bags just over in Chinatown there.'

'Um,' Pat said. He wished he knew.

'Miso!' said Kip. 'That's what it was. Miso soup. Mani lived on that stuff. And he bought me a stripy wool hat too. To cover up the burnt hair.

'I really wasn't used to a situation where I was letting the man do all the work. It was embarrassing. I was really sheepish about it. Like, I just stood there while Mani was saving my ass, and then he was carrying me and everything. It was crazy. And then within a few days, I was doing dorky things like putting my head on his shoulder, walking around the city.

'So, whereas before I was naive and clued out about the asshole-quotient in a given male, afterwards I was not. Or not so much. I knew how to deal with them after that. At least sometimes. I had something to compare them to. Mani did that. Now I don't know what I'm going to do.'

'I'm sure you'll figure something out,' said Pat.

Pat wasn't bragging when he said Lionel's statue was beautiful. The next morning, a skeptical Kip went down the fire escape at 12 Kensington (nearly tripping over a fresh bouquet of field flowers), and travelled east on the College streetcar to Parliament, where she got off and walked north to meet a tremulous and humble Pat at the entrance to St. James Cemetery, whereupon he led her to Plot M,

Section 32. The cemetery wasn't Catholic, but she figured Lionel wouldn't care.

The monument, though: Lionel would have cared about that. A sleek angel holding a long trumpet to her lips, folded wings on the verge of snapping open from the effort of her embouchure. It was the first pre-modernist structure Pat had ever commissioned, perhaps even the first pre-postmodernist structure. He felt strangely altered by it, and Kip had to admit she liked it too.

But it was the inscription that gave her the most to think about:

LIONEL FLYNN, BELOVED FATHER TO KIP,

NEAR SURROGATE FATHER TO ...

And there was Mani's name, chiselled as large as Lionel's, made to look like a mourner, but what Pat had really done, rather artfully (and cannily), was to commemorate him too.

Kip thought, *Well, he wasn't a surrogate father at all but I guess it's okay.* Then she wondered whether her own name should have been carved like that, too, in memory of her gone life. But it was perhaps just as well it wasn't. There was, perhaps, a new life to live.

'I buried your friend's old clothes here,' said Pat. 'It was the best I could do.'

'What do you mean?' asked Kip, slightly alarmed.

'You wanted him to be better dressed,' said Pat. 'You ordered me to get him a suit.'

He explained how it had not been so easy to find the right people to perform such a discreet and delicate task. But such people had indeed been found. Mani had been measured; a suit had been tailored and he had been buried again in better form.

'Where?' asked Kip.

'I thought you might want to know,' said Pat.

She realized she knew where he was taking her: to the landfill beyond the west end of College Street, past where it hit Dundas, on the other side of the bridge that went over the tracks. It was still like summer, despite the cold snap that had brought Mani to take her out of her drainpipe. Kip was a bit stunned. In the long strip of property that ran north and south on the east end of the railroad tracks, directly across from a city park, the backhoes busily smoothed over large lumps of land and there was scrap everywhere. Pat manoeuvred her through the mobile office that fronted the place, giving a discreet wave to the burly Portuguese man behind the counter, and took her to a small patch of new grass, out of the way and fenced-off.

'I'm sorry,' he said. 'This was the best I could do.'

'My father lived right there,' said Kip, pointing across the tracks to the building perched on the bridge. 'There's his window.'

'I know,' said Pat. 'I paid the landlord to put his things in storage.'

Kip cried a bit.

Pat hesitated. Then he said, 'Maybe we should call the police after all.'

He didn't even pose it as a question. Kip looked at him. It was a blustery day, still sunny but with clouds blowing through, threatening to turn it all into fall. Pat's face was pinched and attentive. She realized he wasn't as old as she'd assumed.

'No,' she said. 'Mani already said goodbye to all this. He's gone.'

'Okay,' said Pat, even though he didn't understand.

'He headed up north,' she said.

'Okay,' said Pat. And understood better than he felt he had any right to.

And then he took her to the Mies tower and exposed all his old wounds and scars.

There's a scene in the old French film *La Belle et La Bête*, that story where the beautiful poor girl realizes that the rich monster who won her in a card game is actually the best man she'll ever meet, where Belle comes into Bête's castle of her own free will. The walls all have hands that give her light and food and garments. It's lonely and creepy and strangely romantic. Kip's visit with Pat, back in the offices of the Mies tower, behind the bronze windows this time, was like that. Only there were no disembodied hands. Pat himself was the servant.

First evidence he showed her of a ridiculous and disassociated (you could say monstrous) life was his private portrait gallery, in a room in the Mies tower 5 – all creepy portraits of Pat.

'It's not what it looks like,' he said, as he ushered her in. 'Though I suppose it's pretty close.'

First, the centrepiece: a multiple portrait from a couple of years before which Pat had commissioned and sat for weekly for a period of fourteen months. There were thirty-five faces in the portrait, spanning his infancy, education, youthful travels, all the way up to a projected future in which he found himself surrounded by a throng of loved ones on his deathbed. His face was even in the crescent moon, looking sad. One of the most fully realized small depictions within the larger was an early one wherein Pat, aged around seven, was pointing to his heart as if to say, 'This is where I hurt.'

There were other portraits there too, and he showed them with some embarrassment, though Kip had to admit they were a little bit awesome. A series painted all through his early childhood – full length, frontal, profile and even anamorphosis, meant to be viewed from a sharply acute angle – in which he was dressed as a girl.

'My mother preferred my sister to me,' he said. 'Even though my sister died sometime before I remember, maybe even before I was born.'

'Older sister?' asked Kip,

'I don't know,' said Pat. 'I don't even know. My family always felt it was best to express something other than expression. As I got older, though, I just liked the idea of portraits, and I liked supporting portrait painters. They don't all have to be depictions of me, even though they are. What I really needed was friends.'

'But what do they all mean?' asked Kip. 'Is there a story behind them?'

'There is,' said Pat. 'But it's an ugly story.'

'How ugly can it be?' asked Kip.

Pat explained that his mother's attempt to populate the world with Pats dressed as girls, for reasons he was never able to grasp, failed to produce the result she desired.

'Which was?'

He shrugged. 'Her survival.'

The portraiture interest was conceived as therapy after a certain incident – which would be notorious if J. C. York had not managed to keep it from the press – landed her temporarily in an institution when Pat was about six months old.

Wielding a butcher's knife she had purchased especially for the occasion, Pat's mother had presumably attempted to cleave her child into two perfect halves, using the tip of his nose as a gauge for accuracy. She was stopped by a servant before cutting through much more than cartilage, claiming immediately and hysterically ('and I believe her,' said Pat) that she was only using the knife as a reflective surface so she could close first one eye and then the other, and imagine two babies lying there. And then she had slipped! 'Otherwise,' she asked, 'why would I need a brand-new knife? It was because it was shiny like a mirror! If I was planning to kill him any old knife would do!'

('Why did you not turn the blade upward then?' / 'Well, I should have done that, shouldn't I've!')

Pat turned and gave Kip a childlike smile and she saw again the silver scar. He was perfectly comfortable with the never-credited theory that his mother had lost her balance, leaving her mark on a baby who became prone to screaming, who grew into a child prone to nightmares. For a while when Pat cried after that, tears ran straight into his nostrils. 'But I guess,' he said now, 'something that seemed horrible at first ends up not being quite so horrible when you look at it directly. Like Dundas and Jarvis streets, or something.'

And then, three years later, after her ill health seemed to have been staved off by her interest in portraiture, as well as the gift of a beautiful little dog, Olivia York jumped to her death from the roof of a building. Not the five-year-old Mies tower, as was reported in much of the press, but rather St. Joseph's Hospital, the hospital where Pat was born.

Next constituent of the tour: a small table with an ebony vase holding a single black rose. 'I paid a thousand dollars for it,' he said. 'To a retired schoolteacher, just last month. I didn't mean to pay so much, but she turned out to be a ruthless negotiator.'

'I know some women in Kensington like that,' said Kip. 'They work in the cheese shops.'

Kip looked at the rose, first one she had seen since the days after the tumble to the red carpet. It was perfectly preserved in the tar, every fold and wrinkle.

'I'm sorry I ever doubted the artistry of it,' he said.

Then he brought her into another room and showed her a DaVinci replica flying machine he had once commissioned.

'I can't say I ever actually believed it would fly,' he said. 'But I always wanted one.'

'Me too,' said Kip. 'I've always wanted one too.'

It had never occurred to her before that she had always wanted one. But that didn't make it any less true.

Finally, he showed Kip the rooftop garden.

'It's unbelievable,' she said.

'Maybe I can't fly,' he said, 'but I can still have a place above the clouds.'

'Something to be said about embracing your limitations,' she said.

'There's even a little cottage up here,' he said, 'hidden by the hedgerows.'

He showed it to her.

'It's beautiful,' she said.

'I hate the winter up here though,' he said. 'And in general. But I could have it insulated, if you'd like to stay here sometime.'

'I'd love to stay here,' she said.

'You would?' He was surprised.

'Well why not?' she said.

'Absolutely,' he said. 'Why not?' He looked like a small child. For the second time, Kip saw how young he was. His sartorial conservatism had aged him. His anger had aged him. His being the son of a suicidal mother who had tried to kill him or maybe not had aged him. His protection of a father/murderer had aged him.

But he was not actually aged.

'I'll stay here,' she said.

'It's yours. I'll get you a building pass. Top security. I'll have it winterized. Not the building pass, the cottage. Hell, I'll get the building pass winterized too! And I'll ask your permission if I ever want to come up here.'

'You don't have to do that,' said Kip.

'Yes I do.'

A few nights later, lying alone in her cottage atop the black Mies tower 5, with images from this strange new world swirling around her head, Kip fell asleep and lived a whole strange lifetime in her dream. She woke up in the middle of the night weeping and completely exhausted. Lay there in the dark, not sure where she even was. Then she remembered. Cottage in the sky. Pat York's winged haven. She'd been staying here a week. Still, it all seemed suddenly disconnected. After lying there a little longer, she realized she wanted to feel a deeper earth of the real world between her toes. It required a journey past the great tree and down through the machine rooms and the hollows and the elevators of the building, to street level, where there was still the small strips of green lawn that snaked around the several buildings, with its attendant cows and silences. She squeezed her toes into it and looked up at the October clouds hanging over downtown.

So this is what it's like to feel at home in the downtown, she thought. *Just like they did in the old days.*

For the first time in what felt like a long time (though really not that long), she thought of Nancy. Was she still mad at her? She wondered. Would she ever be able to tell her the truth about what happened to her?

And then she caught a glimmer of light in the corner of her eye. Two worm pickers, with their headlamps and their buckets and their ankles, just around the corner of the wall. They saw Kip and swiftly, quietly fled.

'No,' said Kip. 'Wait!'

She thought of them as old friends. But her cry only made them go faster. And then they were gone. She walked around all the black buildings, snaking double doughnuts, figure eights, unable to tell even what direction they'd gone.

Bereft of friends. Feeling that way, anyway. Well of course. Belle couldn't stay at Bête's castle forever. She had to go back and visit her home.

Four

NOT REVENGE
BUT
A CITY

1

Going back sixteen hours or so, just as Kip was getting on the Mies elevator for the first time, accompanied by Pat and attired in her funereal best from the trip to the cemetery: in that moment, she was spied by an old friend.

Nancy had observed the philanthropic transformation of her erstwhile ally Joseph Luong with a mixture of dismay, pity, dread and, finally, disgust. Anticipating his reluctance to pursue the York vendetta any further, she wondered whether anyone could, in the end, be trusted with getting behind a *cause*. Did everyone place personal comfort and reputation ahead of the best interests of the city? You might think she'd have been pleased about Joseph's unexpected turn towards philanthropy, and her place in it, considering she fancied herself a city builder for the marginalized. But there was no place for fellow-feeling in her narrative. Not anymore. In her all-consuming hunger for revenge, she even went so far as to place one Market gangster square in the other camp – the one that contained the useless, the narcissistic, the criminal, the powerful, the stupid. The target.

More and more, then, she found she had to swoop around and whisper in the ears of the more low-lying citizens of her acquaintance – those who would never catch the attention of anyone (except the police) – while affixing cheaper thorns in Pat York's side. Like graffiti and, of course, arson. These former associates were easy to get to. She didn't have to suck herself up through heating ducts or buzz along fibre-optic wires, or squeeze her way through crumbling sewage pipes snarled with tree roots. Her old friends still adhered to the Kensington Market corners or lounged in the damp grass of Bellevue Park. They heard her voice in the breezes, saw her messages when squinting at the sun. They went and did her bidding and then, often as not, walked over to the fire escape at 12 Kensington and dropped off a bouquet of flowers in her memory.

In the meantime, Nancy had been doing some deep-cover work (the deepest), flitting about the lobby of the black Mies building.

Which brings us back to the moment, sixteen hours and two minutes ago now, depending on how fast you've been reading, when, just coming back from wreaking a bit of harmless havoc on the cow-spotted lawn during lunch hour, Nancy was stopped short. Watched, as if in a dream, as Pat York strolled through the lobby to get onto the elevator.

Beside him, Kip Flynn.

What fairy-tale bullshit was this? What veil of lies suddenly pulled back? What capacity for disregard for anything that resembled human loyalty, or … Nancy lost the capability for even the most whispery speech. This was not to be tolerated.

Kip didn't exactly look like someone who was living in the forest of Arden either. She was wearing nice clothes. Expensive clothes. City clothes. City shoes. All her old adornments were gone, her authentic architectural bits. She'd been ge- … she'd been gentr- … she'd been gentriffffff-f-f-ff … Nancy swooped in close, a cold draft entering the elevator, such as would have knocked the head off the sturdiest rose. Close up, she saw there were no calluses on Kip's hands, no blisters on her elegantly shod feet. Lionel's suppositions had been correct: *obviously* she had accepted a huge financial payoff in exchange for the quietly covered-up death of Mani. And, further, had taken the extended hand of friendship, and even fraternity, from these *Yorks*.

The pair looked surprisingly similar too. They were about the same size. Hair the same colour. Same willowy build, like you could knock them both over with a feather. Nancy was amazed she'd never noticed before how much her friend looked like a silver-spoon, pea-bruised princess.

Fffucking gentri-fffucking fairy-tale twins.

Nancy thought she might just shriek in her ear, grab a discarded newspaper and slap her across the face with it, but anyway the elevator doors were closing and anyway, and anyway …

She would come up with something better. Oh yes. Nancy was nothing these days if not the coil and heat of inspiration. She could feel her presence, generally speaking, in the rage passing between the convertible motorists and the road-warrior cyclists, concealed behind windshields in the former, fatal for the latter; or in the spark of an arsonist's match, or in a thunderstorm in the bay, knocking over sails like so many card tricks, or a sinkhole on Keele Street, another on Sorauren Avenue, shifting the subterranean sand of an ancient Roncesvalles beach. Or, or, or …

She was a lamp. A spotlight, even. She was memory; she was sacrifice; she was truth; she was beauty; she was power; she was life; she was obedience to all these qualities, fixed like astronauts to the juggernaut-fire of her will. There was nowhere to be but here. When she thought long and hard, there finally appeared, rising up from the storm drain of her psyche, an idea of such infernal beauty that she emitted a little shiver and all the lights in the west end dimmed a bit (a phenomenon perhaps really due to a small fire in the Dufferin transformer station, suppressed by a brave worker wielding an extinguisher, but still).

First thing next morning, Kip headed down through the building and up through the city and into the Market and through the black gate, up the fire escape, tripping over another fresh bouquet, to find the Ghost, sitting in his kitchen. He was conducting a panic-stricken conference over the phone with an accountant and was surrounded by several small piles of receipts.

'I have ten thousand of these,' he said, hanging up, so happy to see Kip that he was already babbling. 'I was really dreading it, but really, it's fascinating. My whole life is right here.' (A dramatic gesture.) 'I even made a little paper map of the city. Look. For example.' He held up a squarish bit of paper. 'This is from the Canary Restaurant way out on Cherry Street. It closed a few years ago, which means this piece of paper is practically vintage –'

She interrupted him. 'Do you know where she lives?' she asked.

He didn't skip a beat. 'Nancy? Well, she doesn't keep in touch, but I do have it somewhere.' He replaced his beloved receipt at the lower right edge of his map and flipped open a laptop. 'In case I have to forward any mail.'

The Ghost really was a hoarder of this kind of information. The great statistical substitute for human contact. He had 1528 Facebook friends at last count. That was the proof right there.

He located the address and wrote it down for her on a yellow sheet of paper.

'Yellow is an aid to memory,' he explained. Kip nodded and looked at the address. Her old friend had moved west, to the Junction almost. Sorauren. Just around the corner from where Lionel used to live, as a matter of fact. Near where Mani's body was buried. The place where all the streetcars converged. Kip's new psychic sub-city centre.

Kip was in such a hurry, she forgot to say thank you. But the Ghost understood, it was okay, she was clearly distracted, in a hurry, more important things to think about. He could deal with it. He even forgave her when she opened the door to the fire escape and failed to notice his little paper city fly up into the air.

Sitting in a little café on Dundas Street with a near life-size photo of the view in 1908, Kip felt like she was huddled in a muddy pit, surrounded by crumpled pages, trying to figure out what to write to Nancy. After many attempts, she settled on,

I lied.

Will wait for you at the Boneyard Park.

Adding such-and-such a date and such-and-such a time. Then she folded the envelope and walked out of the coffee shop into the October afternoon. She'd spent three hours on ten words. Her eyes were puffy and burned in the leaf-tinting sun. She continued west, to an address and a mailbox and a rendezvous with the past. Brick the colour of dried blood, with faded prints of chocolate factory signs. The ground-floor apartment looked unoccupied, with closed and dusty blinds in the windows. But Kip did not doubt the Ghost's authority in such clerical matters.

Three days later, when she arrived at the entrance to Guildwood Park, up past the shuttered inn, heart in her mouth, she saw in the middle distance a long-coated figure, standing slightly askew beneath the trees, near the columns of an old bank building designed to convey stability but not holding anything up.

Nancy was buttoned down and pinned up. Much changed. Austere. Taller than her height, almost expressionless. A jacket so tight at the shoulders it might cut off circulation. She lifted her head to greet her old friend with a level gaze that gave away nothing.

All around them, the leaves were changing.

Kip stopped about fifteen feet from her friend, afraid to come closer. Nancy's feet seemed to hover a good half inch off the ground, but Kip attributed the impression to the slant of the light. Somewhere in their peripheral vision, a small family was playing on the autumn grass.

The two old friends kept their distance.

'You look pretty,' said Nancy. 'Trimmed down and spruced up. I probably don't look like that.'

'You look great,' said Kip.

'No,' said Nancy. 'I've piled all my broken little stones together and made a gabion wall. It's not pretty but it will stand forever. You never have to fix what's already broken.'

'Okay,' said Kip.

Kip had expected Nancy to ask about the baby and the flight to the country, or at the very least about the note she wrote: *I lied*. But instead, across the gap, she just got down to business. 'So I'm wondering, since you and Pat York are so close now, has he given you unlimited access to the building?'

It was a bit of a shock. 'What do you mean?' asked Kip.

'Oh, don't bother,' said Nancy. 'I hang out in that black tower sometimes. I see you there, swanning about like you own the place.'

Embarrassed now, Kip couldn't think what to say.

'Do you work there?' she asked, finally.

'I was temping there,' said Nancy. Adding quickly, 'Not anymore, though.'

'What about the tour bus?'

'I lost that job. I was out of commission for a while. Little set-back. A few health issues. You probably didn't hear about them where you were.'

'No,' said Kip, shocked again, thinking of her drainpipe. 'I didn't.' She was getting pushed back on her heels, wondered how she could not have known about Nancy being sick. Why hadn't the Ghost told her? Oh yeah. Trip to Europe.

Now she wanted to express concern – health issues: what did that mean? – but Nancy was behaving just like she had back when she'd first learned that Kip would not engage politically, back when she'd first brought her here to this place and told her this was a cemetery and they were at war, when Kip had said she was a merchant and (therefore) a pacifist.

On the other hand, Kip remembered that, in those days, the chill between them had passed. Differences came to be respected. Friendship was deepened, based on earlier connections. Twindom. Kip had, after all, brought Nancy into the Market, opened the world to her. Nancy would never forget that. She would get over these feelings of betrayal, this dark mood. And then Kip would be able to tell Nancy her seeming-but-not-really-friendship-ending story.

She decided to be patient.

'I'm glad you called this meeting, though,' said Nancy, seeming to warm a bit. 'Because I have an idea.'

'Really?' Kip was surprised, hopeful.

'More of a business proposition, actually,' said Nancy. 'An idea for a bourgeois distraction. I flatter myself imagining that it might strike you as similar to one of your classics, like your funny monogrammed hankies that I remember so well, or the jack-o'-lanterns on spec, personalized seat covers for commuter trains, face-painting stands and knitted penises, stencil kits, homemade paper, rusty-nail jewellery or even the late, great black tar roses.'

'Okay,' said Kip, swallowing hard. 'I'm listening.'

'If you go for it, it might actually remind you of the person you used to be.'

Kip didn't say anything so Nancy went on.

'First of all, I wonder if you were at all aware that your new friend, Pat York, has fallen onto hard times. Financially, I mean? With his business?'

'I –' said Kip, who was not aware.

'No,' said Nancy. 'I didn't think so. Your business instincts are lying dormant, aren't they? How about we wake you up? The building bubble has burst again. There was a poorly timed subway accident in the city last summer. It turned public opinion against that particular mode of transportation just when everyone was putting their eggs in that basket, so then the city's customer service manager – I mean the mayor – put the kibosh on five new lines he had planned and reinstated the height restrictions for buildings in all those neighbourhoods. Nobody on council ever wants to be elitist or anti-populist, so they've fallen into line against the subways, just like they fell into line for them. Emergency sessions. Keystone Kops. Now there are no more high-rises allowed. You can't dig down unless you build up, so the political will for both has collapsed. It's started a bit of a funding backslide. Some of the contractors have lost their shirts, leaving several of these building dudes without workers for existing projects. Lawsuits are pending, blah blah blah, it's ugly. I believe your friend has pulled through but he's definitely got shit stains on his cufflinks. I imagine such blue-blooded noble types do all their suffering in dignified silence though, no?'

'I –' said Kip, who thought, yes, it must be true, like father, like son.

Nancy then explained that York and Associates had begun the development of a big city block, on College Street at the top of the

Market, between Augusta and Spadina, and Oxford Street to the south. They'd dug a pit three storeys deep but then lost their contractor to bankruptcy. So the pit was just sitting there, waiting for the money to come back.

'I know that pit,' said Kip, thinking of the Hoa scrum on College Street.

'Congratulations,' said Nancy. 'Glad to hear you come down from your tower and flit among the living from time to time. But this is not just any pit.'

Then, like the expert tour guide she was, Nancy went on to summarize the history and significance of the site:

Ten feet down (she said), there had, at one time, been a perfectly preserved, late-nineteenth-century dwelling of a young woman who had just recently stopped being a prostitute and was trying to embark on a seamstress business. During discussions of possibilities for preservation at City Hall, the mayor, in his inimitable style, wondered out loud why the city would possibly imperil a legitimate business enterprise in order to investigate a failed one, from the past, run by some stupid hussy to boot? The rest of the councillors voted immediately to plough it under (a few exceptions left spinning in their chairs), whereupon the mayor proudly declared his intention to run for another term.

Twenty feet down had been the remnants of a burned library from an obscure second house on the estate of the Denisons, who had owned all of what would be Kensington Market, leading the foreman of the team who had ploughed it under before alerting the authorities to ask, philosophically (and after he was caught), 'What good is a library that has already been burnt? It's not like you can read the books.' For this he was dismissed, and the excavation team was fined. But nobody could say anything more about the contents of the library.

'Although it was rumoured,' added Nancy, 'to contain an extensive collection of Victorian erotic literature, providing a possible explanation for why it was so far from the main house, obscured by trees, near the wild bank of Russell Smith Creek.'

'You mean Russell Creek,' said Kip.

'That's what I said,' said Nancy.

Thirty feet down were found the skeletons of four horses, buried in a row, all with seeming high honours, bits and everything, but when this burial ground was characterized as nothing more than a mid-eighteenth-century abattoir (to the press and therefore *in* the press), its significance was summarily dismissed.

Forty feet down was all dirt, no remnants of houses at all, but no foliage either, or grasses, as if the land had been tamped down, as if (perhaps) it had been the meeting place of all meeting places.

Fifty feet down was the skeleton of an enormous fish. Not a whale. A fish.

In place of all these histories, Nancy said, there was just a hole now, man-made and full of purpose, a pit of possibility rather than dread. Pat would have argued that the ephemeral prostitute's home (library, etc.) had already been encased beneath all the insignificant warts that had been there before, and if they had stayed, no one would have caught even a fleeting glimpse of the prostitute's house, the abattoir, the library, the meeting place.

But Pat wasn't there to argue his case.

'Sounds like a special place,' said Kip.

'I believe it is,' said Nancy. 'In fact, there's a lot that goes on underground that you don't know about. So my proposal is to do an event down there in the pit called the Meeting Place.'

'What kind of event?'

'The kind of event where the audience is up above, around the edges, and you're below, doing your thing, three storeys down, performing on the surface of the distant past.'

'And what am I performing?' asked Kip, ears tingling, nearly forgetting the chilly detachment of her former friend.

'Well,' said Nancy, 'I thought you could combine one of your fire shows from the old days with a carnival of metal carnage that might reflect our current civic discourse.'

'What do you mean?'

'I mean backhoe fights,' said Nancy. 'When contractors go bankrupt, you can get their machinery for next to nothing. We'll make them perform jousting matches. I mean, come on. Isn't it what everyone's wanted to see on our streets in the last few years? I know I have: construction machines pawing the dust and just going at each other. It'll be like dinosaur wars. They'll be equally matched titans.'

Kip wasn't sure she understood yet, but she wanted to find some common ground with her old friend. 'I think I can see it,' she said.

'See? I thought you'd like it. This way we can really do it, in a safe environment, like, without pulling the telephone lines down. And you can throw in whatever you want in terms of other acts. I have a business associate who might be able to help you acquire the materials, but you'll have to take the idea to him yourself, because, well, I'm kind of furious with him these days.'

'A business associate?'

'I don't know what's come over me.'

'Who is it?' asked Kip.

'Joseph Luong,' said Nancy. 'Our old landlord. He'll be interested, I guarantee it. Because this has the makings of a charity event.' Rolling her eyes. 'And he's become a philanthropist.'

'I've heard that,' said Kip.

'You have?' Nancy seemed impressed. Still, Kip was puzzled by her angle on all this. Why would Nancy be interested in such a spectacle? No idea. But she herself did like the idea. It was a bit scary, a bit bigger than the things from her old life, like Mani dancing out of a laneway from the black-tar weeds then growing to the size of a giant. But anyway, her new life was bigger, and anyway, more importantly, it could be a cornerstone to re-establish a friendship with Nancy.

'I accept,' she said.

'I'm glad,' said Nancy, who conjured a smile from a child on the other side of the park and slapped it over her own gritted teeth.

Kip headed back into the city, through all the golden sections of downtown to the black towers, and up the southernmost one, where she confronted Pat:

'Are you in financial trouble?'

'Um.'

After some hesitation, her new friend confirmed all the challenges that Nancy had described, adding to them the disturbing incidents of arson which had shareholders concerned that his Corp. had become entangled in a vendetta. He'd worried for a while that the arsonist might have been Kip herself and had therefore stalled all investigation into it, hoping she'd get her fill and move on. But the latest incident had happened just in the last few days, while Kip had been staying on the roof; the top of a half-built condo down on Queen's Quay had blazed with heavy black smoke all through the late afternoon, scaring half the city and giving Pat the proof it had never been Kip at all.

Then he showed her the one room he hadn't shown before: full of crumbling maquettes for failed city projects – windmills tilted at quixotically over the decades – and explained that, as had been true in those times, what this was, was merely a downturn.

'What about the big open pit at the top of the Market?' asked Kip.

'How did you hear about that?' he asked.

'Why? Is it invisible or something?'

Pat blushed. 'No, obviously it's not invisible.'

He said he was certain they'd get the money moving again for it in no time.

'How long?' asked Kip.

'Oh ... next spring, I'm absolutely sure.'

'I have an idea,' said Kip, 'for how we could use it in the meantime.'

'Uh,' said Pat.

Kip proposed Nancy's spectacular pitched battle among decommissioned construction machines – excavators, backhoes, skid loaders, road rollers, mobile cranes and even standing cranes – in the old urban tradition of dogfights and bear-baiting, except on a much larger scale and without anybody getting hurt.

'Um, how is it no one's going to get hurt?' asked Pat, going pale.

'Naturally,' said Kip, 'because the operators will be wearing fire-proof marshmallow suits.'

(This was Kip's own enhancement of the idea.)

'Oh,' said Pat. 'I see.'

He didn't. Carnival was not included in his vision of the world.

'We'll be able to exploit the full spectrum of anxiety, ambivalence and rage in the city,' said Kip.

'What rage? What anxiety?'

'The city's changing so fast,' said Kip. 'Haven't you noticed? This is the perfect anecdote.'

'You mean antidote,' said Pat.

'See? You agree with me!'

'I can't say I'm a big fan of extreme fighting.'

'This isn't extreme fighting,' said Kip. 'It's machine fighting.'

'Sounds pretty extreme to me.'

'And we can use it to publicize the challenges of workplace safety.'

'Hardly a natural fit.'

'Don't be a pussy!'

'I'm not a pussy,' said Pat. 'And, furthermore, I find that term offensive.'

'Don't be a killjoy then,' said Kip, 'if you're not a pussy. People are going to love it. It will be terrifying-style carnage in a safe environment. Bread and circuses. Christians and lions. Fun.'

Pat had gone from pale to translucent.

'Just to ride out your building slump through the next few months,' said Kip. 'Otherwise it's going to be a bleak winter. You'll be able to get down to the razing and digging and building again in the spring. Think of it as a sped-up version of what you do every day of your life, but for entertainment purposes only.'

'I'd have to clear it with the board,' said Pat, disliking the killjoy pussy angle.

'Heeha!' said Kip. 'Is that an okay from you?'

'Well ... the mayor might not like it.'

'What does the mayor have to do with anything?'

It was true. Pat didn't like the mayor anymore. He'd mistaken him for a committed friend to big business, but recent events had eradicated that impression. The man had always called himself a customer service manager, but Pat had believed that was all spin. Apparently not. So now maybe it was all right to raise a little hell at the service counter.

'I can appreciate how this type of event is up your alley,' he said, warming to the idea. 'When would it be?'

'Solstice,' said Kip.

'When's that?'

Kip rolled her eyes. Flaky vs. stuffy: the two solitudes of urban culture.

'December 21st,' she said. 'Shortest day of the year.'

'Really? That doesn't give us a lot of time.'

'We've got every day between now and then,' said Kip.

'And who would we get to run it?'

'I'll run it,' said Kip.

'But aren't you going to need access to decommissioned construction machinery? Aren't you going to need access to operators and other manpower?'

'Yeah,' said Kip, 'I know. I have an idea of who I can get to help with that.'

'Okay,' said Joseph Luong, rolling his eyes. 'Tell me your idea for the great urban cultural endeavour and where my name will go.'

As it happens, Kip's former landlord had a bothersome interest in an enormous scrapyard run by a *maa lat lo* associate in Hamilton, to which such kinds of machinery were sent. The same place where he'd stored the storage bins. Kip reminded him of it and he looked at her.

'You were talking about it when I came to see you,' she said. 'You said you weren't Sanford and Son. You said that there are bad people all over the world.'

'*Teen haa,*' said Joseph, '*woo aa.*'

'That's it,' said Kip.

He sat for a few minutes. 'I just sponsored ten guys from Vietnam,' he said. 'They all have construction skills. Can't get jobs though. Nothing's moving. Got them all picking worms. Tell me again though, before we go any further: who's the guy providing the site?'

'I haven't told you the first time yet,' said Kip.

When she mentioned York's name, she added what Nancy had told her to say: 'He wants to establish in a very public way that there are no hard feelings between you.'

'Uh huh,' said Joseph. 'I'll have to think about it,'

'Proceeds from passing the hat,' said Kip, 'to be divided equally between victims of workplace accident and homeless mothers.'

'What about immigration centres?' asked Joseph.

'Fine. We'll add immigration centres.'

Joseph sat in his chair. He was being pushed even further in a direction he'd never expected to go.

Then again, it could be argued he had never expected to go in the first direction he'd gone in. Character is destiny. Kazantzakis after all. Always pulled between earth and heaven. And the devil in there somewhere too, sure.

But then Kip ran into unexpected trouble with the Kensington Carnival peeps, who were accustomed to doing their solstice fire event the same night (of course) in Bellevue Park. Kip was at pains to explain that this was just a temporary move, a farewell of sorts to the ceded upper section of the Market. She eventually won them over by hammering home the idea that the crowd would be able to see better by looking down on the action, rather than merely at the back of someone else's head, and that the fire shows could be that much more spectacular three storeys down from the audience.

Once won over, they insisted that, since Kip herself had been involved in the most notorious, spectacular Kensington Carnival fire act ever, she be at the centre of it.

'But I don't do fire acts anymore,' said Kip. 'I've retired.'

Which statement was summarily ridiculed out of existence. So now she was obliged to get into shape and practise for the curtain-raiser fire show, something Pat was not happy about either, given that the only thing he knew about such events was Kip's story of the old beau Gunthar, with his blind backflips and her burning hair.

'It's usually more professional than that,' said Kip. 'You'll see.'

'How can something be professional when its participants aren't earning any more than pennies for it?' asked Pat.

'Don't knock it,' said Kip. 'Gunthar and me, we made some pretty good coin.'

After getting everyone on board, transforming all former enemies into allies, for a single millennial event, Kip had to cover the complex ground of clearing the event with the Workplace Safety and Insurance Board, which she managed to do by arguing that they were going to present the Meeting Place to raise awareness of issues of workplace safety.

But the city zoning department proved trickiest of all. Kip went in there and encountered behind the counter a pale man who smiled patiently and said no to everything she asked. She argued that it was absurd that a hole in the ground could be considered a zone at all. Where did the city stop after all? The centre of the earth?

'Yes actually,' said the man. 'That hunka hunka burnin' love, right at the core.'

'That figures,' said Kip.

'Don't be sarcastic,' said the man, wagging his finger. 'It's in the citizens' best interest. If a sinkhole were to open up and swallow your home, you would want to have some assurance that what was at the bottom was still yours.'

'Who said anything about a sinkhole?' asked Kip.

'Are you not afraid of sinkholes?' asked the man. 'Seems to me there's very little to fear more these days. Think of all that space below your feet. Think how far down it goes. Think if you're sitting on sand, which could slide away, or slate, that could shift and then crush you. That earth's mantle is unpredictable. Sinkholes opening up all over the place. They're the future.'

'Okay, stop,' said Kip.

'It's just the zeitgeist,' said the man. 'I can't help it.

Kip left the zoning department paranoid and empty-handed. She walked around downtown, wondering whether any buildings would topple over on her, trying to figure out whether there was a practitioner of environmental and site-specific theatre among her acquaintances. Then she remembered a minor detail. Had the Ghost (of all people) not once boasted about serving as an assistant stage manager to a production of *Oedipus Rex* underneath the Gardiner Expressway? He'd been fifteen or something. Always spoke about it, when given the chance, as the best summer of his life. Kip contemplated the prospect of bringing it up with him and enduring the reminiscences. Listed it under suffering for her art. So she made the pilgrimage to the 12 Kensington kitchen, stepping over another new bouquet of dripping flowers on the way up the fire escape.

The Ghost's advice was surprisingly simple and to the point. 'You have to find someone who knows someone,' he said. It was all he said. He was picking up laconic habits from somewhere, which got Kip thinking, not for the first time, *Things never stay the same* …

So Kip went straight back to Pat. Pat raised his eyebrows in the manner of a much older man and then he pulled the magic strings and got the necessary papers within a single afternoon. And his pride in this achievement had the further result of helping to bring him a little closer onside. Beyond irking the city's customer service manager, he was beginning to see the value of the thing itself.

Next there was the finding of volunteers, the renting of bathroom facilities, the securing of generators for lights and sound. And then Kip's discovery at the end of October that she was pregnant, a fact she was planning to keep to herself, more or less buried, morning sickness be damned, until after the solstice.

2

As for Nancy, she stayed away from the business side of things, turning up usually just around sunset to spend time with Kip, regale her with stories about her old activist exploits, as if she were an aged war hero, sitting with her above the rooftops of the city, sometimes telling her about the buildings that used to stand below them, once upon a time, and the lives that unfolded within and around them, employing so much detail that Kip started to believe she'd lived through them and had to remind herself that some of the stories were more than a century old.

'There was a hotel there once,' said Nancy, pointing a few blocks north, 'where the entire police force of the city was mobilized because an Irishman had escaped from his typhus quarantine.' Here she turned around from her tree perch and pointed down at the TIFF Lightbox. 'Here was a bog – that's an Irish immigrant – who'd penetrated the city. The hotel was evacuated even though he wasn't inside it. He was just in the laneway behind it. "I just can't bear the fever tents today!" he was calling. A big crowd had gathered outside, just behind the line. He was shouting that he'd lost his wife and two small children in the tents and he just couldn't face the burlap anymore, and the faces of the sufferers around him. He said he just needed a bit of time by himself. "Please," he was saying. "I'll go back, I swear! Just give me a few hours!"

'There was an exhibit from Venice at the time at a private museum uptown, run by a dude who was friends with the chief of police, who had the idea of co-opting six plague doctor masks from it. The men on the force drew straws and the six who were chosen put on these big overcoats and went in there, six burly ravens, and dragged him out. They were carrying him on their shoulders and he was keening like something you've never heard. They carried him all the way to the Lightbox and left him to the movies!'

'Is that story even true?' asked Kip.

'Every word true,' said Nancy. 'That hotel finally came down when this complex was built, which is funny because the hotel was also built by a prick and the whole thing could have been a lot less rife if there hadn't been a businessman involved, telling the police what to do.'

'But … plague masks?' said Kip.

'I'm telling you. The private museum was owned by the banker, William McMaster, or rather, I guess it was really his wife, which is why the man and his friends could play fast and loose with priceless Venetian artifacts. You can look it up.'

'How do you know the story?'

'It's in the dossier.' Nancy's standard answer.

'What happened to the guy?'

'He went back into the tents, caught the fever and died.'

The two sat in the tree in silence for a while. It was a balmy November evening. All around, the city was growing dark, lights coming on. They were supposed to be planning Kip's fire act, but hadn't spoken of it yet.

'Hey, doesn't he have a flying machine?' Nancy asked, abruptly.

She was talking about Pat. 'How do you know that?' Kip asked.

'Oh, I'm sure you told me. Why don't you use that?'

'But isn't it an artifact?' said Kip. 'Shouldn't it be respected? Wouldn't it be like those policemen using the old plague masks?'

'It's not an artifact,' said Nancy. 'It's not authentic, it's a *copy*. Still, if it was originally designed to fly, then the advantage of a copy is you can use it. It doesn't have to be treated with kid gloves.'

'So, are you saying that, if something is precious, then it can't be used for what it was made to do? So, then, if everything got preserved in this city, we'd all have to tiptoe around old buildings and whisper and close doors carefully and all that?'

'Don't be ridiculous,' said Nancy,

'And, if that's not true, then couldn't those police say those old plague masks should be put to use?'

'Why are you being so contrary?'

But then, Nancy abruptly changed the subject.

'Hey, you know what we're like, though, maybe?' she said, opting to be distracted by the view. 'You and I?'

'No idea,' said Kip.

'Right there,' said Nancy. 'We're like the lakefront.'

'Let me guess,' said Kip. 'You're like the island and I'm like the Expressway.'

'Two solitudes,' said Nancy. I'm like the island, its village aspect protected by municipal decree, keeping beach and shoreline for everyone. Whereas you're more the waterfront of staggered condos above a boardwalk where rich women like yourself go strolling in the morning and which stands otherwise empty.

'Consider,' Nancy went on. 'It's pretty well established that the downtown shores of Lake Ontario have not been conceived for my pleasure. Not that I'm unwelcome, but I'm obliged to walk underneath the Expressway to get there, on narrow sidewalks, with cars whipping by at high speeds. It's a psychological barrier. This, along with the shoreline view of staggered condos, serves only to make us poor citizens feel decidedly poorer. And so the beautiful lakefront of downtown Toronto still stands mostly empty, while rich women like yourself stroll contentedly along the boardwalks in the morning.'

'I don't stroll,' said Kip. 'I zip down the path on my bicycle.'

'Sure you do,' said Nancy. 'As if your bike isn't actually locked somewhere to a pole, gathering rust.'

And Kip thought, *How can she even know about that?*
Was it in the dossier?

And she thought, *Anyway, the bikes aren't locked there. Mani and I went to get them.* Nancy's information was out of date.

'And, in order to get across the divide between island and water-front,' her friend went on, 'you have to swim, sail or take the ferry. So the two solitudes gaze stoically across the bay at one another. Like me and you.'

'If you say so,' said Kip.

They looked out towards the island. October chill in the air. The sky was dark overhead, there were three or four stars, and the western horizon was still pink. To the south, Kip could still make out the two dragon spines of the various spits and islands and landfills that thrust the downtown city into the lake.

'It's like they're sleeping,' she said.

'To me, they look like they're trying to kill each other,' said Nancy. 'Which has the advantage of being close to the truth, since the spit is preventing sand from washing up onto the shores of the island and causing it to erode.'

Kip wondered whether Nancy would ever stop seeing everything as polarities in constant opposition and struggle.

Still, she had a point. She always had a point.

'Don't sigh,' said Nancy. 'I'm sorry. I know, I can be tiresome.'

Kip looked up at her, shocked. Had she sighed? It was like her friend had read her mind.

Nancy's eyes were wet. 'I'd change if I could,' she said. 'I really would. I'm at that age, just about, maybe. To change. I just can't. I really can't.'

'That's okay,' said Kip, overcome by the long-awaited display. 'I love you just the way you are.'

They moved to hug each other but somehow got distracted by the view again and didn't get around to it. Nancy went on to say that she had never seen the island and the spit before. Not for real. She'd never gone buildering quite high enough.

'That's unbelievable,' said Kip.

'True, though,' said Nancy. 'But look at that. The island's not really an island. It's attached.'

'No it's not,' said Kip. 'There's a gap there. See?'

'Oh yeah.'

'It used to be attached,' she said, still not quite believing she was the one conveying information. 'There was a hotel right there. But it got washed away during a storm and then presto: island.'

'When?'

'In 1858. I can't believe you didn't know that.'

'The tour bus can't get down that far.'

'How far down can it get?'

'I'd say about forty metres.'

Kip was confused. Forty metres?

Then she realized Nancy was talking about down, as in down into the earth, not down south. She was on some kind of weird subterranean kick.

'Yeah,' said Nancy. 'Far enough down to take a gander at the big cats and the woolly mammoths and even the Neanderthals. Did you know they used to throw their dead loved ones into crevices they could not see the bottom of?'

'Who?' asked Kip.

'The Neanderthals!' said Nancy.

'I did not know that,' said Kip, thinking of the zoning man.

'I guess they knew that all the mysteries of the world were beneath their feet,' said Nancy. 'Maybe they thought their loved ones would live down there always. Or maybe they thought they would fall forever, divining somehow the idea that to fall and to rise are one and the same thing.'

Pits and crevices and the sinkhole secrets beneath the surface of the earth. Kip looked over at her. Nancy was smiling out towards the islands with her unearthly smile, peering at Kip out of the corner of her eye.

'At least I can still make you think,' said Nancy.

'You make my heart hurt,' said Kip. 'And I don't even know why.'

'It's what I'm here for,' said Nancy.

Though the reclamation of friendship was gaining ground, something still kept Kip from sharing the knowledge of her pregnancy with Nancy. Her friend dwelt on the past, the baby was all future, and anyway Nancy might start making jokes about Kip moving to the country, and she didn't want all that to come up again. Still, she was nearing the end of eight weeks of pregnancy, alone with the news. She didn't want to tell Pat either, he might try and take control of the situation, do something stupid: try and pull the only clear paternal candidate back into his orbit, inappropriately, with his sense of entitlement.

So, after some further lonesome deliberation conducted under the darkness of night, Kip decided finally to put in a spectacularly premature phone call to the receptionist at a certain window-cleaning company.

'Hello, I'd like to leave a message for Wilson Caspi, a cleaner with your company ... Well, I was wondering if I could call back and leave it on the machine ... No? Well, okay, I was just trying to spare you some trouble. Could you perhaps tell him for me then that he's got a expectant mother waiting to say hello to him at 12 Kensington Avenue in the Market, or else the cottage on the roof of the black Mies

tower, like, if he ever wants to stop by? It's an open invitation and he doesn't have to be afraid. He should understand there's no expectation of him. This lady, he should know, too, is not as crazy as he might have reason to believe. If he ever gets over the impulse to flee from this message, he might consider that it's just a message and no one is ever going to show up at his door or your door or anyone's door. And then he might consider making contact. He might just want to know what a kid of his looks like, so I just thought I'd give him plenty of advance warning. I haven't even hit the first trimester yet. All he has to do is count the time from that morning we met and then he'll know when the baby's due. Thank you. Bye.'

The fire act was mostly Kip's, Nancy there to line her up, prop things up, give her thumbs-down or thumbs-up. They spent much of November working on it while Kip trained the worm pickers for the other part of the act. Of course, the construction machinery could not go full out, so it felt more often like gentle choreography, the big rigs dancing around one another, flirting in the twilight. Synchronized swimming performed by pro wrestlers. It was so beautiful, Kip felt compelled to keep things this way, but Nancy insisted people would be hungry for carnage.

By early December, everything was going fairly smoothly, if mostly virtually. But it was better than nothing. And, aside from her entrance, Kip mostly had the fire act down.

There was one night when she was practising down in the pit. The Kensington Carnivalers had packed up their masks and oversize puppets and gone home, but Kip had stayed behind to grab a little more time for crucial after-dark rehearsal. Pat had been there too, trying to do a bit of twirling. 'You know,' Kip had told him, 'It's participatory enough to foot the bill.'

'I want to do more,' said Pat.

'Yeah, but you can't learn this stuff towards a performance. It's process-oriented.'

'It can't be that serious,' said Pat, 'if it doesn't affect the price of eggs.'

'That's a terrible attitude,' said Kip. 'And dangerous.'

Finally he'd gone home to the Bridle Path, carrying the glimmer of an idea for creative input he would keep secret from Kip and bring straight to the Carnivalers the next day.

And then Nancy had come. Nancy had gotten into the habit of climbing up onto one of the support collars on the mast of the abandoned tower crane – an interior platform that sits every fifteen feet all the way up. She was communicating with Kip via flashlight – more to the left, more the right, etc. They'd been at it for an hour and Kip had just about run out of her paraffin supply when a small silhouette emerged from the darkness before her, with buckets strapped to her ankles. A worm picker, actually picking worms, three storeys down.

'Will you even get them down here?' asked Kip.

'Oh yes,' said the woman. 'Migrants. To the world below.'

Her name was Glee. She wore a T-shirt that said 'I speak English' and had come out of the gloom with the warmest smile Kip had ever seen.

As it turned out, there was a reason for the smile. It had not come by chance.

'I think,' Glee said, 'you try to help me once.'

'Sorry?' said Kip.

'It was you, I think,' said Glee. 'In the spring. You try to make them take me to hospital.'

Oh! She was the woman who had fainted so silently.

'You told them to listen to you because you had baby coming!'

'Yes,' said Kip, blushing. 'That was me.'

'Funny!' said the woman.

'I'm not really sure what I meant by that.'

'Do you have baby now?'

'No,' said Kip, trying not to let her expression darken. 'It was a mistaken impression.'

'Now, though,' said Glee. 'Now is no mistaken.'

Up on the mast, Nancy was clicking her flashlight off and on, impatiently. It was time to get back to work with the remnants of the

paraffin and the time before they had to clear out. Kip looked back at the smiling woman. 'No,' she said. 'No mistake this time. How could you tell?'

'You glow,' said Glee, 'is how.'

Kip was unaccountably flattered and didn't want the conversation to end. 'How are you?' she asked.

'I'm fine!' said Glee. 'Except it's a funny thing down here.'

'What funny thing?'

'I see others down here,' said Glee, moving in now, confiding. 'Strange things.'

'What do you mean?'

Glee came in closer to try to explain, but the answer turned out to be beyond the capacity for her English, so she ran and grabbed another picker to interpret.

'She's saying there are ghosts down here,' said the friend. 'She's saying she saw two men fighting a duel with old pistols, and that she thought she would be hit with the bullet, but that it went right through her. She says you cannot have seen them because the fire from your mouth makes them scurry away, like they think you're the devil. But then they come back and pursue their own passions.'

'Two men,' said Kip.

'Duellists,' said the interpreter. 'That's the word, isn't it?'

'Yes,' said Kip, puzzled and worried. 'That's the word.'

She looked around. There were three or four other pickers, taking a break. They didn't seem concerned about the duellists. They were laughing and talking animatedly about something. Kip really didn't know what to say about the alleged ghosts. Up on her crane platform, Nancy had given up with her flashes. So Kip watched a bit of the main event's gentle rehearsal, the machine dancers attempting to be a little less tentative: a backhoe lightly tapped the side of a Caterpillar, knocking the little vehicle over onto its side. Its operator, even from her distance, even in the dark, looked concerned and guilty.

Maybe this event was not actually going to work?

Kip didn't believe in ghosts. It was true, Mani had visited her in her drainpipe. And he'd shown her precisely where he was buried. He had, in fact, saved her life. But that was Mani. Love is not a ghost. Love is the opposite of a ghost.

Then again, perhaps it was just Glee seeing ghosts, just as she saw Kip's pregnancy. Perhaps she just had a special talent for seeing the future and the past.

Kip finally opted to change the subject, pointing to the other worm pickers and asking what it was they found so entertaining.

'Oh,' said Glee, rolling her eyes. 'Story about some funny thing happen in Kensington Market today.'

'What was it?' asked Kip.

'Man in stocks,' said Glee, shaking her head at the barbarity of it all.

'Stocks?' said Kip. 'Really? Was that a ghost too?'

'No,' said Glee. 'He was very much alive. Big man. He got into a fight with someone while still in his stocks. His name was Henry.'

Henry? Kip was thinking. Stocks in the Market. Could it be her Henry?

'Where?' she asked.

'Corner of St. Andrew and Kensington.'

Kip gathered her things together, waved up towards Nancy with *I don't have time* and *follow me* gestures, then ran down the three short blocks to the corner. Kensington had shut down for the night and was as quiet as any suburban street. There were a few splattered vegetables around, but no sign of a big man named Henry. Kip shook her head, puzzled. She waited a half hour for Nancy, who never came, and then wound her way slowly down to the rooftop cottage, to climb up and sleep in the clouds in preparation for the next day's performance.

As it happened, it really had been her Henry, there in the stocks, earlier that day. Here's how that happened.

He'd been released, after five months and fifteen days, in mid-October. But distractions from minor personal demons had prevented him from getting in touch with friends like Kip.

First thing he did when he got out, sixteen days early on account of good behaviour, was go back to the bar to see if the bass was still there. It wasn't, of course. And since it was not the first bass he'd ever lost due to his own stupidity, and since he could not afford to buy a new one and was once again bereft of his livelihood, and since he'd actually killed a man and wasn't going to be getting over that one any time soon, whether through therapy or twelve steps or the power of positive thinking or religion or Facebook or reality TV or irony or sophistry of any kind, and since he'd kept track of all the shitty things that had gone down while he was inside, the next thing that happened was he fell off the prison-imposed wagon. Hard. For several weeks. Feeling more or less buried by the world.

Until one day he woke up, early December, and found himself lying in an alley with vomit all over the front of his shirt. There was a little voice speaking to him in his head, telling him, 'Okay now, Henry, it's really time to come clean.' It was Nancy's voice, very soothing. He heard it, clear as day; in fact he almost even saw her there, shimmering in front of him like tinsel on a tree, wagging a finger.

And Henry said, 'You liked me, didn't you?'

And the voice said, 'Yeah, Henry, I did like you. I wanted to scale you like a building.'

And Henry said, 'I'm such a fucking loser. I never even got to touch you.'

And the voice said, 'Sometimes it's enough for a girl to know when she makes a man weak in the knees.'

Henry said, 'You made me weak in the knees.'

The voice said, 'I know, Henry, it was obvious.'

Henry said, 'You still make me weak in the knees.'

The voice said, 'Are you sure you're not just jonesing?'

Henry said, 'Yeah, I'm jonesing. But you still make me weak in the knees.'

The voice said, 'I know it, Henry. I know it.' And then, 'You have to come clean, though, baby. You're too big to fail.'

Baby.

After that, it became a bigger project. It wasn't enough to just clean himself up, he had to do it in a very public, very self-abjuring, everybody's-got-to-know sort of way. He had to make it so big that even he himself, Henry, would recall it the morning after the day it was done.

Mulling over the obstacles, he rolled through the streets in a four-beat bass rhythm, barely paying attention to where he was going. Ended up in a magazine store, where his eye was drawn to something on the cover of a law-and-order magazine. An article about archaic forms of punishment.

Next day he went to see his friend Grant, proprietor of a large warehouse on Spadina full of junk that had been acquired from old film sets, cleaned up and offered for sale to other film sets. Antique printing presses, latex crocodiles, high school lockers, etc.

'Have you got stocks?' asked Henry, getting right to the point.

'You mean, like, the things they used to put your arms and head into when you broke the law?' said Grant. 'Like in the old days?'

'In the old days, yeah,' said Henry. 'But you're talking about pillories. I want stocks. Stocks are for legs.'

'Oh yeah. Legs. I know what you mean.'

'Have you got them or not?'

'I've got some for rent but not for sale, so I have to know what you're going to use them for.'

'I'll return them the way I found them.'

'But what do you need them for?'

'Just something.'

'Is it a porn movie?'

Henry felt his weather hanging round him.

'No. Man, I don't know why people think I do porn movies all the time.'

'Okay, but that's funny because I thought I saw you just the other da–'

'I don't want to hear about your habits, Grant. I want the stocks because I'd like for you to lock me into them, over in the Market. Just in from the corner of St. Andrew, where the wholesale chicken joint used to be.'

'Really?'

'Yeah.'

'Me?'

'Yeah.'

'Why?'

'Why what?'

'Why me?'

'Because I figure you'll want to keep your eye on them.'

Grant thought about this for a little while.

'When?'

'Soon as you can.'

'How long?'

'Five days.'

'Can I ask what for?'

'Cold turkey,' said Henry.

'No shit.'

'Yeah.'

'Why don't you just handcuff yourself to a bedpost like normal people?'

'I don't like my apartment that much,' said Henry. 'Plus I get claustrophobic even when things are good. Plus I'd break the bedpost or else throw the bed out the window.'

'But you'd be handcuffed to the bed.'

'Yeah,'

'So, like, you'd follow it out the window.'

'Yeah, but it's a bed, Grant; there's a mattress to land on at the bottom.'

'Right,' said Grant. 'So you figure the Market.'

'The Market, yeah,' said Henry. 'It's where they used to do it.'

'The local business community might disapprove,' said Grant. 'Er, unless you think it'll be a draw for them?'

'What's with all the questions, Grant? I'll build them myself.'

He started to go.

'Wait!' said Grant, making a snap decision.

Next day, Henry was all set up in the Market, sitting in his stocks. Grant had even rigged up a portable shitter for him, from an old outhouse.

'Oh that reminds me,' said Henry, looking at the hole. 'I forgot to make arrangements for food.'

'I'll bring you chicken soup on a regular basis,' said Grant.

Henry sat down on top of the hole with two wool blankets draped over him, one for his legs, one for his back. It was mid-December but the cold didn't seem to be a factor. Global warming was in full swing. He laid his legs up in the grooves and Grant snapped the stocks shut and padlocked them. There was also a small reclining board for Henry to lean back on. It looked new.

'You made it look like a deck chair,' said Henry.

'I don't know how else to say this,' said Grant. 'But you'll thank me.'

When Henry started shouting on the third day for Grant to come and get him the fuck out of there, the police came instead and Henry had to calm down and spell out his higher purpose without sarcasm or rage. He managed it, somehow, explaining that he would singlehandedly put several suppliers out of business. 'I was a big consumer,' he explained. 'Their shit was the plankton and I was the whale.'

And then, on the fourth day, physically the worst day, many unexpected things happened. A little girl came up and gave him a flower. 'Like I was fucking Frankenstein or something,' he told Kip later, as if being Frankenstein were a good thing (and it was.) Someone came out of the synagogue and brought him challah.

Old ladies stopped to talk to him. He woke up from a mid-afternoon doze and discovered a bottle of hand cream sitting on the top of the stocks, slightly used.

But then his luck changed again, never a surprise. In the late afternoon he was visited first by the Ghost, who chatted with him for a bit and told him about the big pit event that was going to happen just north of them for the solstice, organized by their old friend Kip. And then he was visited by a pair of Australian brothers for whom he had sometimes worked as a courier. Turns out his trip to prison had left business unfinished and debts unpaid. Sitting there in front of them, he felt pretty much as vulnerable as an ankle-bound baby on a mountaintop, waiting for wolves. As far as the brothers were concerned, Henry was a nice guy, but there were principles and precedents involved. So there was a fight, which did not turn out well for Henry's shins.

As it happens, though, it didn't turn out so well for the Australians either. The fight attracted a crowd, as fights are wont to do, and the people in the crowd were not, it turns out, afraid to hurl the vegetables they had in their hands. Unfortunately for the brothers, it was getting towards the end of the day, and many of the merchants had laid out their boxes of rotting tomatoes and fruits for garbage pickup. So there were plenty of projectiles to go around, even for those who might have hesitated to employ their own dinner's garnish to a greater cause.

All the clattering and cursing, catcalls, cheers and tomato projectiles drew the police again, who cut the lock this time and pulled Henry off his seat, exposing the foul stench of the shitter and triggering some violent olfactory-inspired impulses.

They dragged him away, dumping him into the drunk tank for twenty-four hours, where he sustained himself by running over images of the throng of supporters who had come to his aid. They didn't even know him. Didn't even know he was a musician. He was just some lug in the stocks. And they came to his aid. The sidemen in the best gig he ever played.

Not a lot of time had passed, but these images pulled him over the wall. 'Like I had a guardian fucking angel,' he said later to Kip.

'And you did,' said Kip, later.

When he got out, he felt like being with people. He felt like seeing old friends. He even felt he deserved, a little bit, to see old friends. And that maybe, just maybe, they'd be glad to see him too.

3

As they had all hoped and expected, a huge crowd showed up on December 21st. It was like an early fall day on the first official day of winter, ten or twelve degrees. The full moon was huge and low in the east, competing with the lit-up block of office towers downtown. There was a high fence set up all around the pit, open at the entrances, and the capacity crowd was mostly dressed in windbreakers. Cigar smoke hung in the celebratory air. Many sported costumes; Kip noted some strange translucent masks, the likes of which she'd never seen before – an evolution of papier-mâché? They covered their wearers' heads like astronaut helmets. One featured a lobster playing electric guitar, blinking lights on its antennae. She thought, I could never come up with something like that.

Worm pickers were already running through the crowd with painted hobby horses strapped around their waists. Two lights of an airplane careened at an angle in the distant overhead, as if the pilot were trying to get a look at what was happening down below. And Kip looked for Pat in the place where she expected to see him, sulking up in the lighting booth. She knew he'd gotten special permission to be in there, since he'd always been a little afraid of the outside air, especially at a time of year when things might be falling from the sky, like snow or leaves. She was fully expecting to get a scowl from him, unhappy as he was with his lack of active participation.

But he wasn't there. The lighting guy was alone. Where was Pat? She looked around. There were four follow spots set up high on each corner. As she looked all around the edges of the gathering crowd, the spotlight at the southeast corner suddenly pulled up and flashed her in the eye. Then pulled away again, pointing back down into the pit. She saw splotches. When they cleared, she peered over the heads of the crowd and saw, very clearly the besuited man operating the light. He raised his hand and waved at her. Well, well. Was that an aviator cap he was wearing? In anticipation of her Da Vinci flight?

Kip waved back and started her descent into the pit, just as a collection of animals and big-headed humans began to perambulate down there: several fish, an eagle, a queen with a fiery crown, a polar bear with a blue head, a brown woman with enormous hands.

She recalled that Joseph Luong was supposed to be in the crowd somewhere too, but she had not seen him. And Nancy had climbed up onto the tower crane well before any spectators arrived, so no one would know that she was up in the best seat of the house. Kip twisted around on the ladder, looked up to see her at about the three-quarter mark, crouching on her usual platform inside the mast, a little black dot beneath the sky.

When the horns began to blast, it set off all the dogs in the western part of the city. Kip finished her descent and hurried across the open ground. The riggers had fixed one end of a thick wire about a quarter of the way up the tower, which sloped acutely down at an angle to the east end of the pit, where it was fixed tight to a winch and then pulled taut. Kip was covered with blinking fairy lights (turned off for the moment), powered by a battery pack strapped on one side just above her hip. She hoped her hip would protect it if she fell wrong. As she climbed the tower there was a smattering of applause. Wondering what it was for, she paused and craned her head around, clutching the mast, careful not to kink her neck. Below her, in the pit, the fire spinners had come out among the parade of giants. Now the horns were getting funkier. They always got funkier for fire. And spinners always preceded breathers. It was almost time.

When she got to the platform with the wire, the Da Vinci was there waiting for her. She sensed Nancy's presence too, somewhere above her head. Kip untangled the dangling straps and clipped the wings to the wire.

As she prepared, she remembered a pair of peregrines she had seen, two years ago spring, raising chicks on a downtown building rooftop. She remembered the way they would stoop to street level, chasing pigeons, and sometimes even streetcars. Their swiftness and agility had inspired her in her fire shows at the time. Now she prayed to them for strength, feeling maybe she wouldn't measure up, trying to reassure herself, *It's all just dirt down there, no streetcars to crash into,* as she slipped on the straps of the Da Vinci, double-checked the connection to the battery pack on her waist, switched on the blinking lights, felt Nancy's approving thumbs-up above her head, took a deep huff of breath, clocked the growing roar of the crowd and jumped.

Boom. It was over before she knew it. Landing by the small pail of paraffin at the bottom, pulling off straps, scooping up tools and running barefoot to the centre, rolling, blowing plumes, diving through hula hoops held up by Kensington compatriots all blowing their own fire too. Boom. The rhythmic blast of horns everywhere. With her peripheral vision she could see twenty Carnivalers spinning fire around her, with ropes and quarterstaves, four men doing backflips among them, blowing plumes up towards the moon just like Gunthar used to do. And Kip was doing it too, over and over again, rolling, torch away in the tumble, keeping her cheeks ballooned and her throat shut up against the paraffin – of all the tasks, this was always the hardest, she absorbed a bit, swallowed a bit, but blew most of it out, flames arching towards the high, smiling faces.

Now she was covered with sweat, chin glistening with paraffin and dripping with applause, though she'd lost the fairy lights some-where along the line. For the first time, she felt the heat of the spotlight on her (hi, Pat) as she stepped into a four-point curtsy, pulling a sweatshirt over her shoulders, her bare midriff. She could see by the lights of the torches that the people up around the periphery were happy. Excited. Once in a lifetime. City transforming. Change for the better. Nancy had been right. This went beyond psychogeography, it was psycho-killer-qu'est-ce-que-c'est-geography.

And then, among all the faces up there, Kip saw Henry.

Henry!

Last time she'd seen Henry she'd been cross with him. In the Market with the laundry, stuck inside his bass case, so long ago. Spring. Things always change. They never stay the same.

Kip ran to the west-side ladder, past the worm pickers on the side-lines holding up blankets soaked in fire retardant, ready to quench any trouble, past a man shouting, hoarsely, 'If you want to go on, line up here!' and 'We need to keep this spot clear!' and 'Go! Go!' He was wearing an orange reflecting vest but he reminded Kip of Nancy's story of the typhus victim. She paused to watch him for a moment, mouth open, until he shouted, 'Shit or get off the pot, lassie!' And so she scurried up.

When she got to the top, there were some people who wanted to lay their hands on her to see that she was real, and others who would never recognize her as the performer they had just watched even though she glowed with the remnants of all the fire that had come out of her. Behind her began the sound of powwow drums. She turned to look down just as a vast thunderbird came into the centre of the pit, right at the foot of the tower, and performed a war dance all the way around its base, to the sound of cries, yelps, sometimes shrieks, Kip's favourite kind of singing. There were other dancers too, special guests from Wikwemikong masquerading as Mississauga.

She turned back again and pushed through the crowd, wanting to see if she could spot Henry again from the back. As she came out into the open again, she noticed a bunch of kids, ten or eleven, twirling flameless hula hoops. Emulators, thought Kip: future Gunthars, Nancys, Josephs, Manis, Kips, Glees, Pats. And Henrys.

It took another five minutes before she spotted him again.

'Henry,' she called. 'Henry!'

Henry saw her. 'Yeah,' he said. There was a smile under there somewhere, she could see it.

'It's so good to see you!'

'Good to see you too, babe,' said Henry. He looked surprisingly clear-eyed. She reached up to give him a big hug and a greasy kiss on the cheek.

'Did you, did you …?' Kip wasn't sure what to say, what she was allowed to ask, what might be thoughtful and what might be wounding. But what had happened to Henry?

'Tell you later,' he said, divining the bulk of it. 'I heard you were up to something over here. Thought I'd head up, say hello.'

'I'm glad you did, I'm glad you did!' said Kip. 'I'm glad you're okay!'

'I'm okay,' said Henry. 'I'm too big to fail.'

'Have you seen Nancy?' Kip asked, excitement growing, ready to turn and point to the festive little black dot up there on the tower crane. For some reason, the spectators directly around them were all wearing headlamps, giving them illuminations instead of faces, bright ghosts.

'Nancy?' Henry looked uncomfortable.

'She'll be thrilled to see you,' said Kip. 'Look.' She turned and pointed. 'She's up there. About halfway up.'

Henry looked. Saw a small dot where Kip was pointing, about halfway up the tower crane. There was someone there for sure, but ...

He said, 'Kip, what are you talking about?'

Kip stopped and turned around to face him. Henry didn't usually ever say a person's name. It wasn't his style. Too intimate. 'Kip' sounded weird coming out of his mouth.

'What do you mean what am I talking about? She's –'

'Nancy's dead,' said Henry.

Kip hadn't heard right. She looked up at him, uncomprehending. 'Yeah,' he went on. 'She died in a subway accident in the summer.'

'What?' said Kip. 'No.' She stuttered a bit. 'I heard there was a subway accident, yeah, but –'

'She lived for a few hours,' said Henry. 'I was in the fucking jail. I couldn't go see her. And then she died. She fucking died. Nancy died.'

With each repeat, the idea dropped further in. And below it, the undeniable (no: deniable, fully deniable) flicker of knowledge (the image of Nancy in Guildwood Park, her feet half an inch above the ground; flower bouquets on fire-escape steps; the powerful detachment, deference to the daytime; stories from a century ago, told with authority (denied, all denied).

And there was undeniable weary grief in Henry's voice; Kip nearly burst into tears. But she still wouldn't believe any of the words, no matter what she felt or didn't feel. She was looking up at his eyes.

They looked black in the bright solstice night. His cheeks were stubbed too, but he was lucid; he'd never looked so serious.

'Nancy died, Kip,' he said again, softly.

'But – ' said Kip. 'But I talk to her. I talk to her all the time. She razzes me but she's had some brilliant ideas. I mean, it's true, she's angry. They're angry ideas. But good ideas, really good ideas. She talked me into putting on this –'

'Yeah,' said Henry. 'She told me to clean up my act –'

'No, I mean for real!' said Kip. 'For real!' Almost angry now. Insistent. 'That was probably just your own –'

She was going to say *idea* again. Or *subconscious*. Or *will*. Or *power*. Or *desire*.

But whose idea was the Meeting Place anyway? One might as well ask whose idea was the shipping-container homeless shelters? Whose idea the psychogeography, the philanthropy? Whose idea? And this show too? The one that was even now gearing up for its main event. Whose idea was this?

'Nancy's,' said Kip, answering her own question.

'Yeah,' said Henry. 'She always had a lot of pop. I'd rather have the girl than her advice, though, you know?'

It was an undeniable truth. But Kip was not about to agree with it. She had both.

'But –' she said.

Kip looked away from Henry, up at the dot on the scaffold. It couldn't be true. Not really. Nancy had spoken to her. And, for god's sake, Joseph Luong had spoken to Nancy, hadn't he? Nancy said she'd been furious with him.

Kip was going to have to find Joseph and talk to him. That's what she had to do. Dismiss this drug-addled bullshit of Henry's once and for all.

On the other hand, Henry's eyes were so clear. No need for the eyedrops anymore. She was slandering the man who was trying to help her; she might as well be yelling at him, leaving him with his broken bass case. All over again.

No. She had to talk to Nancy. She had to get over to the tower crane, up the mast and talk to Nancy.

Trumpets were sounding again now, signalling the main event. Kip turned back towards the pit, ready to dive in.

But what she saw there was another surprise. Not quite on the level of confirming the death of a friend, but enough to disorient her. The machines were all gathered north of centre, just as they were supposed to be. But they didn't start up. Instead, all eyes were drawn to a brand-new, beautiful aubergine Saab, driving with barely a purr up from the south corner, past the foot of the tower crane and into the centre of the pit, where, calmly, it began to proscribe a gentle circle.

Kip registered the change and hesitated. She'd had the layout of the action mapped out in her mind, ready to negotiate her way around it on her journey to the tower crane. But this was different. Confusing. It was going to slow her down. She looked up at the fourth follow-spot operator, who flashed her in the eye again. Something told her that's where the answer lay, though she didn't have any time for questions.

You might, though, have time for questions. And so we will provide one final pause in the action to patch over the gap and allow you to proceed safely.

For too long, Pat had, he felt, embraced the brutal outlook of the new civic politics, pretending the haves were have-nots and the have-nots were elites. He'd played the whole stupid game of masquerading as one of the great unwashed, as if the little people were somehow preventing him from getting home to his mansion on the Bridle Path. Literally too: the campaign against the war on the car suggested that if the rich man wants to get home faster, he shouldn't have to buy a helicopter, no, he should rather force the poorer people to clear a path for him by travelling underground.

This position – spectacularly good for business, spawning a building boom whose like had not been seen since the sixties, permitting him to build the cockroach towers of tomorrow – had led inevitably to entitlements, oversteps, escalation, the immolation of a house (more than one, actually), the death of a boy and the near-destruction of a girl who happened to be – he was realizing more and more every day – dearer to him than his own self. This feeling was so foreign, he barely knew how to deal with it. He certainly didn't want to burden Kip Flynn with it, either, considering all his past sins.

But he did want to do something to mark his transformation.

Sure, it was true, business wasn't so great right now, and the mayor was not as reliable a corporate villain as he was supposed to be. Not since that subway accident, both tragic and unlucky – devastating for business. But still, Pat had benefited from the doubled-down empowerment of the already powerful. What he wanted, with all his heart, was to restore some balance. Or to acknowledge the need for balance, with a celebration rather than a tragedy.

For weeks, he'd resisted (and feared) the inherent chaos that would preside over this solstice event, before it occurred to him that it was providing an opportunity for the very gesture he was seeking to make.

(Either that, or else some anarchic spirit, or force, or sprite, or barely corporeal presence, had whispered in his ear …)

No matter the inspiration, it was a simple thing, really: the Saab, which had been presented secretly and shyly, by Pat, to the members of the Kensington Carnival, now calmly proscribing its modest circle, quietly, quietly, there in the pit.

The calm only lasted a few moments, though. Then someone drew aside a curtain and thirty Carnivalers riding mountain bikes appeared at the south end. They sprang forth and, rushing up through the space, past the tower crane, arrived at their destination, moving into a pattern of dizzying circles, both directions, around the accelerating little car, no vehicle ever touching another. For a little while, there was almost no sound, as if all that machinery were emulating the internal workings of an old pocket watch. Then, at one point, a man jumped off his bike and, using the momentum from the ride, spun it aloft, over his head as he leapt, miraculously, up onto the front hood of the now-fishtailing Saab. Some force kept him there as the rest of the cyclists continued their tightening circle and he continued to spin with the bicycle aloft. The circle flowered outward, making space in the middle as the aubergine sports car abruptly braked, the driver's door flew open and someone tumbled out just as the man on the hood let go of his bike and leapt to the ground as it smashed through the front windshield.

Up at his position as fourth follow-spot operator, Pat took it all in, he had to admit, with a pronounced lack of ease. He'd decided in advance that this night would represent a kind of liberation for him, an expulsion of all his sins and those of his father. But the fire down in the pit was just a little too bright, and he was disturbed to note that this whole business reminded him of the little house that blew up in the Market last spring. Sure, these people were professionals, apparently in control (despite working for pennies and lacking investment plans and RSPS), but he was feeling queasy.

Then, as if to underscore his sense of the growing pandemonium, one of the worm pickers holding a fire-retardant blanket abruptly fainted on the sidelines down below. There was no way for Pat – or anyone else for that matter – to have known that this particular worm picker, who had a fondness for T-shirts that said *I speak English*, was simply prone to fainting spells. There was a man standing beside her who probably should have known but didn't. What's more, the noise and the crowds and the whirling sense of danger had augmented a habitual anxiety within him. So, unfortunately, Glee's faint tipped him over into a burst of panic, and he took off for one of the ladders, ankle-buckets going *clang clang* CLANG CLANG CLANG, so loud they could be heard above the bicycle business in the centre.

Still, the worm picker kept running and then climbing and everyone in the audience held their collective breath, thinking he might slip and fall. But then he got to the top and was pulled into the crowd. And Pat breathed a sigh of relief, thinking, *I have to cede control if I'm going to survive this night.*

Down below, the cyclists finally dumped their bikes, descended on the little car and jumped onto the hood, stomping with crack-brained glee, their rhythm taken up by the drums and horns of the band members who brought it up to a crescendo and called out the backhoe that finally came rolling. Finally now, with the appearance of the promised construction machine, the audience applauded and there was a palpable release of tension. They were all looking towards the centre, where the driver of the Saab, looking calm and healthy, had just jumped into the cab of a small Caterpillar and bee-tled it out to the centre, raising and lowering its shovel in a comic display of defiance against the tyrannosauric backhoe that was making its way.

The main event was finally underway. All surprises were done.

Except they weren't done. No sir. In the space between the backhoe and the Caterpillar, a little man suddenly appeared. He had his hand up and was wearing an orange reflector vest, which caused the machine operators to shut down their engines, just like that. He was stooped and thin, though – thin as a rail – and beneath the orange vest he seemed to be wearing the threads of another era.

In his upraised fist, he clutched an old hat.

He turned, strange Carnivaler he was, in a slow circle, and then made a dramatic presentational gesture with his open hand, which the spotlights tried to follow, twirling around and up, and up again, towards – it finally became clear – the little black dot on the mast of the tower crane.

Nancy.

The main event.

Nancy had an old-fashioned megaphone, and her words were uncannily clear and loud, spoken in her most professional tour-bus mode, for the whole city to hear:

'I just have one little question,' she called, 'for all you builders out there, you acquisitive big-pants builders and the politicians that back you. It's a small question, intellectual, one might aver, but it also happens to be the central one right at the origin of all our building, or, really, our civilization: what are you going to do with all that wood? By which I mean for you to cast your minds back to occupy the crania of early historic peoples standing all ashiver in the tall forest of yore. Do you use the forage you find to build a fire or do you use it to build a house?'

She paused, dramatically, as if she thought someone were going to try to answer the question. Long enough to provoke a murmur that ran through the crowd.

And then she went on.

'There's little doubt that the first specimens of architecture in this part of the world were ephemeral. They were made of fire and lasted only through the darkness of a single night! There's no better warmth than a wall of flame, my friends. And yes, too, there have been a few times in the history of our city when we have honoured that earliest of all traditions with our emulation! The first was in 1849, when the whole small city burned, and the second was in 1904 when the downtown got gutted at Bay and Front and Wellington! It was spectacular, glorious, far more celebratory than the way these buildings get taken down these days. So I ask you: what better way to honour the ghosts of the past and salute the solstice than to burn it all down again!'

And then, as if it had been doused with fifty barrels of gasoline, as if it were a crack opening in the earth's crust holding back a cauldron of magma, the collection of decommissioned construction machinery gathered together just north of her in the pit blew up, just like that, on cue, bursting into flame and creating a black-tipped plume that swooped up six storeys and nearly licked the faces of nine hundred startled spectators, who did not stampede so much as take a single collective step back. The man in the orange vest had disappeared and the two drivers of the vehicles jumped out of their machines and made a run for the south end in their marshmallow costumes. Everyone was going for the ladders.

Kip, barely comprehending the shock of what was happening, turned and saw Joseph Luong standing near her, his expression confused and afflicted. Then she turned back to Henry, who looked worried and grim but not the least bit surprised.

Then she made a decision. There was no map to follow except her own wish to lay it out.

Henry tried to stop her, 'Hey!'

Too late, as she swung over the barrier and began to climb down the ladder, pausing to let several of the worm pickers, Carnivalers and a couple of emergency medical practitioners climb over her on their way up. She could feel the heat of the fire licking her spine, the wind swooped around and above her. She wondered whether this inferno would leap the three storeys and spread.

Nancy was still speaking into her megaphone as Kip got to the bottom and started making her way across the pit. She could hear her even though the audience had begun to clamour, words that were becoming less coherent, more angry and nonsensical, at least to Kip:

'One man hears a knock on the door, assumes it's next door, assumes it's not for him. For another man, the knock could be as far as half a mile away and won't he just shout, "Who is it!" What do you think the difference is between these two men? Why, the first is a poor man and the second is a rich man! But when the fire comes, it won't knock on the door, it calls no name at all. It breaks down the door, rather, swoops down the hall, makes each face it equally. Still, some of the victims are inevitably remembered more than others who are merely swept into the ashes and forgotten! Buried in some stupid landfill and recalled by none who outlive them!'

My god, thought Kip, stopping short. *Mani was buried in a landfill. Was she talking about Mani?*

People were screaming and fleeing now, pulling away from the fence and dispersing into the city. Several more stuck to their places, though, confident to the last that this was all part of an act to celebrate the darkest night of the year, traditionally a time to confront your fears of poverty and change and death. They stood mesmerized by the flame and the tour bus barker's words coming from upside the tower crane and bouncing back and forth among the buildings to the north of them, beyond College Street and up through the Annex, where even those who'd stayed home came to their windows and porches to listen.

Now Kip, as she ran, heard a pistol shot, felt the heavy flight of a ball whizzing past her ear. And then a bike courier zoomed past her, a skinhead with the hot ember of a piercing in his chin, reflecting the roar. He rode nearly as fast as the bullet, straight into the inferno; she saw his shadow licked by flame in there, still spinning even as it crumbled into creosote and slid away. That was not the trick of the living. Was he a ghost too, then? Like Nancy?

And where had the presenter come from, with the orange vest and open hand?

The fire was redoubling its breath, spitting flares over the heads of the crowd like misfired pyrotechnics. A restaurant on the west side of Augusta caught a lick and started to burn. Nancy was shouting something about how nothing ever changes, everything stays the same, at least beneath the surface, where Sam Jarvis can fight a duel with John Ridout, jamming not his pistol but the clutch of his sports car, and the court of public opinion will then report that Ridout was a hothead and had it coming, in 1817, and then again in 2009, as if no time has passed between them. 'And it hasn't!' she shouted. 'That's the beauty of it!'

So, Kip thought, as the tower crane loomed in front of her, *was this the performance that Glee had seen a glimmer of in rehearsal? And was Nancy really, truly dead then? Had she engaged the services of her fellow dead? The forgotten, as she called them?*

The concrete base of the tower was in front of Kip now. She scrabbled up onto it.

'The rich man will never stand with the poor man!' Nancy shouted. 'They can never be brother and sister. Not in this city! They might live side by side, but they're not related except in a best-forgotten fairy tale!'

On top of the concrete foundation, Kip saw a ladder rising up through the centre. Far above, another ladder ascended through the pivot hinge and around the cab. Kip crawled inside the mast and began to climb, thinking to herself, Nancy wants to burn down the whole city, something's not right about that. She's mad because – who knows! Maybe she's just mad because she's dead. But how could she want to destroy a city she loves?

She couldn't, Kip thought. She didn't. That had to be the only answer. She didn't.

4

Kip was above the crowd. From all around came the smell of kerosene. It burned the inside of her nose, so she breathed through her mouth until it burned her soft palette and the back of her throat. She felt the inferno's heat against her ankles, her bare soles. The little girlboy inside probably felt it too, she thought. But she had no time to worry. And she knew her girlboy was going to be tough, primed for a life of tumbling and kerosene, fleeing all the infernos of peak oil, end of oil, short-haired from all the singeing. She was distracting herself with the thought of it, her little daughterson's survival heroics, but she had to lay that aside and get on with the here and now. She heard the *thunk thunk thunk* of Nancy above her head, cutting off her speech to climb higher and away from Kip. *Thunk thunk thunk*. It reminded Kip of something. Took her a moment to realize it was the fire escape at 12 Kensington. It gave her confidence for some reason. As if it meant she'd been climbing tower cranes after so-called ghosts all her life.

She ascended silently in her bare feet. Above her, Nancy was pulling away, fleeing her contact, climbing higher. The silent living chasing the heavy-footed dead. *Thunk thunk thunk*. Till Nancy had climbed past the operator's cab and up and into the jib, stepping out and away from the mast, her flight moving from the vertical plane to the horizontal, a balancing act over the city.

'Hey!' shouted Kip as Nancy climbed up into it. 'You'll fall!'

Nancy responded by turning and throwing her megaphone at her. It bounced with a clang to her left and tumbled into the fiery pit below. Wow. Did her friend mean her harm? Not possible.

'Oh shoot!' called Nancy, as if in answer. 'I missed!' And then she turned and continued her balancing act out onto the jib of the crane.

There was a hardness and a brokenness at the centre of Nancy that Kip had been unable to confront. The gabion wall. It scared her and made her sad. But she had a potent desire to salve it. Still, how can you salve a stone? If it's a blister, it needs to be pried off; if it's a callus, it needs a file. Whatever was beneath that stone was all that remained of their friendship, and the reason she was going to get up to Nancy, even step out onto the jib if she had to.

She stopped and looked up again, right inside the pivot hinge now, an enormous mechanism that could turn the whole jib of the crane, high above the city. There was a polished red emergency button just above her head. She wished it said *Abort*, would have pushed it if she knew it would bring any relief. Instead, she kept going up and around and came out on the roof of the cab. She had a good view of Nancy now, who had almost reached the end of the jib, itself swaying ever so slightly, up and down. It gave Kip vertigo and she had to look away for a moment, down through the window into the cab. She could see the operator's winter coat, left open and splayed across the creased vinyl seat. She couldn't tell what colour it was in the dark (maroon maybe?) but she could see a clouded Mason jar sitting at the foot of it, probably for pissing in, and a small assortment of photos and heirlooms fixed to the chair and the glass and the bracing. Here was a home, contained, like Kip's body used to be, but hanging here in midair. No vertigo, then, for the crane operator. If he could be a bird in a nest up here, then she could too.

She looked up again. Nancy had stopped near the end of the jib and was peering back at her. Then she turned away again, took the last few steps till she was crouching at the tip in the cramped space beneath the steel bars. In front of her, the triangular walls of the truss tapered away, leaving only the tip of the base to poke out over the world like the blade of a leaf. She climbed through, tip of the diving board above a pool of fire.

Now that they were both stationary, Kip didn't know what to say. Decided to cut to the chase. 'I know you're dead!' she shouted.

Nancy stiffened, straight up on her leaf blade, dark coat rippling away from her tight shoulders in the wind. Then she turned slowly, step by carefully placed step, to face Kip.

'Oh, you heard that, did you?'

'I'm sorry!' shouted Kip. 'But you could have told me!'

'Ha ha ha!' called Nancy. 'It's not true anyway! I'm way too pissed to be dead.'

'No!' called Kip. 'You're dead! I know it! Henry told me!'

'What would Henry know?'

'He heard about it when he was in jail!'

'Guess I just got lucky with my choice of friends!' called Nancy. 'Henry in jail! Kip gone missing and maybe rich! Mani dead and disappeared!'

'I'm sorry!' called Kip.

'Gee, and look at that! It's all coming back to me now, the horror of it, that first moment, and all the loneliness that followed. Thanks a lot, old friend.'

Nancy seemed to be speaking in a normal register, no longer shouting, though braced with bitterness, her voice carrying across the gap straight to Kip's ear.

'Forget about it!' Kip called.

'I can't,' said Nancy, her low tone buoyed by the whirlwind. 'When I was underneath those wheels, beneath that car, I got really scared. I tried to pull myself out but nothing was working and I was just lying there in all that steel, helpless and cold. And do you know what I found myself thinking?'

After a moment, it became apparent that Kip was expected to reply. She shook her head.

Nancy went on. 'I was thinking, *I need civilization! I need to be safe!* I realized for the first time that maybe I had a vested interest in being on the same side as those city bastards. *Those guys,* I thought, as I lay there listening to the grunts of the firemen, *they're not after beauty or memory or culture. They want safety, aided by efficiency and clean lines. A place where we can live our lives and then die painlessly and be swept away by city cleaners, at least as long as they're making slave wages.* I looked down at my body and then I said to one of those firemen guys, "I'm sorry I made such a mess."'

She paused again, expecting Kip to speak.

'And what did he say?' she asked.

'He was crying. He said they were going to get me out of there. He said I was going to be okay. He didn't get the point.'

'What was the point?' asked Kip.

'I was trying to tell him that I finally understood how the other half thinks. I was equipped with understanding for my enemy, and the big drag of it was that my life was over!'

'So you chose for your life not to be over.'

'You betcha,' called Nancy. 'I fight on! See, it's better that I'm dead because while I was still alive, in those last moments, I was thinking I would grow old and fearful and frail and let all my conviction go to pot, whereas then at least I could just get it over with in one big gulp of horror and pain. It was pretty bad, though. I mean, I guess I was lying to myself a little bit by thinking I knew now how the enemy thought. It was consolation for dying, not so much before surviving. *Go ahead,* I was thinking, *eradicate everything, just don't eradicate me, let me live, let me live, remember me!* God, I was pathetic!'

To Kip's surprise, since it was all coming out hard and cold like stones and dust from a falling building, Nancy's voice broke.

The gap, Kip thought. The gap was too big between them. How do you shout about your loves, your shames, your failures? How can anyone do it? But more, how can we do it, here in this city?

And, distressingly now, Nancy was turning away again. Raising her arms like a conductor.

So Kip made a decision. Her responsibility was too big to deny. She had introduced her friend to this world Nancy was now trapped in. Kip had brought her to this place of chaos where she herself had always lived. Kip could absorb its changes, steady on her sea legs. Nancy could never be like that. She was sensitive.

The jib of the crane was not quite broad enough to stand upright inside and not really designed for walking. Once Kip was inside it, though, making her way along, bent over and finding handholds in the steel-cast beams that slanted sharply on either side of her head, stepping from angular slat to angular slat, she was able to find a rhythm for her bare feet. It was tricky for her to make her way, the wind stronger up here than she expected, affecting her balance. She wished she were wearing dance shoes and motorcycle gloves.

Below her, the flames had leapt over the heads of the watchers on the north side and had begun to burn College Street. There was a fire station not a block away, one of the only originals left in the city. Kip could see the clock tower out of the corner of her eye – a second full moon to reflect the real one. The garage doors were opening, the trucks were screaming out, turning onto College Street, to the sound of sympathetic sirens starting to howl with the dogs all over the city.

Then she faced forward again and started to make her way along. Hand foot foot hand foot. The bars slanted below her as well, disorienting a bruised pair of feet. It was difficult to place them with any regularity. Still, she managed it. Nancy continued to ignore her, so Kip thought she should wait to speak until she got at least halfway. Her tights were pulling against all the muscles in her legs as she moved out onto the sway, high above the remnants of the crowd, people who were staying because she was in danger or because the flames had hypnotized them or for their own reasons. As she moved, she sensed the city before her, ranging off to the north in the glittering night, white and yellow and green and red lights, blinking and still, smudged by the force of hard tears standing in her eyes. There was a breeze rising again, from the south, and clouds rolling in. The jib swayed beneath her body, up and down. Maybe her sea legs were not so perfect after all. It was stable, though, it was stable! Meant to hoist far greater weights than two small women! It was like climbing to the crow's nest from the deck of a ship, rising and falling ever so gently in the sea.

Then again, the sea, too, is an obliterator, if you fall into it. Just like the fire below.

She took a breath and then another step. Then another and another.

'I'll remember!' she called, finally, vaguely, feeling desperate inspiration and then regretting it as inappropriate. And then, what the hell, again: 'I'll remember you!'

Nancy whirled.

'Evidence against you there, my friend!'

'What do you mean?'

'I mean does the name Mani ring a bell to you?'

Mani.

Kip called, 'You don't understand what happened.' She wished she could have made her reply more suggestive, speculative, not this imperative.

'Oh I think do!' called Nancy. 'You and the whole city! So worried about your own survival that you let everything go to oblivion around you! So blinkered about your own history that you don't even know who your real father is!'

'I know who my father is!' called Kip, confused.

'Do you? Crawl out of your case, kiddo. Talk to Henry about it. I don't have the patience for this fairy-tale bullshit. All I know is, like everyone else, you took the money and let the memory get ploughed under. Just like the whole, fucking —'

'I'm not the city!' called Kip. 'Fuck off!'

'Good one!' shouted Nancy.

'I'm sorry I didn't tell you about Mani!'

'How could you have?' asked Nancy. 'After what you did to him?'

'I cried so hard for Mani,' called Kip. 'I nearly died myself. I lived in a drainpipe on the Humber River for months —'

'Where?' asked Nancy, brought up short. 'What part?'

Well, that was annoying. Nancy: impressed, in the middle of an inferno, by the evidence of Kip's former city-rat authenticity.

'That one was installed after Hurricane Hazel,' said Nancy.

'I'm glad you approve!' shouted Kip.

'You could have been washed away!'

'I was looking to be washed away!' called Kip. 'Don't you get it? I'm not like you, I could never stick around, I'm just so much fish food, in the end, and that's okay! But then Mani came. He told me he was okay. And he told me the dead don't seek revenge! But I didn't believe him. So then, to get me out of there, he told me to get up and to seek revenge.'

'Sounds good,' called Nancy. 'When do we start?'

'His point was just to say that I was cold and so was revenge.'

'It is cold,' said Nancy, who shivered above the heat. 'The coldest.'

'But it was what he said first,' said Kip, 'that I believe now. The dead don't seek revenge.'

'Look below, babe,' said Nancy. 'That's just so not true.'

Kip looked. The whole top of Augusta was burning now.

'Yeah, see,' said Kip, 'That's what doesn't make sense to me. Why would you want your city to burn? Your own beloved city?'

'Because it's not so beloved, maybe?' called Nancy, coattails swooping. 'Because it's crushing and hurtful and full of people who just want to survive and nothing more. Well, I'm here to show them they don't even have to survive! They should fall into the burning Neanderthal hole and join the party we're having. It's fun!'

'It doesn't look like fun!' called Kip.

'It doesn't?' Nancy pushed up and down like she was on the tip of a diving board, cackling bitterly like a murder of crows in High Park. 'I'm shocked you think so!' she called. 'It's fun all right! Take my word for it!'

'Is it as much fun,' called Kip, clutching the jib, 'as getting the gun that killed Mani?'

'Oh!' said Nancy, clutching her mock wounded heart. 'Good one! Here I am, deceased, with the fires of rebellion burning below me, and you're going to compare it to a little pop gun? How lame!'

'It wasn't little,' said Kip. 'It did the trick.'

It was making Kip angry to be ridiculed like this. What she was becoming aware of, though, was how her whole body was shaking from it; and the jib was swaying now perhaps more than it really should. It was scary. She had seen videos of destabilized tower cranes spinning in the wind like tops. That would not be good for anybody.

Maybe she should give up. Maybe she should turn around and go back, leaving her bitter friend in midair.

'You should really be careful,' said Nancy, softly somehow, seeming suddenly aware of Kip's change of mood. 'You wouldn't want to fall.'

It was a shock. A reversal. Kip's mouth fell open. She looked across the gap to see Nancy, still swaying there, calmly, sky-high, still telling Kip to hold on.

'But I'm so angry with you!' called Kip.

'Now that,' said Nancy, 'is a feeling I can understand.'

Then she sat down out on the triangle, facing inward, legs dangling, and looked down over the inferno below. 'Anyway, what difference does it make?' she asked, and there was regret in her voice. 'I made a mistake. I can't undo it.'

Kip was still struggling to catch up, caught between fury and a long-sought-after conversation.

'What mistake?' she asked.

'Oh come on. Do we really have to belabour it?'

'I –'

Was she talking about the gun?

'You were so mad about it,' said Nancy. 'I didn't understand what was going on. And you told me Mani was okay, you told me you were moving away. How could I know he was dead! Otherwise I would have understood!'

'I'm sorry,' called Kip.

'I would have understood!' said Nancy. 'I was your friend! That was a horrible thing that happened. You punished me without any reason. It felt so arbitrary, like everything else, like everything I hate. Why didn't you just tell me?'

'I was trying to –' Kip couldn't quite believe she'd hit pay dirt somehow. Couldn't quite bring herself to say she'd been trying to protect her. Nancy would never understand that. She believed she was so much tougher than Kip. Which is tougher, though: the gabion wall or the tiny newt that scuttles around and makes her home in all its cracks?

Anyway, it was all so absurd and meaningless now. Enemies had become friends and friends enemies. Things changed. For Kip, the misunderstanding between them had already sifted away to nothing. Or not nothing, but something more complex and meaningful and rife, something to hold like a little diamond at the top of her spine. While for Nancy it had grown to a city-size inferno.

How do people ever understand one another?

'It's too late anyway,' said Nancy, as if answering a question Kip had not asked. 'I wouldn't know how to undo this.' Indicating the fire. Again, Kip heard the sound of regret in there.

'But look what you're doing to the Market,' said Kip. 'Don't burn it.'

'I have to,' said Nancy. 'Revenge must be both bitter and sweet.'

'Why are you seeking revenge?' said Kip.

'It just comes out like that.'

'I should have told you about Mani,' said Kip.

'You're right, though,' said Nancy. 'Maybe it was my fault.'

'He,' said Kip, 'was angry.'

'I was angry too. I got him a gun.'

'All gone now,' said Kip. 'Water under the bridge.'

'Breaking the banks is more like it,' said Nancy. 'Bursting the dam. Sweeping away the whole neighbourhood.'

'Don't think about it anymore,' said Kip.

'How can I not?' said Nancy. 'Death is nothing but memory.'

'You're telling me you want to burn the Market down,' said Kip, 'because you gave a gun to Mani?'

'I'm sorry I did it,' said Nancy.

'I don't know what to say.' Kip was realizing she might have a hard time letting this one go.

Ah, what the heck.

'I forgive you!' she shouted.

Nancy sat and swayed and blinked.

'Oh come on!' she called. 'It can't be as easy as that!'

'It isn't easy!' shouted Kip. 'Are you kidding me? It wasn't easy. I nearly killed myself with anger and fear and regret. It wasn't easy!'

'Well,' said Nancy. 'In that case …'

Her feet were dangling up and down and up and down. The jib was swaying more but Kip had got used to it. Nancy was looking down but now she looked up at Kip and her eyes were full and big, still full of hurt and sarcasm, but brimming, water at the top of a dam about to go.

'Okay,' said Kip, gently. 'Can we stop burning the city now?'

'Can't,' said Nancy, suddenly playing up that she was swaying like an old doll on a swing. 'Can't do anything anymore. Dead, remember?'

'Hasn't stopped you so far.'

'No …'

'Seems like a pretty dynamic state for you.'

'Well, I mean,' said Nancy, perched out on the leaf tip of the jib. 'I *could* cry.'

Kip barely heard her. 'What can I do to help you?' she called.

'Remember me,' said Nancy.

'I already said,' called Kip. 'Without a doubt.'

'What could you possibly remember?' asked Nancy, softly, sarcastically. 'I always burned away tenderness. What's there to remember with a life like that?'

'Well,' said Kip, 'it might take a bit of an adjustment, since you're still here. I mean, you're still here!'

'I am still here,' said Nancy, softly. 'But not for long.'

The rage was seeping out of her body, a gabion wall too narrow to hold back the sea.

'Well,' said Kip, 'I'd like to point out from experience that I won't always remember properly. But when I forget, I'll have the pleasure of remembering again, all of a sudden, like, "Oh yeah, that!" like your face popping up in front of me, right out of the sidewalk!'

'Like saying, "Remember, this was where that after-hours club used to be?" Except with me.'

'Yeah, like that,' said Kip. 'You've always been an after-hours club to me.'

'I can do that,' said Nancy. 'I can have that arranged.'

Kip was finally sitting now too, halfway down the jib, her legs dangling too, like they were two girls on the seesaws in Bellevue Park. Although the soles of her feet were burning.

'I'll be a bourgeois distraction,' said Nancy.

'If you say so,' said Kip. 'But I'll remember us in the Market for sure. Our apartment. The way it used to be, with the music blaring up from below, as if we lived in the vibrating ashtrays on the bar. As if we were the flowers in the jars.'

'We *were* the flowers in the jars!' said Nancy. 'Ornaments on the table. The rhythm of the city. That's always been me.'

'And I'll recall the little family out back and the bowling shirts and Cuban shirts and top hats of Courage My Love. But I can't be all memory, Nancy. I've got the future to think of.'

'Yeah, yeah,' said Nancy. 'The future. I know.' She looked anxious when she said it, and Kip realized, by some instinct, that in the etiquette book of speaking to the dead, it was inappropriate to bring up the new life that would appear in their absence. Impolite. So she did not bring up the other thing that was happening inside her, just entering its second trimester, bathed in paraffin, fire, gasps of air, tears, rage, love. Love.

So then there was an awkward pause, still rife with resolution, despite some withholding. Nancy sensed the missing piece, realized she didn't want to know about it. The future more terrifying than all the fires she could ever set.

'Tell Henry,' said Nancy, 'he looks good.'

'You've seen him?'

'Tell him I'm proud of him,' she said. 'For sure his luck has turned.'

'I'll tell him,' said Kip.

'Tell him just don't answer the door in his underwear and he'll be okay.'

'I'll tell him.'

They were regarding each other warily across the gap, still sitting, feet dangling, seesawing, or at least seeing. Kip the shoreline with its spit. Nancy the island with its beaches. They'd be connected if not for one fierce storm that took out a hotel with its bourgeois distractions.

'So what now?'

'Now,' said Nancy, 'I guess I try to squeeze out a few tears.'

And then she pouted and raised her open hand to Kip, who did the same, trying now to stand up.

'Careful,' said Nancy. 'Don't lose your balance.'

And she came to her feet in one fluid move and turned all the way around at the tip of her jib and, like a diver, she raised her hands up in the air.

'Hold on,' she called back.

'Are you going to be all right?' called Kip.

'What do you think?' called Nancy, over her shoulder.

And then she leapt. Swan dive.

As she ascended, there was a thunderclap. And then much rain.

Kip looked down through the bars of the crane, way, way down, and saw, at the bottom of the tower, Joseph Luong, standing on the concrete base, about to start climbing. He hesitated though, when he saw what happened. Watched Nancy go.

He had something raised in one hand. Kip couldn't make it out.

It was a little statue. 'Buddha icon,' he told her later. 'The law of give and take. I had to go all the way into Chinatown to get it. Sorry I took so long.'

'That's okay,' said Kip, puzzled. Still, understanding better than she felt she had any right to.

It was still before eleven p.m. The sun had been down for six hours. Pat had been taken to hospital suffering from nervous exhaustion, leaving his follow spot shining on the smouldering construction machinery. He was still wondering if he'd gone too far by suggesting the Carnivalers celebrate the war on the car. Was it all his fault? This inferno? Was it? Kip would have to assure him that, although he could undoubtedly take his share, the allocation of blame was certainly much more complicated.

When Henry and Kip, still shaken and covered with damp soot, arrived at the gate of number 12, there was a young round-headed man sitting on the curb in front of the building. He'd been waiting patiently since around five o'clock.

'Are you trying to get to the back?' asked Henry. 'Gate's open, you know.'

'Oh, said the man. 'No, I –'

And then he saw Kip. Squinted a bit, uncertain. And then more certain.

'I'm here about some babies,' he said.

They didn't know what he meant by 'some babies.'

'No idea,' said Henry, 'what you're talking about.'

'Me neither,' said the man. 'But I heard something about some babies. I heard I was the father.'

It was hilarious. Where he'd got the plural idea. Like there were ten or eleven babies in behind the gate somewhere, playing in a sandbox, and they were all connected to him.

He was offering a sheepish smile. More of a half smile. Kip took a closer look. Despite it being the end of the first part of the longest night of the year, she saw the sun reflecting off a bronze-tinted window and glinting in his eyes. Grateful for the sudden insight that memory can sometimes overwhelm the present, she tipped her invisible hat to Nancy.

And then she smiled back.

'Okay,' she said. 'Come on up. We'll see if we can't find some common ground.'

Acknowledgements

The debate about fire vs. shelter in architecture comes from Luis Fernández-Galiano's book *Fire and Memory*, in which he attributes the idea to Reyner Banham.

Martin Dixon and criminal lawyer John A. Renwick helped with Henry's charges and probation. Kent Dixon helped too.

The typeface used in Nancy's nightmare visions is from Quadrant's Toronto Subway series.

The card game summary of *La Belle et La Bête* is a quote from Damian Rogers. Nanika Hart taught me how to make the black-tar roses. Margaux Williamson read an early draft and gave good notes. My editor, Alana Wilcox, challenged me to fix it. Ker Wells told me to draw pictures. Clare Hey offered early faith and guidance. My wife, Kat Cizek, stood by me through a trying period. Amy Lavender Harris pointed me to the book *Toronto of Old* and also provided inspiration with her own excellent book, *Imagining Toronto*, especially the revelations about St. John's Ward. *Concrete Toronto*, by Michael McClelland and Graeme Stewart, expanded my understanding of urban preservation.

The character of Henry appeared before in a story, *Sic Transit Gloria at the Humber Loop*, published in the collection *Toronto Noir* (Akashic Books, 2008). The story depicts his crime as it unfolds, moment to moment, from Henry's point of view. I have a manuscript, written in verse, in which Henry solves a crime swiped from Hesiod's *Theogeny*, but I'm not sure it works.

'The cut worm forgives the plough' is an aphorism from William Blake's *Proverbs of Hell*. As is 'Everything that is is holy.'

Two of the drawings – one of two flying hands (p. 104) and another of a spirit following a travelling man (p. 208) – were copied into a notebook from petroglyphs carved into the white marble rock of Petroglyphs Provincial Park, northeast of Peterborough, Ontario, some time between 900 and 1400 AD.

Bruce Beaton, current resident of number 12, and his flatmate Cara Goldberg, let me come and crash in the room that was once my office, looking over the roof of the Temp and the house in the back that later blew up. He also taught me about rats. But even though I used to live there, I am not a ghost.

About the Author

Sean Dixon is a playwright, novelist and actor. His plays have been produced in Canada, the U.S., Australia and the U.K., and collected in *AWOL: Three Plays for Theatre SKAM.* Sean's first novel was *The Girls Who Saw Everything* (*The Last Days of the Lacuna Cabal* in the U.S. and the U.K.), named one of the Best Books of 2007 by *Quill & Quire.* He is the author of two books for young readers, *The Feathered Cloak* and *The Winter Drey.* He occasionally plays banjo with the Toronto glam rock band tomboyfriend.

Typeset in Albertina, CA Ginger Mint and Kavaler

Edited and designed by Alana Wilcox
Cover design by Ingrid Paulson
Author photo by Anna van der Wee

Coach House Books
80 bpNichol Lane
Toronto ON M5S 3J4

416 979 2217
800 367 6360

mail@chbooks.com
www.chbooks.com